Mrs. Covington's

K.R.R. LOCKHAVEN

For everyone who pledged or helped this project come to life in any way.

CHAPTER 1

New Dawn

Jacob would have been excited when the small bay fronting New Dawn became visible, but he was far too busy steadying his wobbly legs and trying to stave off the churning in his stomach. He gripped the starboard rail with both hands and focused on the skyline, taking in deep breaths through his nose and out through pursed lips.

"First time, eh?" said a large, sunbaked brute of a man as he slapped Jacob's back, nearly sending him overboard.

"No," Jacob said as he turned to face the man. It was his second time on a ship at sea. "I just...it must have been something I ate."

"Oh, okay." The man suppressed a knowing smirk, but not before a hint of it broke through. "What brings ya to New Dawn? If ya don't mind me askin'."

"A fresh start."

"Nothin' wrong with that." The man held out an oversized hand. "Cyrus is the name."

Jacob hadn't known his name but already knew the man was the captain of the ship. He had watched him from afar throughout the trip, imagining what it would be like to be him.

"I'm Jacob." Luckily, Cyrus didn't squeeze his hand too hard. "Jacob Bright." The last name was a false one, a name he'd picked out as part of his *fresh start.*

The word *bright* embodied everything his father was not. The life he had left behind had been one of spiritless luxury. He had mindlessly followed in his wealthy father's footsteps, even though his heart had longed for something else.

"What does this fresh start entail?" Cyrus asked.

"I'm not sure. I was thinking about joining a ship's crew, but..."

"Oh, don't worry about bein' a little green about the gills. You'll get yer sea legs in no time." Another slap on the back pushed the wind from Jacob's lungs.

"You think so?"

"Sure, but if I'm being honest, which I'm known to be at times, I don't think yer quite ready to be on a crew yet."

"Why not?"

"Well—how do I say this without soundin' cruel? —yer a bit of a dandy, and a bit on the sensitive side for any crew I know of."

Jacob looked down at his clothes. He had specifically worn his least fancy suit to avoid such labels. He was clean-shaven, so the burn scar on his right cheek and neck was clearly visible. He always liked to think that his scar, earned the first time he'd ever set foot on a ship, gave him a tough, rugged appearance. His black hair was messy on top, with random curls falling over his forehead and temples, which was in the modern style of the working man. Apparently, he wasn't quite pulling it off.

"Most crews would have you in a pot, choppin' vegetables in and lickin' their lips."

Jacob scrunched his eyebrows together.

"I mean they'd eat you alive, my boy." Instead of slapping his back again, Cyrus gripped his shoulder and gave it a fatherly—Jacob guessed some fathers did such things—squeeze. "No. You need to get a bit more life experience under your belt, I reckon. Toughen up, first. Then maybe you'd stand a chance out here."

Cyrus must have noticed Jacob's forlorn face, because he added, "I'm not sayin' it can't be done. With the right amount of grit, most things are possible." He looked Jacob in the eye with what was definitely a fatherly look. "You're kind at yer core, I can see it in yer eyes." He flashed Jacob a warm, gap-tooth smile. "I'm in a position where I can appreciate that for what it is, but some will see it as weakness and aim to take advantage.

"Be wary, but don't let 'em kill the kindness in you. It isn't weakness. You'll just have to trust me on that."

"Okay..." Strangely, Jacob found himself on the verge of tears. Since he was a kid, he had always seen himself as weak. The ship's captain was cutting to Jacob's core within the first minute of meeting him. Clenching his fists and jaw, he managed to keep the tears at bay. "Why are you telling me this?" he asked, concentrating on keeping his voice steady.

Cyrus looked around as if to see if anyone was listening to them. "Fact is, I see a lot of myself in you." He held up his thumb and forefinger about an inch apart. "I came this close to letting a harsh life at sea crush the kindness in me as a lad. I nearly..." He trailed away, eyes trained out at the offing, then shook his head and chuckled. "Anyway, I reckon someday you'll look back and thank ol' Cyrus for the advice. I'm not usually one for dispensin' it, but you've caught me in a good mood. Got a gal here in New Dawn who I can't wait to see, and I'm giddy as a schoolboy."

Jacob didn't know what to say. He tried to process all Cyrus had told him while gazing across the deck of the ship where some kids near the port rail were feeding fruit to the ship's capybara.

"So," Jacob started, suddenly feeling more like a kid than a twenty-year-old man, "what should I do, then?"

Cyrus thought for a moment, scratching his patchy beard with dirty fingernails. "Challenge yourself," he said. "It's not exactly going to be a cakewalk in town, but there will be opportunities that are on the easier, more comfortable side. Bypass those and find somethin' where yer in over yer head. Best way to learn how to swim, that." He nodded at Jacob.

"That's it?" Jacob had been hoping for something much more specific.

"That's all I got for ya. But I promise you'll be confident and ready to tread the timbers in no time if you overcome a few proper challenges on yer own."

Jacob nodded as if he thoroughly understood.

"Alright, I'll leave you to it, now. I've been a right bag of hot wind.

There's just somethin' about you. You got this sparkle in your eye. I'd hate to see it extinguished right out of the gate, is all."

"Thank you, sir, for all your advice. It's a lot to take in, but I think it'll probably do me some good." He wished he could take Cyrus into New Dawn with him.

"Just don't forget about me when you've hit it big." He flashed another warm smile.

"I won't." The idea of hitting it big stirred something inside of Jacob. If it actually happened, he would finally prove himself worthy. He could show his family—his father—that he could be successful on his own, in his own way.

"Good lad." Cyrus turned and began barking curse-laden orders to a small group of sailors.

Jacob looked up at the Ring, making its constant arc across the bright, azure sky. It was the exact same view of the ring around the planet as it was back home. That thought was comforting. As he followed the Ring's path down to the horizon, Jacob smiled. He may have already gotten himself in over his head, but *this* was a proper adventure.

CHAPTER 2

"Welcome to Mrs. Covington's"

The bustle on and around the docks was loud and overwhelming. On all sides, people were conducting business by way of shouting at each other and waving things over their heads. The people were mostly human, but there were several purple-skinned ciguapa people and at least one faun that Jacob could see. There didn't seem to be any orcs, which wasn't all that surprising. He had thought he might see one on this new island but realized the chances weren't that good. He had never seen an orc in his life.

With nothing but a small suitcase stuffed with clothes, Jacob pushed his way through the crowd and onto the main street, which ran parallel to the bay. All along the street were buildings made of stones of all different sizes, held together by some kind of cement. He'd walked many a cobblestone street, but these were his first cobblestone buildings, and he loved them.

The buildings were homes to all the businesses one might expect; a mercantile store, a butcher, a blacksmith, a gunsmith, a livery, a bakery, and too many pubs to count. Fish vendors sold their catch from stands along the seaside of the street

Jacob moved with the ebb and flow of the crowd until he found a side street that led west, toward a tall steepled building in the distance that could only be the First Church. This street, home to an inn and what he assumed to be a brothel, was much less crowded. He stopped to catch his breath and get his bearings, trying his best to avoid eye contact with the beautiful girl smiling at him from the doorway across the street.

He gave the girl an awkward wave, then hurried west to the next cross street. There he took a right and wandered for a while, eyes exploring all that New Dawn had to offer.

As he walked, he became more and more parched. Beads of sweat began to dot his forehead.

There was a pub just ahead, with a wooden sign hanging from a pole over the door that read *The Dripping Bucket*. He peered inside through the wedged-open door and found that it was loud and completely packed. Unwilling to immerse himself into a rowdy crowd quite yet, he continued on.

After the next block, the road crossed what was either a small river or a large creek on a rickety bridge that was missing a board, then turned from cobblestone to dirt. The buildings on the other side were made of mostly wood instead of stone and were much further spaced out. This section of town had a much more laid-back, almost pastoral feel.

Alongside the creek—Jacob decided he would think of it as a creek —was a slightly rundown building that seemed to house two businesses. The far business had a sign written in another language but looked to be some sort of restaurant. The closer business was a pub called Mrs. Covington's, which had a sign with a painting of a capybara in a modified evening gown over the door. Something about the capybara sign drew him to the pub. It was alive with whimsy, something his life had been devoid of for far too long. A smaller sign, propped up against the building near the door, read:

There's Always a Keg of Beer and a Block of Cheese!

His mouth feeling as if it were filled with warm sand, Jacob threw open the door to the pub and stepped inside.

The place was dark, lit only by a small window on the creek side, and a few candles behind the bar. It smelled of stale beer and the vague scent of horse manure. A ciguapa woman—tall, beautiful, and indigo-skinned—was setting down mugs of beer for two shady-looking human patrons who sat at a small table in the corner. A human, with his elbows on the bar and his face buried in his hands, barely looked up as Jacob entered.

"Welcome to Mrs. Covington's," the ciguapa woman said, her voice musical.

As if on cue, a capybara someone had dressed in an evening gown waddled in from a back room.

"Hey! It's Mrs. Covington, herself!" Jacob tried to say this with energy, but his mouth was so dry it came out barely intelligible and accompanied by strange popping noises.

"Yep." The ciguapa woman forced a smile. "That's her."

"Does she own this place?" Jacob said, trying his best to be funny.

"No." The woman gave him a compassionate look, as if he was the dumbest person she'd ever met, and she felt bad for him. It was either that, or this was the thousandth time she'd heard that joke. "She's a capybara."

"Oh."

"Anyway, my name is Cora. Can I get you anything?"

"A beer, please." Saying it aloud gave Jacob a thrill. This was going to be his first ever alcohol, aside from sips of fancy wine at formal dinners.

"Sure thing. For a copper, you get a beer, and we can get you a clean knife so you can cut yourself some slices from the cheese block." She pointed to a cube of yellow cheese as big as Jacob's head sitting on the bar. The man behind the bar lazily waved a hand to scare a group of flies up from it.

"Uh...sure." Jacob's stomach turned, but he didn't want to be rude.

As Cora poured his beer, Jacob took a seat at the bar, holding his suitcase in his lap.

The man behind the bar wiped off a knife's blade with a rag and handed it to Jacob. "If you find any mold, just cut it off and toss it behind the bar." the man said, his voice monotone.

"Thank you." Jacob tried to address both bartenders at once. "My name is Jacob, and I arrived in New Dawn only moments ago."

"I'm Tadrick." The man gave a half wave and an attempt at a smile.

"Nice to meet you two." Jacob felt Tadrick's eyes linger for a moment on his burn scar, but it was so quick, and he was so used to it, it barely registered.

Both Tadrick and Cora seemed to be around eighteen or nineteen, just a couple of years younger than Jacob, but Jacob's style of dress made him look older than he was. Both of the pub workers wore simple clothes. Cora's dark blue blouse perfectly matched her hair, which was tied into a ponytail with a leather strap. Tadrick wore a button-up white shirt. They both wore dark brown breeches.

"Welcome to town." Cora nodded and set his beer on the bar in front of him.

Jacob gripped the mug's handle, raised it as if about to toast, then took a swig. He squeezed his eyes shut as the warm, bitter liquid went down, then shuddered in his seat. It was much more intense than he imagined.

"Is this considered...good beer?" he asked, trying not to sound rude.

"It's not bad." Cora shrugged. "Middling, I'd say."

"There are worse beers," Tadrick added.

Jacob steeled himself and took another gulp. He found that after the initial shock, it really wasn't so bad. Before he knew it, he had finished the mug and ordered another.

"Where you coming from?" Cora asked, although her eyes flitted around the pub as if watching butterflies only she could see.

It was strange for Jacob to be sitting there talking conversationally with a ciguapa person. He'd had limited talks with both ciguapas and fauns, but mostly just about business. He welcomed the idea of befriending people from any race, but his father was much less open to such things.

"First Frontier," he said, before taking a drink from his second beer. He was already feeling the effects of the alcohol. He felt lighter, like he might float away on a breeze. Most of his worries about being alone in a totally new place began to melt away. He found himself unable to stifle the smile on his lips.

"Wonderful mountains on that island," Cora said, looking at Jacob for a moment, then looking past him, toward the door as if she expected someone to arrive at any minute.

"Yeah. I suppose there are." He had never fully appreciated how wonderful those mountains really were until this moment. He had always been taught that things like beauty and nature were nothing more than distractions.

"How long are you staying?" Cora's eyes remained on the door.

"I'm not sure. Maybe forever." Jacob shrugged and took another swig. "I've got everything I own with me. All my money, too. I might just set down roots here if I can find something I enjoy."

At the mention of money, the two shady characters in the corner took a sudden interest in Jacob. He subtly rolled his eyes, wishing he had started a little slower with the drinking. As inconspicuously as possible, he turned a bit on his stool so he could keep a better eye on the men.

Jacob picked up his knife and sliced a chunk of cheese from the block, making sure they noticed that he had a weapon, although the thought of actually using it dulled his buzz. He had never even been in a fistfight, before.

The cheese, for its part, was a lot better than it looked. A hard cheese from the mountains, if he wasn't mistaken.

As Jacob lifted his mug to his lips, the door burst open, causing him to spill a quarter of the beer down the front of his shirt. A tall, handsome ciguapa man came in backward, pulling a wooden cart stacked with random supplies.

"Hey, Cora, hey, Tadrick." He stopped the cart next to the bar. "Got a delivery for you."

"Let me guess," said Cora, "beer and...cheese." Her face positively shone with interest in the delivery man, and she seemed to stand at least two inches taller.

"It's like you're a psychic or something," the man said.

"No," Cora replied, "it's just that nine times out of ten, the only things you bring for us are beer and cheese." Her expression lost some of its shine as she spoke. It was as if she knew her words were somehow killing the moment, but she couldn't stop making the obvious point. "It was just a logical guess, based on the odds. And if I had got it wrong, it wouldn't have been all that embarrassing anyway, right?"

"No, you're not embarrassing, er, it wouldn't have been, I mean." The man had come in hot and full of confidence but was immediately awkward and unsure of himself.

"Hey, Yandro," Tadrick said with a half-wave. "I'll go get the boss for you." He disappeared into the back room.

Yandro and Cora spent an uncomfortable twenty seconds looking at each other—eyes flicking away, then back again. Jacob took a drink, then tried to ease the awkward tension.

"Hello, Yandro." He stuck his hand out. "I'm Jacob."

Yandro, whose shoulders visibly relaxed once distracted, approached Jacob and shook his hand. "Pleased to meet you, Jacob." Up close, the guy was even more handsome, from his perfect indigo skin to his well-manicured, dark blue hair. He looked down at the suitcase. "Are you thinking about buying this place?"

"Huh?" Jacob didn't have enough time to say anything else before the owner came out from the back.

"Shit," the owner, a short human man, said. "I forgot to cancel my cheese order. We got enough here for another week at least."

A thought popped into Jacob's head as he watched the interaction. They didn't need the cheese delivery because there hadn't been enough business. This place must not be doing very well. He pushed the thought away, trying not to see every little thing through a business lens anymore.

"I can see if they'll take it back," Yandro said.

"Oh, no. It'll be fine. I don't want to trouble you." The owner lifted the cheese from the cart. "You haven't gotten any bites on my idea, have you?"

"No, Mr. Davies." Yandro shook his head. "Sorry. No takers, yet."

"Damn." Mr. Davies sighed. "I'm getting way too old for this. I'd rather be on a beach somewhere, spoiling the grandkids while my daughter works." He stared wistfully into the corner. "Why don't you start putting it out there that I'd be willing to part with this place for ten gold?"

"Ten gold?" Jacob almost spilled his beer again. Mr. Davies must have been absolutely desperate to sell for that price.

"Yeah!" Mr. Davies took an intense sudden interest in Jacob. His eyes lingered a little longer on the burn scar, but he shook it off and re-engaged by staring into Jacob's eyes. "You in the market for a well-established pub? I'll even throw in one and a half blocks of grade-A cheese and two kegs of beer."

"Uh...I don't know about all that." The price was much cheaper than Jacob would have guessed. Still, if he were to buy the pub, which he wasn't really considering, it would take nearly all the money he'd brought with him.

The idea was ridiculous, but something about it actually kind of appealed to him. It could be a chance to run a business his way. For far too long he had tried to force himself into his father's way of thinking, almost starting to believe that profit really was everything. It had never *felt* right, though. He believed it could be done differently, and would love a chance to prove that.

"Do you got that kind of money on you, sir?" Mr. Davies asked.

"Well, yeah, but I don't want to be too hasty to part with it."

The two men in the corner stood and began to approach Jacob, not bothering to hide their ill intent, but Mr. Davies waved them away emphatically. "I saw him first! Back off, you two!"

The men sat back down, faces forlorn.

Jacob mentally kicked himself for showing his hand. It was bad business. He knew better than that, but the beer had worn down all his ingrained business sense. He barely knew how he had gotten himself into a discussion about money to begin with.

"Would you let us stay on?" Tadrick asked Jacob. "I mean, this job bores me to tears, but it's all I got at the moment."

"Of course, you could stay on," Jacob heard himself say. "Er, I'm not buying this place, though."

"But why not?" Mr. Davies patted Jacob on the back. "You look like a man who knows his way around money and commerce." He pinched the fancy lace on the front of Jacob's shirt. "This could be just the thing a young man like you needs to get his start on this island."

"But I'm trying to branch out from all things business. My family owned a shipping company back home, but I wanted...I don't know... more of an adventure. I wanted to join a ship's crew at first, but that's on hold at the moment. I'd much rather do something adventurous like that than run a pub."

"Oh, but running a pub is an adventure in itself, I assure you." Mr. Davies's finger shot up in the air and his eyes opened wide. "Ah! I tell you what. If it's adventure you seek, I'll throw in my original copy of the Fenton Treasure Poem!"

"Fenton Treasure Poem?" Something stirred inside Jacob at the mention of whatever that was.

"Do you not know of the Fenton Treasure?"

"No."

"Can I tell him?" Tadrick said, looking alive for the first time since Jacob met him.

"Sure, Tadrick. Go ahead."

"Okay, so about five years ago, this old rich woman named Virginia Fenton buried a treasure somewhere in the vicinity of New Dawn. She wrote a poem that was a clue as to the whereabouts of the treasure and posted it around the town. There were less than ten original copies, and Mr. Davies was lucky enough to snag one of them."

Jacob sat up in his chair.

"Although," Tadrick continued, "I should probably mention that most people think the treasure is unfindable."

Mr. Davies shot Tadrick a stern look as if to shut him up. At least that's what Jacob thought he saw. His head was still a bit woozy, so he couldn't be sure.

"I tell you what," Mr. Davies said. "I'll give you some time to think while I go rustle up the parchment with the poem."

"Hmm." Jacob couldn't get anything else out. His mind churned like a sea in a storm considering the possibilities. He hadn't ever dreamed of being a pub owner. The idea resonated with something in him, but it wasn't what he had in mind, at all, when he moved to New Dawn.

Then there was this treasure thing, which, if he was being honest with himself, was probably nothing.

But what if it really existed?

What a triumph it would be to return home with vast riches, earned entirely on his own.

His eyes were drawn to Yandro as he pulled a mango from his cart, knelt, and held it out for Mrs. Covington, who scuttled across the wood floor and took it from his hand. This place did have...something about it. Even though it was appallingly dull inside, it had potential. The location next to the creek was fantastic, and the—

Shit. He wondered if he was letting the alcohol cloud his judgment. This kind of decision wasn't one he should make in a rush.

Suddenly resolute, Jacob stood from his barstool.

"How much do I owe you for the beers and cheese?" he asked Cora.

"A copper and a half." She watched Yandro feeding Mrs. Covington as she spoke.

As Jacob fished the coppers from his pocket, Mr. Davies came back out from the back room holding a roll of weathered parchment.

"I will consider your offer," Jacob said, projecting as much confidence as he could. "I will be back tomorrow with my answer. No earlier."

"But—"

"Good day to you all. It was very nice to meet you, and I hope to see you all again tomorrow."

Clutching his suitcase to his chest, Jacob walked out of the pub with his head held high, only glancing at the scary men in the corner once.

CHAPTER 3

The Decision

After hurrying away from the pub and back over the rickety bridge, Jacob made his way to an inn, where he booked a room for the night.

Once inside the room, he threw the deadbolt, slid his briefcase under the small bed in the corner, and lay down on his back, staring up at the cracked plaster ceiling.

His mind raced as he considered the pros and cons of buying the dilapidated pub.

In a straight-up battle, the cons were sure to win. They had the bigger numbers, and each of them was solid and strong.

If what he had intuited was right, and he had little reason to doubt his assessment, the pub was failing. Jacob had zero knowledge of the local economy, so there was no good reason to believe he could correct the lack of success.

He let a depressing scenario play out in his head—one in which he bought the pub, slowly bled all his money, and was forced to crawl back home defeated. This was the most likely outcome, and it would be devastating. He envisioned his father's face when he first saw Jacob walk in the door—the certainty in his eyes that this had been a foregone conclusion as he tried to hold back a smirk. "I told you," his father would say. "You're too weak. Not cutthroat enough to make it out in the world."

Jacob pushed the image from his head and tried to focus on the pros. They were weaker than the cons and stood on far less steady ground, but they had a different quality to them—the exciting, almost mystical quality of the unknown.

Jacob thought about Cyrus' words. "Find something where you're in over your head," he had said. Well, this would definitely qualify as being in over his head. He would hardly be able to see the surface from how far under he would be. But as Cyrus said, it might be the best way to learn how to swim in these new waters.

He thought about Cora, and Tadrick, and imagined becoming friends with them. He pictured them all hanging out after closing, drinking a few beers together and laughing, knowing it was an unrealistic fantasy, but still enjoying the idea of it.

Then there was the map, which was exactly the kind of thing he had left home for. The notion of searching for a hidden treasure was the most appealing thing in the world to him, with the possible exception of kissing a woman.

His head still fuzzy from alcohol, Jacob drifted off to sleep with vague thoughts of the pub before the sun had even dipped below the horizon.

~

When Jacob opened his eyes to the bright morning sun, he knew what he was going to do.

Somewhat embarrassed that he had slept in his clothes, he changed into a slightly more expensive suit than he had worn the day before because it was all he had.

In a move that would have made his father keel over, he ripped the white-laced frills from the ends of both sleeves and tossed them in the wastebasket. And although he immediately felt guilty for the erratic and spontaneous behavior, it was also freeing. With a grin across his face, he left the room and headed back toward Mrs. Covington's.

Once back at the bridge, he leaped over the missing board with a spring in his step and a whistle on his lips. He flung open the door and found Mr. Davies counting money at the bar. As soon as Mr. Davies saw him, he turned over the paper he'd been writing on.

"Jacob!" His eyes lit up. "It's great to see you on this fine morning."

"It's great to see you too, sir."

"Oh, you can forget the sir stuff." Mr. Davies waved a hand as if brushing the word *sir* away. "Have you come to a decision on my offer?"

"I have."

Mr. Davies stood, straight-backed and wide-eyed. "And?"

Jacob audibly gulped. He'd thought he was confident in his decision until it was time to say the actual words. "I..." Another gulp. "I'll take it."

Mr. Davies rushed around the bar, grasped Jacob around the waist, and lifted him off his feet. "You're a good man, Jacob! I hope nothing but the best for you in your new endeavor!"

"Thank you." Jacob leaned back in an attempt to keep from falling on top of the excited old man.

Eventually, Mr. Davies set him back down. Jacob opened his suitcase on the bar and took out his coin purse. He opened it and began to count out ten gold.

"Hold on just a minute," Mr. Davies said. "Let me get you the deed first." He turned and headed for the back room, but stopped just short of it. "And your poem, of course."

A thrill shot through Jacob's body.

While Mr. Davies was away, Jacob scanned the pub. Mrs. Covington had just come in from outside. After waddling across the floor, she crawled up onto a little four-poster bed someone had made for her behind the bar.

In no time at all, Mr. Davies flew out of the back room holding two rolls of parchment.

As he unrolled the deed on the bar, Jacob found that he couldn't take his eyes off of the other roll.

"Just sign right here and she's yours." Mr. Davies handed him a quill.

Jacob dipped the tip into an ink pot and let it hover over the spot he was supposed to sign.

Was he absolutely sure about this?

The answer was clear—no.

Would he ever be absolutely sure about anything in this new life he intended to make for himself? Probably not. He thought he'd been sure about being part of a ship's crew, but between the seasickness and Cyrus's words, his surety had been shaken.

He looked down at Mrs. Covington, who was still laying in her bed, but his eyes darted back to the rolled-up poem.

The ship's crew could wait. This was an adventure in itself.

With sweat beading on his brow, he touched quill to parchment and signed his name. He handed ten gold to Mr. Davies and took the poem in his other hand.

"Great doing business with you." Mr. Davies shoved the coins into his pocket.

"You, as well." Jacob couldn't have described exactly what he felt for all the treasure in the world.

"Alright, now I hope you're not going to be sore at me, but I do have a few things to tell you."

Jacob's heart raced and his eyebrows pinched. Mr. Davies had seemed like such a good, honest man, but this seemed nefarious.

"How do you feel about fauns?" Mr. Davies asked.

"I suppose you could say I don't have much of an opinion, as I haven't had the chance to get to know any of them before."

"So, you don't have any negative feelings about them?"

"No. Not at all."

"Well, that's good to hear."

"Why do you ask?"

"As you probably noticed, this building is home to two businesses. The other one is a faun restaurant owned by a faun woman named Juniper. We don't talk much, aside from the normal niceties, but she's a good person, and I wouldn't want there to be any trouble."

"But you didn't want to avoid trouble enough to tell me before we closed the deal." Jacob looked him in the eyes, unblinking.

Jacob was annoyed with the man's skullduggery but was more annoyed with himself. He hadn't even investigated the adjoining building. What if it had been something that discouraged commerce in the area, like a thieves' guild or something? He hadn't inspected the pub itself, either. It could be ready to collapse around him for all he knew. His business sense seemed to have been left behind when he set sail.

Mr. Davies blushed. "You didn't seem like the bigoted type. And..." He looked down. "I'm sorry. That wasn't very honest of me."

"So, what else do you have to tell me?" Jacob steeled himself.

"Well, business has been slow lately. To be honest, I've barely been getting by after paying the help. I should have told you that before. I've just been so desperate to get it off my hands and get out of here. I don't think it's anything a smart young man like yourself couldn't overcome. I've been stagnant for far too long. The cheese block thing used to be a hit, but this new generation finds it kind of disgusting."

"Yeah, it's not the most appealing thing."

"So..." Mr. Davies glanced up at Jacob sheepishly. "No hard feelings?"

Jacob felt like he should be more upset with the man, but he just wasn't. He still reserved the most scorn for himself.

"I tell you what," Jacob said, "if you throw in Mrs. Covington herself, I'll forget you ever said anything."

"Oh, I wouldn't dream of taking her from here. She's yours. Or rather, you're hers. You'll find she pretty much rules this roost. Cora and Tadrick will get you caught up with her routine and feeding expectations. I recommend keeping her happy at all times."

Jacob smiled, any lingering negative feelings melting away.

"What about that dress she wears? Isn't that uncomfortable for her?"

"For most capybaras, you're absolutely right. But go ahead and try to take that dress off Mrs. Covington. She won't let you. In fact, the only person who can coax it off of her for washing is Cora. If not for her, that thing would get pretty ripe." Mr. Davies crouched and scratched under Mrs. Covington's chin. "We got this little lady's grandma as a pup for my daughter. She was the one who started putting the capybaras in dresses. We always kept one female around, and my daughter kept dressing them up. I think it becomes comforting to them." Mr. Davies shrugged.

"Oh." Jacob shrugged back. "What can you tell me about the Fenton Treasure?"

Mr. Davies' eyes lit up. He stood and quickly unrolled the parchment flat on the bar. "Have a look for yourself first."

Most of the parchment was covered with a vague drawing of the island of Landfall. Inside the island were the following words, written in beautiful calligraphy:

Hail to all explorers with adventure in their hearts
Let me regale you of the place where this adventure starts
It's easy if you work together, what I say is true
Just boat a creek on rainy main to all afloat for two

"That last line seems like nonsense," Jacob said.

"You have no idea how much time I've spent thinking about that line." Mr. Davies stared off in the direction of the creek, a wistful gleam in his eyes. "I have explored this creek from silt to surface, source to mouth, and come up empty-handed. I've gone out to sea on rainy days and tried to find a clue, but not a one has ever revealed itself."

"Hmm." Jacob scratched his head as he tried to decipher the enigmatic sentence.

"It says you have to work together with someone, and mentions the number two, so there's that. I haven't been able to work out what that means either."

"Hmm," Jacob repeated, fascinated by the mystery of the clue.

"Well," Mr. Davies said, "I suppose I'll be off, now. You seem like a decent person, so this probably doesn't need saying, but I'm saying it anyway. Take care of Cora and Tadrick. They're good kids, and they're both in situations where they need the money right now."

"Of course," Jacob said. "I have an idea for them that they might like quite a bit."

Mr. Davies was obviously intrigued, but his eagerness to leave overpowered his curiosity. "I hope you're right, sir. I wish you nothing but the best of luck."

"Thank you." Jacob rubbed his palm over the smooth surface of the bar.

His bar.

CHAPTER 4

Neighbors

After Mr. Davies left, Jacob stood behind the bar and looked over the pub. He couldn't get over the fact that it was his, now, all on his own. He took a deep breath in through his nose, getting hints of mustiness and cheese. The place wasn't much to look at, but it was something tangible, something apart from his father.

With a smile on his lips, he began to explore. His first stop was the back room, which turned out to be both an office and a bedroom. A single bed sat in the back corner, and a large oak desk covered most of the opposite wall. There was a small but heavy-looking safe tucked under the desk. Much like the pub, there were no decorations of any kind in the room.

Jacob sat down at the desk and rummaged through the drawers, finding records of supplies and sales dating back at least twenty years. From what he could tell, the pub had been in a slow but steady decline for about half that time. He wondered why Mr. Davies hadn't done more to try and reverse the trend, but figured it was nothing more than an old dog and new tricks kind of thing. Jacob's father had been resistant to change in the social world but was quick to accept innovations when it came to business. He would have had this pub earning several times as much money, but probably wouldn't have had Cora working behind the bar. He likely would have bought out the other side of the building from the faun woman, too, whether by a large sum of money or increasing levels of coercion.

Jacob pushed back from the desk and waltzed into the bar area. Mrs. Covington was asleep on her little bed. Her gentle snoring was the only sound inside the pub.

"I'll let you get your beauty sleep," Jacob whispered. "Hopefully Cora and Tadrick get here before too long so they can show me what you like to eat. I'm guessing it's not cheese."

In a little alcove around the corner, he found an answer to the question of Mrs. Covington's food. A feeder of sorts had remnants of dried hay in the bowl part on the ground. He still didn't know where they kept her food, though.

Jacob crept around the bar and inspected the tables and chairs set throughout the pub's floor. Counting the stools at the bar, there was seating for twenty-one people. Four tables with four chairs each, and five stools at the bar, although one of them was balanced precariously on three legs. Jacob wondered when the place had last been at capacity. Judging from the dust under most of the tables, it had probably been quite a while.

His next stop on the tour of his new place was out through the back door. The sound of rushing water greeted him as he stepped out. The creek made a sharp bend behind the pub, running roughly parallel to both the side and back walls. Not twenty feet from the back door was a pool of still water the entire pub could have fit into. The pool was slowly fed by the creek, and a trickling stream seemed to slowly return water back to the creek on the other side. Jacob couldn't tell if it was a natural water feature, or if Mr. Davies had made an artificial pond for Mrs. Covington. Either way, it was a fantastic garden area.

A wooden box sat just outside the back door. Jacob lifted the lid and found it to be full of hay. He grabbed a handful and wandered back inside. After setting the hay in the bowl, he leaned against the bar and wondered what he was going to do first.

A soft knock sounded from the adjoining wall between the pub and the faun restaurant. Something metal fell to the floor with a clang, and a woman's voice said something unintelligible.

"I think I'll go meet my new neighbor," he said; whether to himself or the capybara, he wasn't really sure.

As he stepped out onto the street, he found a world alive with activity. Most of it was from across the bridge, on the cobblestone streets, but there were people coming and going on the dirt road, too. The babbling of the creek could just be heard above the hubbub of town life.

Jacob took two steps toward the other business, then stopped short. He couldn't introduce himself to his building mate without bearing some kind of gift. At least he thought that was the appropriate thing to do. His parents had always brought some kind of gift when they were invited to someone's house. Maybe it was nothing more than a tradition between rich humans, but Jacob preferred to be safe rather than sorry when it came to the first meeting with someone he'd need to get along with for the foreseeable future. He also wanted to show her that he was not bigoted against her in any way. But would he be going overboard just to prove he wasn't someone like his father?

Jacob shook his head. Getting a gift for someone was a nice thing to do, regardless of traditions. He probably shouldn't overthink it.

He searched the area for anyone selling anything gift-like. Finding nothing besides a stray dog doing its business in the middle of the dirt road, he hurried over the bridge and immersed himself in the bustle. Many wares were being hocked— everything from pastries to wands to shoes—but nothing jumped out at him. He was about to give up when he noticed a small stand on the corner of an intersection selling potted plants. Most of them were tiny trees, meticulously pruned into wonderful shapes. They looked like majestic evergreens but were no more than six inches high.

"How much for one of these trees?" he asked the woman running the stand.

"One silver." She gave him a warm nod with her eyes closed.

Jacob held back his surprise, but that was a lot of money for a little plant. He tried to decide if he could spare a full silver for something like this. The answer was that he really shouldn't, but the little tree was just too perfect to pass up.

He fumbled through his coin purse, produced a silver, and took the best-looking tree.

"Thank you," the woman said. "They bring good fortune, you know?"

"I hadn't heard that," Jacob said. "Thank you." With a nod, he headed back over the bridge. He deftly side-stepped the present the dog had left in the road and stopped in front of the restaurant door.

After knocking, he ran his free hand through his tangled hair and tried out different standing positions in hopes to discover the friendliest way to stand. He ended up with legs awkwardly crossed and one hand behind his back.

The door opened and a woman about two heads shorter than Jacob appeared. She had curled horns on either side of her head, both surrounded by curls of long brown hair. She wore glasses and a plain white blouse over britches that cut off at her knees. The bottom halves of her legs, including her hooves, were unadorned. The scent of something unfamiliar, but wonderful wafted out from inside.

"Hello." Her accent was thick but clearly understandable. If she noticed Jacob's burn scar, she didn't let it show.

"Hello." Jacob thrust out the potted tree. "I am the new owner of Mrs. Covington's pub. I have brought you a potted tree that brings good fortune as a gift. And I probably should have led with this, but my name is Jacob." The words came out in a stuttering rush.

The woman took the tree with a smile. "Well, thank you so much! My name is Juniper." Two kids peered out from behind her legs. They looked to be about ten years old or so, but Jacob was horrible at guessing the ages of children. "This is Aspen and Ceda." She gestured at the kids with the potted plant. "They both just turned five last month."

"Good to meet you all."

"Would you like to come in? I could serve you a little breakfast in return for this beautiful gift."

"Sure." If whatever she was cooking tasted half as good as it smelled, he wasn't going to pass it up.

She led him into the restaurant, the kids continuing to use her legs as a place to hide.

"You can have a seat right here and I'll bring something right out."

Jacob smiled and sat at a table draped in a dark red tablecloth. The fabric was extremely smooth— a rare silk from the southern islands.

The restaurant's seating area was small and cozy. The walls were adorned with paintings of forest scenes, and each table had a glowing candle hanging over its top in an ornamental sconce. A fireplace was tucked into the back corner but looked as if it hadn't been used in years.

While Jacob looked over the place, Juniper disappeared into the back and returned with a small basket full of little triangular things.

"In the human tongue, these are called corn chips." She set the basket down in front of him. "You can try a few while I get your proper meal together."

Jacob picked up one of the corn chips, sniffed it, then took a bite. The crunch was a bit startling, the salty flavor fantastic. He popped the rest of it into his mouth and crunched happily. He had never eaten anything quite like it. Before Juniper returned, holding a steaming pie on a plate, Jacob had eaten the entire basket.

"You like the chips, then?"

"They're amazing!" He had licked the salt from two fingers before becoming self-aware enough to stop.

"I'm glad to hear it." She set the plate down.

His proper meal looked like an elongated meat pie of some sort. There was a crust, or more like a wrap, of something around a generous helping of filling. When prompted, he picked up a fork and cut into it, finding that it cut rather easily. The inside was strange, but not unappealing. Cautiously optimistic, Jacob shoveled a forkful into his mouth.

At first, the taste was both overpowering and delicious, but after a few chews, a flavor that could only be described as dirt came to the forefront. Jacob tried to keep his expression impassive, but Juniper could read his displeasure.

"It tastes like soil to you, doesn't it?"

Jacob took some time chewing and swallowing to compose an answer. "It definitely has a flavor I'm not used to, but I'm not sure if I'd say soil."

"No, it's okay. A lot of humans seem to get that." She flashed a knowing, and slightly disappointed, smile. "It's the beetroot. Fauns absolutely love beetroot, but apparently, not everyone shares our enthusiasm for it.

"I've tried to sell pies without beetroot to humans, but it's been tough to get the word out. I think most humans around here have already made their minds up about faun food." She took the plate from the table. "I should have made you one without beetroot, but it would have taken longer. I had this one ready to go."

"Oh, that's okay," Jacob said. "The chicken is really good. And those chips were incredible."

"Thank you." She looked as if she wanted to say more, but stopped herself short. When Jacob also remained silent, gazing awkwardly at her, she let it out. "I'm afraid that business has not been good. I'm sorry about getting too serious, here, but if things don't turn around, I'm going to be forced to close soon. I just thought that maybe you should know that since you're my new neighbor."

"I'm sorry to hear that. I..."

"It's okay." She forced a smile.

"But what about the kids? Is their father around to help?" Jacob immediately turned a deep red. "I'm so sorry. That's none of my business at all."

"It's alright. Their father died when they were very young, in a mining accident."

Jacob had a vague awareness that a disproportionate number of fauns had been put to work in various mines across the islands. He had heard the working conditions were awful, and that it was one of the most dangerous jobs in the League. The fact that his father's company had profited because of such things made him sick to his stomach.

"We'll get by, one way or another," Juniper continued. "I don't mean to trouble you with our problems. I just wanted to make you aware you might be getting a new neighbor before long."

"Is there any way I can help?"

"I don't think so." Juniper smiled. "Thank you, though."

Jacob wracked his brain, but couldn't think of anything he could do to help. This woman was so kind, and she had two little ones to look after. She deserved all the success in the world.

"There used to be a lot of fauns here, back when the iron mines were operating," Juniper said. "You should have seen this place back then. We had a line out the door at times! I don't know if you've seen them, but the old iron mines are just up the road to the north. Unfortunately, about two years back, the mines were tapped, so most of the fauns working this island moved on. It's not exactly easy for fauns to thrive outside of mining operations here in the League. Not all humans are as welcoming as you are." She pointed to her potted plant and forced another smile. "I should probably try to relocate to whichever mines are flourishing these days, but I don't want to uproot the kids. This place is all they know, and they like it here. They've got friends here."

"Mrs. Covington's has been struggling as well. Do you think the two are related?"

"I couldn't say for sure, but I don't think New Dawn has fully recovered from the loss of the mining operation. It seems to be bouncing back, but the process has been painfully slow."

"Gods, I wish there was something I could do to help you." Jacob stared at the floor.

"I appreciate the sentiment, but we'll be alright. I'll do what I need to do to keep these kids healthy and happy. I have done, and I will do. Simple as that."

Jacob envied her resiliency.

Mrs. Covington stretched out her front feet after climbing out of bed. She shuffled over to her feeder and sniffed the fresh hay there. It was appetizing, but something else was more appealing this morning. There was a dense cluster of water hyacinths growing toward the back of the pool, and that would be the perfect breakfast.

In no hurry, Mrs. Covington made her way through her capybara-sized door in the back of the building. She walked through the grass to the edge of the pool, wiggled her backside, then leaped into the water, submerging her entire body.

She came up near the middle of the pond and paddled to the hyacinths. Without delay, she began munching on them. The crunchy stalks and leaves were filling, and the blooms added a little bit of sweetness to make the perfect meal.

After getting her fill, she lazily swam out into the middle of the pond. She submerged everything but the very top of her head and just floated.

The babbling of the creek was soothing, but there was still an edge of uneasiness in every waking moment lately.

Mrs. Covington wasn't used to being alone.

She longed to be among other capybaras.

Time drifted by as she floated in slow circles. At some point, a small bird alighted on the top of her head. She changed nothing, unbothered and even welcoming the tiny visitor, who eventually flew off toward the rising sun.

Feeling physically refreshed, she dipped her head under the surface, performed a few graceful rolls underwater, and made her way back to shore.

CHAPTER 5

Partners

When Jacob returned to the pub, Tadrick was there, wiping the bar with a wet rag.

"Good morning, Tadrick!" Jacob's voice must have been too loud, as it provoked a cringe.

"Hey, Boss." Tadrick's voice had its usual gloominess.

"Hey, I know it's probably awkward, but would you mind telling me a little bit about yourself?" Jacob realized, too late, that his voice had been getting higher and higher as he asked the question. "What kind of things do you like to do?"

Tadrick looked up from his work with an expression of mild annoyance, but then the faintest hint of a smile appeared. Jacob liked to think it was his own genuine interest that elicited the change, but he couldn't be sure.

"I'm writing a book." The smile grew, still subtle, but definitely there.

"Seriously? That's fantastic."

Now Tadrick's smile was in full bloom.

"What's it about? If you don't mind me asking."

"Well..." He hesitated, as if unused to this kind of question. "It's about a dragon from a different world that comes here and wants to rule over the islands." His face reddened. "And there's this guy who works at an old pub that kind of falls into the job of being the only person who can stop the dragon."

"That sounds fascinating." Jacob never would have thought of writing a make-believe book in a million years.

"Thanks." Tadrick turned even redder. "It's not like anyone will ever see it or anything. It's just...my real life is so uneventful. It's nice to escape into an exciting story sometimes."

"Yeah." Jacob nodded. Although he wanted to nudge Tadrick into having real adventures, he figured nodding was more appropriate for someone he'd just met.

The door of the pub swung open and Cora came in backward, holding a small box filled with fruit. She greeted the two men with smiles, then set the box down for Mrs. Covington, who had come out from behind the bar to see her. The capybara sniffed it, then took a nibble from a dragon fruit.

"Good morning," Jacob said as Cora playfully slapped Tadrick on the back of his head.

"Hello, Boss."

"You're the second one to call me that this morning." Jacob was torn on the subject. On one hand, being called boss filled him with a sense of pride, of worthiness. On the other, it didn't fit with the plan he'd devised for turning the pub around.

"Well, you *are* the boss, now." Tadrick shrugged.

"Actually, I wanted to talk to you two about that."

Both of them looked confused.

"You're not going to fire us, are you?" Tadrick switched from confusion to anxiety in a blink.

"No, no." Jacob held his hands up. "I have a proposition for you."

Cora remained confused, while Tadrick didn't seem to know which emotion to convey.

"I was wondering if you'd have any interest in being my partners, here."

"What do you mean by that?" Cora was clearly skeptical.

"I mean that the pub would be owned by the three of us. We would make decisions about it together, and share equally in the profits if there were any."

No one responded.

"It would be a bit of a risk for you because I would no longer pay you a wage. But if we can get this place going again, the potential for you to earn much more than you're earning now is there. The more the pub succeeds, the more we all succeed." He gave them his best I'm-not-bull-shitting-you-and-I-hope-you'll-agree grin. He wasn't bullshitting, but his motives weren't completely altruistic. Bringing them in and giving them a stake in the fate of the pub was, first and foremost, a business decision.

"But we haven't paid anything in," Cora said, eyebrows still pinched.

"We'll start on slightly uneven ground in that regard, but I think you'll make up for it with your knowledge of pub business and this town in general." Jacob shrugged.

When another span of silence ensued, Jacob said, "So...what do you think?"

"You're completely serious about this?" Tadrick's eyes narrowed.

"Absolutely."

"Are you just trying to get out of paying us a wage?"

Jacob laughed, having not thought of that angle. "No, I promise you. In fact, if you want, you can immediately take charge of our finances. I have seven silver left that I'm willing to use for improvements, but after that's spent, we can start at zero and split all future profits, and costs, three ways."

Tadrick gave Cora a questioning look. As they shared a long moment, Jacob realized how close the two of them were.

At some unseen cue, they both looked back to Jacob.

"I'm in." Tadrick was the first to answer.

"Me too." Cora still had a bit of skepticism in her voice.

"Great!" Jacob shook hands with his two new partners. "I'll draw up a contract for you to read and, if it's agreeable, sign."

Jacob hurried to his office and wrote a simply worded contract on a piece of parchment. When he brought it out, Cora read it at least three times, then signed her name. Tadrick was clearly satisfied if Cora was because he signed it without even perusing the document.

As Cora read the contract, Jacob had filled three mugs with beer. When they had both signed, he distributed the mugs.

"To a successful partnership." He held his mug aloft.

Tadrick and Cora clinked their mugs into his, and they all drank.

"Now," Jacob said, wasting no time, "our first order of business is improvements, if you'll agree?"

"Yes!" Tadrick agreed, then immediately looked down as if embarrassed.

"Absolutely." Cora vigorously nodded her head.

"I know you've got ideas, so let me have 'em."

"We need more natural light in here!" Cora was the most animated Jacob had seen her. "A bigger window, or a big door we could keep open on the creek side. And maybe even some outdoor seating by the creek."

"That all sounds wonderful," Jacob agreed. Already this gambit seemed to be paying off. He wasn't sure he would have thought of something like that.

"And decorations," Tadrick added. "It's so...depressing in here. We need a theme. I was thinking maybe nautical? Like ships' wheels and paintings of krakens and stuff like that?"

"Yes!" Nothing could have appealed more to Jacob.

Cora and Tadrick both blurted out a comment at the same time.

Cora said, "The cheese block has got to go."

Tadrick said, "No more cheese block."

Jacob wrinkled his nose. "Yeah, it's not the most appetizing thing, is it?"

All three of them turned their heads to face the cuboidal monstrosity on the bar. As if on cue, a fly landed on its corner.

Tadrick raised his hand like a schoolboy in class, then brought it back down quickly, face reddening again. "My partner plays in a band that does sea shanties. Mr. Davies was never into the idea, but maybe they could...play here? I think it would drum up a little business. They've got a small but loyal following on the island."

"Sure." Jacob nodded. "That sounds great."

Mrs. Covington bit into a particularly juicy piece of fruit, making a squelching sound that drew their attention. Jacob smiled at the sight, but Cora's shoulders slumped.

"She's a shell of her former self," she said, shaking her head.

"Really?" Jacob said. "Why?"

"Lonely, I suppose. Ever since Arthur left."

"Arthur?"

"Her husband. Well, we called him that anyway. He used to belong to me and my betrothed, but my betrothed took him when we broke the engagement, just to be spiteful."

"The guy doesn't even have Arthur anymore," Tadrick added.

"Yeah, he recently moved off island, so his parents took Arthur in. Now the poor little capybara is neglected, and just sits in a small pen on the edge of their farm."

Jacob wasn't used to assessing the moods of capybaras, but now that Cora had mentioned it, Mrs. Covington did seem a little down in the dumps.

"I think the pub has suffered ever since Arthur left," Cora said.

"The pub?"

"Yeah, you know how on a ship they always have a capybara aboard for good luck?"

"Yes."

"I think it's kinda like that with pubs...maybe." Cora was struggling to get words out, looking to the floor as she spoke. "But maybe having a sad capybara is bad luck, too?" She gave an over-exaggerated shrug.

"You don't seem like the type to believe in luck." Jacob hoped the comment wasn't too familiar.

"I don't," she said, matter-of-factly. "I'm just trying to convince you two that we should get her husband back. I think Mrs. Covington's gloominess is reason enough, personally."

"How would we get him back?"

"Take him." Tadrick's eyes widened as if he just realized this was an option.

"Exactly." Cora and Tadrick performed a strange handshake, or more like a hand slap, above their heads. "It's not like they would even know Arthur was gone."

"So, what are we talking about here?" Jacob held his arms out, a quizzical look on his face.

"I'm talking about a capybara heist," Cora said, positively shining.

CHAPTER 6

Capybara Heist

Jacob was torn. On one side, the adventure and justice of the idea was filling him with joy and excitement. On the other, he absolutely did not want to get in trouble with any authorities before his time on his own could even get started.

A dispiriting fantasy took shape in his head—one in which he went to jail, was bailed out by his father, and was never truly free again.

However, this whole thing seemed like the perfect opportunity to bond with his new business partners. Helping them steal the capybara back could potentially make him one of them. They'd be like a pirate crew in a way; a small way, but still a way. If they were to bond, the business could only be better for it. They would be united in the common goal of making the pub succeed.

"You sure they won't notice?" he asked.

Cora and Tadrick were going over a tentative plan using beer mugs to represent people on the bar, which functioned as the farm in question.

"I'm positive they won't give a shit." Cora, using her hand to represent a fence, jumped a glass from one side to the other.

"Why don't we just buy him back?" Jacob asked.

"Tadrick already tried that," Cora said. "They told him they were holding on to it for their son, and it wasn't for sale."

"What if...a constable is around and sees us?" Jacob nervously rubbed the burn scar on his cheek.

"There's only one constable in New Dawn, now, and he's only interested in matters of money," Tadrick said. "He wouldn't bat an eye at the humane rehoming of an unhappy capybara."

"And I've been staking the place out," Cora added. "The constable is never out that way."

"Staking it out?" Jacob wondered just how much criminal activity Cora was into.

"Yeah. Just getting an idea about how a heist might go. The place is pretty quiet. I probably would have already done it, but Mr. Davies asked me not to."

"Oh."

As Jacob pondered the idea, he watched Cora and Tadrick continue to form their ridiculous plan. He couldn't seem to keep a smile from his lips.

"What will you need me to do?"

~

The fact that they didn't get one customer that night would have been worrying, but on this occasion, Jacob was glad for it. He found that his concern about the lack of customers was paling in comparison to his anxiety about the impending heist.

The night was fairly dark. The Ring's soft silvery light was dulled by a thick layer of clouds, letting through just enough light for Jacob to see his feet as he padded toward the edge of the farm.

His job was simple. He was to be the lookout and to give Cora and Tadrick a signal if anyone crossed their path during the operation.

On the walk over to the farm where the capybara was being kept, Jacob became increasingly troubled with the lack of seriousness his partners were showing. They seemed completely unbothered by thoughts of getting caught. Jacob, on the other hand, was already sweating through his shirt.

After five minutes of anxiety-riddled travel, they arrived at a small wooden house sitting just inside a two-rail fence that also surrounded a large pasture. At least twenty goats were in differing degrees of wakefulness throughout the pasture.

"This is it." Cora waved them forward, past the house until it was barely visible. She turned to Tadrick, giddy with excitement as they approached the fence. "You ready?"

Tadrick nodded.

Cora looked at Jacob. "You ready, boss?"

Jacob shot her a disapproving look.

"I mean, you ready, Jacob?"

"Sure." It was definitely more of a question than an answer.

"Alright."

Jacob watched as the two of them scaled the fence onto the property of Cora's one-time betrothed. Tadrick caught a foot on the cross rail and face-planted into the pasture, prompting Cora to break into an uncontrollable giggling fit. The goats began to take notice of the invaders. Many of them standing and staring.

"Shh," Jacob scolded, eyeing the house, but they were too far away to hear him.

Heart bounding in his chest, he continued to watch them until they disappeared through the groggy goats into darkness. He turned and tried his best to act nonchalant. The act couldn't have been very good, though, because he was constantly scanning up and down the road.

A nightbird sang to the east, causing him to flinch and curse under his breath.

Feeling ridiculous, he took a long breath in through his nose and let it out slowly.

A fat brown toad hopped onto the road, then proceeded to cross it in two big leaps. Jacob was momentarily proud of himself for not flinching at its appearance until he considered how absurd that was.

He did flinch again when something caught his eye from down the road to the north. He squinted in the dark, trying to make out what could have been a figure in the middle distance.

A twig snapped behind him. The sharp sound echoed across the pasture. He looked, but couldn't see any indication of what made the sound, figuring it was Cora or Tadrick somewhere beyond his sight.

Jacob focused his attention back on the place he'd seen movement.

It was, in fact, a figure. And it was moving in his direction.

"Shit," Jacob said as a clearer image of the approaching figure took shape. It looked to be a man wearing a dark coat with oversized buttons down the middle. The figure wore a hat that was rounded but came to a point on the top. A metal badge on the man's chest caught the Ringlight.

It was the town's only constable.

Jacob encircled his mouth with his hands and made his best crow caw—the agreed-upon signal. Jacob had practiced before they left the pub, but the caws had sounded much better then. The sudden dryness in his mouth made this crow sound sick.

The constable kept coming.

Jacob looked to the sky, pretending to search for crows.

"Whatcha doin' out here?" the constable called as he neared.

"Just trying to catch a crow." The words spilled out before he could give them any thought.

The constable stopped in his tracks for a moment. "Why in the world would you be doin' that?"

"Well, I...think they're delicious." He tried to fight the urge to glance in Cora and Tadrick's direction, but couldn't help himself. They were still nowhere to be seen.

"You're not from around here, are you?" The man continued walking toward Jacob.

"I just moved here."

"From where?"

"First Frontier."

"Do they eat crows in First Frontier?" The constable was standing very near Jacob now. His face was scrunched up in confusion. He had a thick mustache that curled up on the ends and kind but suspicious eyes.

"Yes. Some people do. Have you never had crow noodle soup?" Jacob had no idea where this nonsense was coming from.

"Can't say that I have."

"Well, you should try it. My mom's crow noodle soup is delicious." He glanced at the pasture again. This time the constable did the same.

"So, you're trying to tell me that you're out here in the middle of the night cawing to random crows in hopes to catch one so you can make soup?"

"Yes?"

"Hmm." The constable scanned the entire area, a look of mild concern on his face. "What are you really do—"

The door to the house flung open, and a ciguapa woman stepped out onto the porch. "What's going on here?" she asked the constable.

"I'm trying to figure that out, Miss." The constable removed his hat.

Out of the corner of his eye, Jacob saw Cora and Tadrick jogging toward him, awkwardly holding a capybara between them. Without thinking, he encircled his mouth again and let out a forceful caw.

"Sir!" The constable furrowed his brow as he slammed the hat back on his head. "Please refrain from this nonsense in the presence of this woman." His tone was much more authoritative, now.

"I'm sorry," Jacob said. "I thought I saw one on the house."

When the constable looked up at the house, Jacob hazarded another glance to the pasture. Cora and Tadrick had set the capybara down, then fallen to their hands and knees, trying to blend in with the goats.

As if the gods were taunting them, there was a break in the cloud cover, and the pasture was suddenly bathed in silvery Ringlight.

"Have you ever seen this man before?" the constable asked the woman.

Tentatively, she came closer. "No, I haven't."

The capybara was meandering in their direction, stopping every few steps to nibble on grass.

"What did you catch him doing out here?" the woman asked.

"He claims to be trying to catch crows, but I'm not buying what he's selling. He keeps glancing into your pasture. Does he look anything like the person you reported the other night?"

"No. Not at all. That was a woman. A ciguapa if I'm not mistaken."

The capybara shuffled up to the woman while making soft grunting noises.

"How did you get out?" she asked the capybara.

The creature tried to nuzzle her leg, but she took a step back in disgust.

"That have anything to do with you?" the constable said to Jacob, pointing at the capybara.

"I didn't let it out. I swear."

Either annoyed or spooked by Cora and Tadrick among their ranks, the goats began to wander away, leaving the would-be thieves exposed.

They tried to crawl along with the herd, but that only prompted the goats to run away faster.

"Miss." The constable pointed. "There are people crawling in your pasture." He put his hand on the baton at his side.

The woman turned her head and gasped.

Cora bleated.

"Cora?" the woman said. "Is that you?"

Cora refused to break character, remaining on her hands and knees in the grass.

"I can clearly see you, Cora," the woman said. "What's going on here?"

Finally admitting defeat, Cora and Tadrick stood and sheepishly made their way to the fence.

"Well?" The constable's baton was halfway out of its holster. "Tell us what's going on here."

Cora sighed, then looked at the woman. "We were trying to take Arthur back, Mrs. Juno."

"Arthur?"

"The capybara." Cora pointed.

Mrs. Juno looked thoroughly confused. "So, you're out here in the middle of the night with two humans trying to sneak it away? Why didn't you just ask me for it?"

"Uh... I didn't think you would give him to me. When your son and I broke our engagement, it wasn't exactly pretty."

"He never treated you the way he should have. I don't blame you at all for getting rid of him."

"Oh."

In the silence that followed, Jacob watched with relief as the constable slid his baton back down where it was supposed to be.

"But to see you out here in the middle of the night pretending to be a goat..." The woman shook her head. "Maybe I understand his side, too."

Cora maintained eye contact with the woman, flashing a hint of an apologetic smile.

"Was it you I saw out here a few nights ago lurking around?"

"Yes, ma'am."

"Hmm." Her head never stopped shaking.

The constable took a step closer to Mrs. Juno. "What would you like me to do with this lot?"

The woman looked each of them in the eye, an expression of vague pity on her face.

The constable tensed an almost unnoticeable amount. His hand moved slowly back to his baton.

Jacob's heart bounded even harder.

"We never wanted that thing here in the first place," Mrs. Juno finally said. "We were holding onto it for my son, but the goddess knows he's never going to take responsibility for it. So, go ahead. If you want it that bad, it's yours." She flicked a hand as if shooing them all away.

"You sure?" There might have been a slight note of disappointment in the constable's voice, but Jacob may have been imagining it.

"Yes. Just get everyone out of here, please. I would like nothing more than to get back to bed."

"Alright, you heard her." The constable's voice boomed with authority. "Collect the capy and get moving."

Cora rushed to the capybara, picked him up with both arms, and passed him to Jacob on the other side of the fence. The creature's feet were wet and muddy, and he squirmed with an unexpected strength, but Jacob held onto him and immediately walked away. "Thank you," he called behind him, quickening his pace.

"I'm sorry, Mrs. Juno," Cora called as she leaped the fence.

Tadrick gave the constable an awkward salute as he passed, smearing a line of mud across his forehead.

The two younger conspirators caught up and hurried away on either side of Jacob. None of the three looked back.

Only when he was back within the safe confines of his new pub did Jacob allow himself to smile. Until then, he had been hyper-focused on getting away from the scene of the crime before anyone changed their minds.

Cora and Tadrick had been holding back giggles the entire way. Now, inside, they burst out laughing.

Tadrick set the capybara on the floor and it started sniffing along the wall, heading slowly toward the place where Mrs. Covington slept.

"How in the world did we just get away with that?" Cora said between guffaws.

"We must have had the worst luck in the world, then the best luck in the world, within minutes of each other." Tadrick rested his palm on his forehead, grinning.

Jacob chuckled along, caught up in their carefree mirth.

"And then you bleated!"

All three of them doubled over with laughter. Tadrick put a hand on the bar to help himself stay upright, while Cora plopped down in the middle of the floor.

"What did you think?" Tadrick said. "They were gonna say, 'Oh, I thought I saw someone crawling on their hands and knees, but that was such a perfect bleat, it must be one of the goats'?"

Tears were forming in Jacob's eyes. His abdominal muscles were starting to ache. He didn't think he had laughed like this his entire life. For the first time, he felt like he belonged on this island with these people, and that maybe everything was actually going to be alright.

From the floor, Cora bleated again.

Tears streamed down Jacob's face, now. He folded his arms on the bar next to Tadrick and rested his forehead on them, trying to catch his breath.

Strange chattering and squeaking sounds came from behind him, so he turned mid-laugh to find that Arthur had reunited with Mrs. Covington. The two of them were nuzzling each other and excitedly chatting in their own language.

The laughter slowly faded away, but smiles remained plastered on everyone's faces.

"Oh, Arthur needs something!" Cora jumped up from the floor, hurried to the bar, and began rummaging through some drawers that Jacob hadn't known were there. In a matter of seconds, she held up a fancy black bowtie. "He's got to be presentable for his wife." She crouched down and clasped the tie around his neck. He didn't seem to mind at all.

"It's good to have him back," Tadrick said. "It's been too long."

Cora nodded as she scratched behind Arthur's ear. With his eyes closed, the capybara leaned into the scratch, purring.

CHAPTER 7

Renewal

The next morning, Tadrick showed up early holding a crate that was almost too big for him to carry. After backing through the door with considerable effort, he dropped the crate on the nearest table with a crash.

"What do you have there?" Jacob said as he rounded the bar.

"Just some decoration ideas."

The biggest, most noticeable object in the crate was a framed painting of a ship at full sail cresting a giant swell.

"I had an idea that I could paint a tiny Mrs. Covington on the ship," Tadrick said as he pulled it from the crate. "Like maybe with her front feet on the rail, peering over the side? Unless that sounds stupid?"

"Not stupid at all. But I didn't know you were a painter, too."

"I'm not a very good one, but I could make it work."

"I absolutely love the idea of filling these walls up with paintings of ships with Mrs. Covington added on."

Tadrick brightened.

"I've got this, too." Tadrick heaved out a brass ship's bell with a mounting bracket attached. "I figured we could ring it when it's time for last orders...if we have customers at closing time."

"Fantastic." Jacob took the bell when Tadrick handed it to him and began polishing it with his sleeve.

"All that's left is this old compass and a few smaller pictures." He

revealed a compass as big as a dinner plate, and two small framed paintings—one of a capybara with a monkey on its back, and another of a
palm tree.

"Perfect. It'll be nice to liven this place up a little."

They found a hammer and some nails in one of the drawers and
began strategizing about where to hang the various decorations. While
they tried different ideas out, Jacob asked Tadrick about the Fenton
treasure.

"I wish I had something for you, but I don't," Tadrick said. "I feel
like I've spent so much of my life thinking about that damn clue. I'm
kinda done with it." The corner of his mouth turned up. "I mean, I say
that, but it's not completely true. If some new insight revealed itself, I'd
be right back in."

"You said Mr. Davies got one of the ten posted copies of the poem.
How many people even know about this treasure?"

"Not as many as you'd think. Those ten poems were snatched up
pretty fast, and not too many people were willing to share the information on them. Mr. Davies kept his pretty close to the vest. He eventually
showed me and Cora, but we couldn't figure any of it out."

With their mouths busy talking about the treasure, they used only
looks and nods to decide that the compass and small paintings should go
up on the wall behind the bar. Jacob hammered in nails, and Tadrick
hung the decorations.

"Is the old woman who wrote the poem still alive?" Jacob asked as
he hammered.

"Nope. She orchestrated this whole treasure hunt when she got
really sick. She had her kids hide it for her, and promise her they'd never
reveal its location. There's a rumor that she had a crisis of conscience
when she was near death. She felt she hadn't done enough with her
money to make the world a better place."

"Are her kids around anymore?"

"Also no. After Mrs. Fenton died, her property was supposed to go
to her children, but there was some kind of legal trickery her ex-husband
—a previous marriage, not the kids' father—used in order to pull the
land out from under them. A guy named Mr. Lowell owns the entire
estate now. I think I've heard that the kids moved to Paradise Island."

"Huh... Do you know anything about this Mr. Lowell?"

"Just that he's a prick. I haven't met the guy personally, but that's the overwhelming majority of the gossip about him." Tadrick shrugged. "He's the commissioner of the city council, too. What do you think about right here?" He held the large painting up in the middle of the north wall. "That way it's the first thing people see when they come in."

"Perfect," said Jacob.

There was a knock at the door, and Juniper poked her head in. "Hello. Alright if I come in?"

"Of course." Jacob waved her inside with exaggerated movements.

"I heard some hammering over here and thought you might like a snack." In her hand was a plate of those corn chips.

"You thought right. Thank you!"

She set the plate down on the bar with a smile. Jacob immediately grabbed a chip and crunched into it.

"Have you tried these?" he asked Tadrick.

"Yeah. They're great, right?"

"I love 'em," Jacob said while crunching.

There was another, louder, knock on the door.

"Come in," called Jacob.

Yandro, the ciguapa delivery man, opened the door and stepped just inside. He scanned the pub and was visibly discouraged by Cora's absence.

"Hey, I...heard this place had a new owner, and I was just wondering if you'd like to continue ordering supplies from me."

"Of course, I will," Jacob said. "But I do have some questions. Come in."

"Alright." Yandro entered and let the door close behind him.

"Do you do shipments to other pubs in town?"

"Yeah."

"Could you tell me what some of the more popular pubs are serving as far as food?"

"Mostly meat," Yandro said. "Pork chops and leg of mutton are really popular right now."

"Hmm." This pub didn't have the means to cook such things unless they used the fireplace, which was a silly idea. Jacob pictured himself reaching into the fireplace and turning over legs of mutton. The chances were better that he would accidentally knock them into the fire or burn himself again than cook them to perfection.

"I gotta warn you, meat prices are pretty high." Yandro pointed his thumb toward the ceiling. "Mr. Lowell just raised his prices again."

"How can one man control the price of meat?"

"He owns pretty much all the farmable land on the island. And getting meat from off-island has its own costs. So, people buy it because it's really the only game in town."

Jacob's thoughts went immediately to his father's business. They were in different lines of work but had very similar tactics. They would use their wealth and influence to dominate the shipping market in their area, then raise prices to get as much as they could out of people. Jacob never really thought about how it affected so many people in so many ways. A sudden surge of self-loathing washed over him, but he tried his best to ignore it.

"What about fish?" he said. "There are countless fish vendors down by the docks. That much competition should lead to some pretty decent prices."

"True," said Yandro, "but I think people get their fill of fish at home. It's pretty much the main staple here, just like any of the islands, but people want something different when they're out at a pub." He shrugged.

"Oh." Jacob saw truth in that. He had grown up on not much else besides fish. He still liked it but could see the appeal of something different. "What about chickens?" he offered. "Couldn't people raise their own chickens for meat?"

"Sure." Juniper pointed in the direction of her restaurant. "I raise chickens in the back of my place. Most of the food I serve has chicken in it."

"So why don't they just do that?" Jacob asked Yandro.

"I don't know, sir. It's just what people want right now. I think it's a social status thing. I still have a hard time figuring out how humans think. No offense, sir."

"None taken. And you can call me Jacob. I struggle quite a bit with how most humans think, too. So, we've got that in common." He flashed a hopefully-warm smile.

Yandro smiled back. "Mr. Davies was pretty stuck on the whole cheese thing. You're kinda overloaded with the stuff. Maybe you could figure out something to do with it?" He shrugged again.

"Yeah..." Jacob pondered the idea but had nothing.

Yandro scanned the pub again, possibly wondering if he'd missed Cora the first time. "Well, I've gotta get going. More shipments to make and all that."

"Thank you for stopping by, Yandro."

Everyone waved to the disappointed-looking Yandro as he left.

Not five minutes passed before Cora showed up at the pub.

"You just missed Yandro," Tadrick said, with just a hint of teasing in his voice.

"Really?" She instinctively looked back at the door. When she turned back around, her cheeks had darkened a shade or two. "Oh, well." She did her best to seem unconcerned, but Jacob wasn't buying it.

"You like what we've done so far?" Jacob held his hands out toward the decorations they had put up.

"I do." Cora's eyes widened. "Looking a lot better already."

The pride Jacob felt seemed disproportionate to the amount of work he'd done.

"But it would look a lot better with some natural light coming in from over here." She pointed to the unadorned west wall.

"How do you propose we go about doing that?" Jacob asked.

"I don't know. Chop the wall down with an axe?"

Jacob wasn't yet sure how to take things Cora said. Most of the time she seemed very literal, but now it seemed like she was joking. Maybe.

"I had some renovations done when I first bought my place," Juniper said. "The orcs who renovated my place did excellent work."

"Orcs?" Jacob didn't know there were orcs on this island.

"Yes. They live in a cave to the northeast, not far past the mines. They're very skilled, and do work for reasonable prices."

Fear took a strange physical form in Jacob's chest. It was a tingling, as if someone had just told him there was a ghost in the room. On a conscious level, he knew this fear was unfounded. If Juniper had recommended them, they must be perfectly nice people. But all his life, Jacob had been taught to fear orcs. Stories read to him as a child depicted them as bloodthirsty monsters.

Of course, he was told less than flattering things about ciguapas and fauns, too, but all those turned out to be untrue.

That kind of thinking was exactly what he was trying to get away from when he moved here. He wasn't going to let fear of the unknown influence his decisions anymore.

"Let's see if they would like to give us an estimate," Jacob said.

CHAPTER 8

Orcs and Doors

Juniper wasn't able to take Jacob to the cave because she couldn't afford to miss any potential lunch customers. Cora knew of the place, though, so she volunteered to take him.

"Their names are Shelu and Korga," Juniper said as they left. "Shelu is the older sister, and Korga is the younger brother. They don't speak the human tongue perfectly, but enough to get by."

Jacob thanked her and they headed north. He was nervous but thankful he was going to see more of the island.

The town of New Dawn didn't extend very far past Mrs. Covington's. After two blocks of modest houses and businesses, the town gave way to nature.

They followed the creek that ran by the pub upstream for two hundred yards or so before it disappeared into a heavily jungle-laden rise to the west.

"So..." Cora kicked a pebble, sending it tumbling down the dirt road. "What did Yandro want at the pub?"

"He was just checking to see if we wanted to change anything about the usual orders."

"What'd you say?"

"I asked him about what other places were doing. Just trying to figure out how we can change our menu."

"Oh." Cora stared straight ahead.

As they continued on in silence, a pandemonium of blue and yellow parrots soared across their path overhead.

"Did he say anything else?" Cora asked, still looking out ahead.

Jacob struggled with a response. He knew what Cora was really asking, but his relatively small amount of interaction with women made him unsure of what to say. It was painfully obvious to anyone who had seen the two together that they had feelings for each other. But Jacob didn't know if he would be doing Yandro a disservice by letting Cora know he'd been looking for her. One of the very few pieces of advice Jacob's father had given him was, "Never forfeit the upper hand, with women, or in business."

Jacob never took much stock in his father's words—they just never felt right to him—but he assumed the man knew considerably more about women than Jacob himself did. In Jacob's limited experience, he never felt he was close to having the upper hand with a woman, or if he even wanted it. Actually, he knew he didn't want it. The idea of trying to dominate anyone in that way cheapened the idea of love.

But what if Yandro wanted the upper hand? Or, on the other side, what if Cora wanted it? Cora was his friend and business partner. Shouldn't he favor her in such things?

After overthinking everything, Jacob decided not to intervene.

"Nope. That was it."

Cora didn't say anything, didn't change her stride or her facial expression, but Jacob could somehow tell that she deflated a bit.

They must have been passing the mines because the hills to the left were mostly barren and had wooden structures built into them. As the two of them walked in silence, Jacob examined the mines—dozens of tunnels bored into the hill at all different levels, with the remnants of roads coming from each one. All of the tunnels had been boarded up, and the roads were barely visible under the saplings trying to regain their proper place.

The scent of wildflowers wafted in on a gentle, cooling sea breeze out of the east. Birdsong filled the air around them as they strolled in between swaths of swaying verdant grasses.

What should have been an enjoyable excursion exploring his new island was slightly tarnished as Jacob worried if he was hindering things between Cora and Yandro. He also couldn't seem to push away the fear of meeting actual orcs. Up until this morning, he would have told anyone he'd be delighted to meet an orc, and he wouldn't have been lying. But now that the meeting was imminent, a visceral unease refused to go away. He hated the feeling. It was proof that, despite his best efforts, he must be bigoted. Guilt and anger roiled in his chest. Most of the anger was directed at his parents, who read him stories like *The Twins and the Snarling Orc* as a child, but the guilt overpowered any of the blame.

Jacob looked at Cora, wondering how she was doing. He cried out and stopped in his tracks. One of the blue and yellow parrots that had flown overhead had somehow landed on Cora's outstretched arm without him hearing it.

"What?" Cora said, stopping and turning to him.

"Sorry...I just. That was unexpected." Jacob could feel his face turning red.

The parrot performed a head-bobbing dance on Cora's arm.

"Can ciguapa...commune with animals?"

"Not any more than anyone else can." Cora gave a half-smile. "This is just an illusion."

Jacob studied the bird more closely. There was absolutely nothing he could see that would indicate the parrot wasn't real.

Cora whispered a word, and the parrot vanished.

"See," she said as she started walking again.

Jacob stood dumbfounded for several seconds, then ran to catch up.

"That was amazing."

"Oh, thanks. I'm actually pretty decent at them. I can do bigger, more elaborate illusions, too, but they drain me quite a bit. I used to practice a lot as a kid." She shrugged.

Up ahead, the path diverged. To the left, it began a set of switch-backs heading up into the hills of the mining operation. To the right, it veered east, toward the sea.

"We go right." Cora pointed.

Jacob followed her down a gentle incline until they reached the edge of a rocky beach. As Cora looked both ways, pondering which way to go, Jacob glanced down and gasped. There was a footprint in the dirt going south from where he was standing. The footprint was at least twice as big as his boot.

"I'm guessing right, again," he said after involuntarily gulping.

"Yeah," Cora pointed to an area along the beach where the rocks rose about thirty feet high, "There it is."

She led him through a stand of palm trees just past the rocky rise, then turned toward the ocean. As they came out from the trees, a fantastic cove opened up in front of them. Black rock cliffs jutted up on either side of a picturesque beach. The cliffs curved toward each other, forming a horseshoe shape that encapsulated all but a ten-foot inlet for water to enter or exit the bay. To the left, about fifty feet away, a cave was carved into the cliff at ground level.

"Hello?" Cora called. Her voice echoed around the cove.

As they approached the cave, tentatively on Jacob's part, a voice called back to them from out in the bay. "Hello," a booming gravely voice called.

Out on the cliff, standing on a ledge about ten feet up from the water, two orcs held fishing rods, their lines bobbing in the gentle waves.

The bigger of the two set the fishing pole down, yelled, "Cannonball!" and leaped from the cliff, curling legs and arms to make the rough approximation of a ball. The splash was huge, as if a real cannonball had plunged into the sea.

The other orc followed the first into the water, preferring a front flip instead of a *cannonball*. The two of them swam surprisingly fast and were stepping onto the beach in moments. As they emerged, something about their demeanor and the smoothness of their gray skin made it seem like they were very young. Jacob had never met an orc before, so he couldn't be sure, but he thought they might be kids, or teenagers at most. They still towered above him; at least two feet higher than the top of Jacob's head. Their arms were bigger around than his legs, shoulders broader than most doors. Still, they weren't as intimidating as he had expected. They seemed to be trying hard to not appear threatening in any way. Their tusky smiles radiated nothing but kindness. Jacob remained tense, however, unable to push away the images that were burned into his mind as a child.

Cora took a step toward them.

"Hello," she said. "I am Cora, and this is Jacob. We are friends of Juniper."

"Juniper." The bigger orc's face lit up with recognition. Her smile exposed the full length of the tusks sticking up from her bottom jaw. "Pleasure to meet you, Cora and Isjacob." Her—the bigger orc was undoubtedly a her—human tongue was slow and heavily accented, but easy to understand. Her voice was gruff, but not unpleasant.

"It's just Jacob," Jacob said, instantly wishing he hadn't.

"Hello, Justjacob, I am Shelu, and this," she pointed, "Korga."

Jacob was done correcting her. He was Justjacob now.

Shelu held out a giant hand, and Jacob did his best to shake it. Her grip was gentle, and she smiled at him as she shook his hand. As he looked up into her kind eyes, the tension he'd been holding throughout his body relaxed.

After all the introductions were made, Cora said, "We need work done at our pub." She spoke slowly and annunciated each word clearly. "How much money to tear out wall and replace with doors?"

Shelu looked to Korga. They discussed something in Orcish. Korga shrugged.

"How big wall?" Shelu asked.

"About twenty feet across and eight feet tall." Jacob tried to walk the line between talking slowly enough and sounding condescending. "The wall is part stone, part wood."

Again, the orcs discussed. They seemed to have a disagreement. The younger brother jerked a thumb into the air several times while the older sister waved a flattened hand back and forth at him.

"Two silvers for work," Shelu finally said. "And you buy wood for doors. Will be...about one silver."

Now it was Jacob and Cora's turn to discuss.

"Is that a lot?" Cora asked.

"It's about half of the money I, or we, have left." Being left with only four silvers was risky. If any unforeseen expenses came up, and the pub continued to not turn a profit, things could get bad in a hurry.

"Hmm." Cora rubbed her shoulder as she pondered.

"Do you think it will increase business?" Jacob asked.

"I do." Cora nodded. "Our pub is like a dungeon, and I don't think the younger crowd is into it. I mean, on cold or stormy days we could close the doors and light up the fireplace and it'd be pretty cozy in there, but on a Finiday night when the weather is nice, a more open concept will be so much better."

Jacob didn't need to think anymore. He was all in on this venture, and he trusted his business partner's judgment. "Let's do it, then."

Cora beamed.

She turned back to the orcs. "Deal."

Again, they shook hands.

"When can you come look at pub?" Cora asked.

"Can we look now?" Korga spoke up from behind his sister.

"Sure."

"We'll be right back." Shelu waved her brother forward.

The orcs hurried to their cave and came back wearing matching brown tunics and black pants. Their feet remained bare.

"Ready," Shelu said.

As they passed through the trees, no one said a word, but once on the road, Jacob felt the urge to break the silence.

"How long have you lived on the island?" He hoped it was as anodyne a question as any.

"Almost year, now," Shelu replied.

Jacob wanted to ask why they were here, but that seemed much too invasive.

"We come here to work for Mr. Lowell," Shelu offered up without him having to ask. "He...recruit orcs from Torsals to work on his...estate."

"So, you work for Mr. Lowell?" Cora asked.

"Not anymore." Korga didn't bother hiding the spite in his voice.

"Are you friend of Mr. Lowell?" Shelu asked.

"No!" Cora was quite animated in her answer.

"Mr. Lowell not treat us good," Shelu continued. "Pay not what he said it would be. Almost nothing. So, we quit and found our cave."

"How old are you?" Jacob just had to know. "If you don't mind me asking?"

"I am...fifteen," Shelu said. "Korga thirteen."

"And you moved away from your parents to work?" Jacob felt he was being too familiar, but his curiosity was enough to push him past that.

"Yes." Korga this time. "Orcs can go to war at this age. Can go to work, too."

"We try to make enough...money to go home," Shelu said. "To

family. Mr. Lowell say we work for one year, then he take us home with lots of coins in our pockets. But that was lie."

"How much do you need?"

"Three gold for each."

"That seems outrageous." Jacob had only paid a few silvers for his passage to New Dawn. Sure, the Torsals—the place where most of the orcs on the islands had settled—was much farther away, but not *that* big of a difference.

"Orc price on human ship," Korga said with a slight scowl.

Cora raised an eyebrow. "Why not take a ciguapa ship?"

"Ciguapa ship same price."

Cora looked both shocked and disappointed at once.

"We already save...five silver." Shelu did her best to make her words sound positive, but they still had fifty-five silver to go if they were both going to buy passage back home. It seemed insurmountable. "Up to... seven after this job."

Jacob hated that orcs were being treated like that. If he had his own ship, he'd charge the same for passage no matter what someone's race.

But what if these orcs hadn't been so kind to him initially? They had every right to distrust humans, and they could have chased Jacob and Cora away; maybe even snarled. If that had happened, would he be as open to the idea of orcs booking passage on his make-believe ship? He liked to think he would, but his ingrained prejudice was stronger than he'd like to admit.

For the rest of the trip up the hill to the main road, he let the fantasy of owning his own ship take over any thoughts of his own shortcomings. He pictured himself as a benevolent captain, standing tall at the ship's wheel—not seasick at all—while everyone looked up to him. His crew was a mix of humans, ciguapa, fauns, and orcs. They were all singing a shanty together.

It took far too long for him to realize the conversation had continued while he was daydreaming. He shook the fantasies away and refocused.

"...a Kraken almost take us down." Shelu mimed an eight-tentacled creature with her hands.

"But we make it to Torsals," Korga added. "Whole family make it."

"Well, that's good," Cora said.

The orcs nodded while looking at their feet.

It seemed that they had been discussing their journey from the Continent, but the conversation was apparently over. Jacob mentally kicked himself. He had wanted to ask about the war on the Continent, and the orcs' voyage across the seemingly never-ending ocean to immigrate to the islands, but he felt he'd missed his chance, now.

They traveled for a while in silence. Every now and then, they would pass someone on the road. There were no major incidents, but humans, fauns, and ciguapas all acted similarly—giving them wide berths and keeping a watchful eye on the orcs as they passed.

Once at the pub, Jacob brought them inside to show them the wall in question. They had to duck their heads while inside but made no complaints. Tadrick was there, and he shook hands with the orcs like it was nothing special.

Korga knocked on the wall and gave it a little push as Shelu measured its dimensions using her hands. While they worked, Jacob and Cora filled Tadrick in on the plans and the amount of money for the job. Tadrick agreed that it was a good idea.

"Do you want us to use extra wood to build a...covered area, for sitting outside?" Shelu asked after measurements were made.

"Of course!" Jacob said. "That would be great. We would give you another silver for that." He turned to Cora and Tadrick, face reddening. "I mean, right?"

"Absolutely," Tadrick said.

Cora nodded vigorously.

Jacob worried that they were playing a bit fast and loose with what little coin they had left, but this just seemed right. When he had formed the partnership, he kind of hoped his partners would reign in his instinct to take risks, but apparently, they liked to gamble, too.

"We come back tomorrow." Shelu held out a massive hand. "We need one silver now for...materials."

Jacob reached into his ever-shrinking coin purse, pulled out a silver coin, and handed it to Shelu.

"See you tomorrow."

∼

The orcs arrived very early. Their knock awakened Jacob from a strange dream about chasing his father, who was riding a horse, through a thick fog. Jacob had been awkwardly riding a capybara. He shook off the dream and rushed to the door, finding that it was still dark outside. There was the slightest band of light on the horizon to the east.

"Too early, Justjacob?" Shelu asked.

"No, it's fine." Jacob rubbed his eyes. "Come on in."

"We start on outside if okay."

"Sure."

Half asleep, Jacob wandered out the back door and picked up an armful of hay for Mrs. Covington and Arthur, who were both still asleep. He set it in their little hopper and crawled back in bed.

He lay there and thought about money, and what they were going to do if and when they ran out. It was troubling, and the orcs' work was extremely loud, but he still drifted back to sleep, this time dreamless.

When he awoke, he jumped out of bed, momentarily unaware of what the racket was outside his bedroom. When sense returned to him, he stepped out into the main area of the pub, which was now bathed in sunlight. Shelu and Korga had completely removed the west wall, installed two overgrown doors, each big enough to cover half of the new opening, and were working on the outside covered area.

"Good morning." Shelu wiped the sweat from her brow and wiped it on her pants.

"Wow. You guys are fast!"

Shelu grinned and proceeded to show Jacob how the doors worked. There was a post in the middle of the opening, and the doors, when closed, would latch onto either side of it. When open, the doors would fold into thirds on hinges and tuck into place on the north and south walls, barely taking up any space. It gave the pub a wonderful, wide-open feel.

Outside, they had set two posts into the ground and were building a cover over the area from the doors to about twenty feet out. It would be enough space for two to three tables.

Jacob wondered how much tables cost.

This was great, but they were going to be cutting it very close.

"Great work, you two." Jacob handed Shelu the three silver he owed them.

CHAPTER 9

Free Beer and Bilge Rat

Not long after the orcs headed home, Cora and Tadrick showed up at the pub together.

"Holy shit!" Cora stared wide-eyed at the new layout from the bridge over the creek.

Jacob heard her and came out from the new doors smiling.

"This is better than I could have imagined," Cora called. "And they did it in one morning?"

"Yes." Jacob nodded, still in disbelief. "I've never seen anything like it."

Jacob gave his business partners a tour of the improved pub. He showed them how the doors worked and discussed buying more tables for the covered area outside.

"This is great," Tadrick said, his voice much more reserved than the other two. "I don't want to kill the mood or anything, but I wonder if we should hold off a bit on any more spending."

"But people are going to want to sit outside." Cora pointed at the idyllic scene along the edge of the new covered area. "The creek babbling by, the breeze making the temperature perfect in the shade. Who wouldn't want to sit here?"

"Possibly true, but we could move tables from inside if that happens." Tadrick seemed disappointed in himself, but resolute.

Mrs. Covington waddled nearby. Her dress had slipped down around her hind legs, just barely holding on to her back.

"Come here, girl." Cora knelt beside her.

"Again," Tadrick said, "I don't want to scrape the jam off your toast, but I think we should temper our expectations a bit. I've worked here a long time, and I've literally never seen more than five customers in here at one time. It's usually somewhere between zero and three. I can't help but be skeptical that even this," he motioned to the covered area, "will change much."

"That's a wise thought," Jacob said, sobered a bit. "We're dangerously low on funds at the moment. We probably shouldn't put the cart before the horse, here."

Cora worked the dress back up Mrs. Covington's body while looking at Jacob. "I don't know what this has to do with horses and carts, but I think there's reason for optimism," she said. "We ciguapa believe that you can manifest change in the world with positive belief. It's not ciguapa magic, just the way the world works. If you believe you're going to fail, you probably will, because your actions will be driven by that belief. But if you go into something knowing you'll succeed; your odds are much better." She shrugged. "Isn't that right, Mrs. Covington?" She twisted the dress around the capybara's body until it was back in the perfect place.

The covered area was silent. Jacob could see Cora's point but still didn't think it was a good idea to spend the last of the money on more tables that may never be used. Averse to conflict, he wanted to change the subject but support Cora at the same time.

"We should do a grand reopening," he said as hopefully as he could.

"Yes!" Cora agreed, standing up so fast that she nearly came off the ground. "That's the spirit."

Mrs. Covington waddled away, looking very proper.

"I actually talked to my partner about Bilge Rat playing here," Tadrick said. "He said they would come play for free—one time—whenever we wanted them to."

"Bilge Rat?" Jacob raised an eyebrow.

"It's the name of his band." Tadrick shrugged.

"Could they do tomorrow?" Cora asked. "Finiday night would be perfect for our reopening."

"Yeah. They're free tomorrow. We already discussed the idea a bit."

"Perfect! We could make some flyers and post them around town." Cora hopped an inch or two off the ground, crossing her legs while in the air. When she landed, she pivoted a quarter turn on the balls of her feet until she was facing Jacob with legs uncrossed again. The little move was completely effortless, as if she'd done it a hundred times before. "Do you have any paper we could use?"

"Let me check." Jacob hurried to his office, or bedroom, or both, unsure why he was hurrying. He supposed he was caught up in Cora's excitement. What if this grand reopening was a success? He couldn't help but believe.

After rummaging through the papers in his desk, he couldn't find anything blank. There were, however, around a hundred full-page receipts from Yandro's employer. Each one had the same order—one keg of beer and one block of cheese. He couldn't think of a reason he would ever need these receipts, so he took ten of them back out to the pub area.

Cora was waiting for him at the bar with a feather quill and an inkwell already open. When Jacob handed her the paper, she wordlessly began to write on one of them.

As she wrote, the front door swung open and two men walked in. Jacob's heart picked up its pace as he recognized who they were. It was the two shady-looking characters from the first time he had come to Mrs. Covington's. The men who would have robbed him if Mr. Davies hadn't intervened. One of them carried a suitcase that seemed the perfect size for a crossbow.

"Hello." Tadrick waved. "The usual?"

Both men nodded and took seats in the back corner of the pub. The suitcase was placed on the table between them.

Tadrick poured two mugs of beer and grabbed two knives, which he brought to the men.

"This is interesting." One of the men pointed at the place a wall used to be.

The other man couldn't keep his eyes off Jacob, whose hand went instinctively to his coin purse.

"Yeah," Tadrick said. "What do you think?"

"Eh, I don't know." The man shrugged. "I'm sure the younger crowd will like it, but we two kinda like to lurk about in the shadows until we're ready to strike." He gave Tadrick a smile that was either playful or pure evil. "You know what I mean?"

Tadrick was about to answer when Jacob cut in. "That work didn't come cheap, either," he said from behind the bar. "We barely have a coin to our names, now." He nervously rubbed the back of his neck. "Nope, we're pretty dead broke around here."

The men and Tadrick seemed confused by his statements and carried on as if Jacob wasn't there.

"You know the drill," Tadrick told them. "A copper apiece, please."

Both men reached into their pockets and produced payment.

"Thank you, gents. Let me know when you're ready for another."

At the bar, Cora crumpled up the piece of paper she'd been writing on.

"We need something else if we're going to make this big." She gazed up at the ceiling, deep in thought.

"What do you have in mind?" Jacob took an awkward route to the bar that allowed him to keep an eye on the two customers.

"What do you think about giving out free beer?" Cora asked.

"Not bad." Tadrick nodded to her.

"How much free beer?" Jacob's mind immediately went to the cost of another keg, which he knew well from the myriad receipts in the drawers to be forty-two coppers—damn near half a silver.

"Well..." Cora pursed her lips. "What if we advertised free beer between, say, seven and eight o'clock tomorrow night? Then Bilge Rat could start at eight? That way we could get people in here drinking, but they'd still have to buy beer once the band starts. I know it's a money-losing proposition, but we have to get people to come and see the new and improved place if we're ever going to get new customers, right?"

"I think it's a good idea," Tadrick said. "We've already put most of our money into the pot on this venture. I think going all out for this grand reopening might be our only hope. We might as well push all in and call hoard."

Jacob knew this was a Dragon's Hoard reference, but he didn't really understand it. Dragon's Hoard was the most popular card game on the islands, but he had never learned how to play. Wanting to seem like he did understand, he said, "Yeah, I get that. We either succeed or fail spectacularly."

Cora seemed heartened by the idea, but Tadrick took on a decidedly disheartened look.

"We won't fail, though," Tadrick asked, "right?"

"I sure hope not." Jacob did his best to sound hopeful.

Cora, who had been writing on and off ever since the free beer plan was floated, held up a sheet of paper with beautiful writing that read:

FREE BEER!
From 7-8
Then
BILGE RAT!
At 8
This Finiday Night at
Mrs. Covington's Pub
Just Across the Bridge on 3rd Street

Jacob gulped. "Alright," he said. "Let's do this."

When Jacob awoke the next morning, it was still dark outside. He tried to go back to sleep, but his mind was far too active. Instead, he got up, put out hay for the capybaras, and headed for the beach.

The town was still asleep, apart from a stray dog or two and several fishermen setting off from the docks. There was a slight chill in the air, causing Jacob to cross his arms and occasionally rub them. The Ring above was unobstructed, its silvery light guiding his way to the sandy beach just north of the docks.

Once on the beach, he took off his boots, dug his toes into the cool sand, and sat against a smooth black rock. The sun was close to peeking over the skyline. A brightening brushstroke of orange light painted the horizon to the east.

Jacob sat and listened to the waves break and roll onto the sand. His gaze unfocused, he stared out to sea. Like usual, it pulled at him with invisible strings. An unexplainable longing resided somewhere in his being. He felt like he belonged out there among the swells.

A two-masted ship was barely visible to the south. He imagined himself aboard—the flutter in the sails, the creaking of cordage, sea shanties sung together with the crew. Why did these things appeal so strongly to him? There was something mystical about the sea, almost numinous, but it wasn't just that. He supposed, at his core, it was a yearning to belong. A ship's crew seemed like it might be the family he never really had, but had always wanted. Or, at the very least, it seemed like a group of close friends, united in common cause and bonded for life.

Jacob was aware that these thoughts might well be naive, but he liked to think them anyway. He loved the moments when he became lost in daydreams, imagining himself amongst a crew singing songs at the top of their lungs, or searching for lost treasure.

Thoughts of treasure brought him out of his reverie. He recited the Fenton Treasure Poem aloud. "Hail to all explorers with adventure in their hearts. Let me regale you of the place where this adventure starts. It's easy if you work together, what I say is true. Just boat a creek on rainy main to all afloat for two." He still wasn't able to make any sense of the last line.

Pondering the poem, his mind wandered from the treasure to the pub. Today was their grand reopening. It could be the day that made or broke the entire venture.

Blowing out a deep breath through pursed lips, Jacob stood and brushed the sand off his butt. Boots in hand, he gave the sea a final glance before turning back to town. But as he turned, something caught his eye from up the beach. A piece of wood with a strange shape had washed ashore and lay just outside the waves' reach. He altered his course to get a better look.

It was a ship's wheel! Three-quarters of a ship's wheel, anyway. A fourth of it was broken away, leaving jagged edges. Barnacles were covering two of the handles opposite the break.

"Perfect," he whispered to himself, grinning.

~

Jacob had only been admiring the placement of the ship's wheel on the wall behind the bar for ten minutes or so when Cora and Tadrick showed up.

"That's perfect!" Tadrick ran up closer to the wheel for a better look.

"That's what I said," Jacob responded. He raised his hand like he'd seen his partners do before, instantly mortified that he was doing it wrong. But, thankfully, Tadrick slapped it. The strange little handshake thing was actually pretty fun.

"It really does look great." Cora smiled, set down a crate she'd been carrying, and held her hand up toward Jacob. But when he tried to slap it, he missed. Cora guffawed, then said, "Go ahead, give it another try."

On his second attempt, Jacob made gentle contact, his face red with embarrassment.

"I've got something for tonight," Cora said as she pulled a rope from the crate.

The rope had sea-green glass balls as big as a fist attached every two feet or so.

"I've got about fifty feet, here. I figure we can hang them on the ceiling in a big square from the bar to the front door."

"Nice," Jacob said. "That'll look really good."

"Just wait." Cora flashed him a smile.

Jacob didn't have a clue what she was talking about, but he let it go as he helped nail the rope to the ceiling while standing on tables.

When it was all up, Cora hurried to the big folding doors and closed them. When Jacob shot her a quizzical look, she pointed to the ceiling above him. As he looked up, his eyes widened and his jaw dropped open. The glass balls were all glowing with an aquamarine light.

"What...er...how?" Tadrick asked.

"There are caves along the west coast of the island near the ciguapa villages where I was born that have glowing algae we call *luscen*. My people use it for special occasions, like fourteenth birthday parties, or what you would call weddings. We collect water from the caves and put some into each ball, then after the party, we put it back where we found it. I had to beg my mother to use ours, but she finally relented."

"How do you get the water in these glass balls?" Jacob asked, admiring one of them up close while standing on the bar.

"Ciguapa magic."

"Like with rune tattoos?" That was the extent of Jacob's knowledge about ciguapa magic.

"Yes." An ephemeral shadow passed over Cora's face, almost as if she was ashamed of something. "I don't have that ability, but my parents do."

"They're spectacular." Tadrick gaped up at them.

"I love them." The brightness returned to her smile as if it had never left.

Jacob couldn't help but notice how much different Tadrick was now than when he had first met him. He had seemed so depressed then, but now it seemed he had broken out of whatever shell was holding him back. It was nice to see.

"They're going to look really good tonight, even with the big doors open." Cora opened the folding doors, tucking them into their places. She walked over to the front door and turned to look at the bar. "Come here." She motioned them over to where she was standing.

Jacob and Tadrick obeyed. She took each of them by the shoulder and spun them around. "Look at this place."

The pub was unrecognizable from the one Jacob had first walked into. The glowing glass balls, the paintings, the ship's wheel, and the other improvements had given the place personality. The pub had life, now.

Mrs. Covington and Arthur waddled in through their little door, soaking wet, and lay down on the floor next to the bar.

"This might really work," Jacob said.

"I sure hope so," Tadrick added, a note of skepticism in his voice.

"It will." Cora nodded. "The flyers are out there. Bilge Rat is coming. This is gonna be good."

CHAPTER 10

Grand Reopening

At seven o'clock, customers started to trickle in and ask for their free beer. Several drank their beer and left, but some stayed. One man would chug his glass, then ask for another, repeatedly. Since they hadn't specified the rules of the promotion, they allowed him to continue, hoping he would slow down sooner rather than later.

The number of customers was a bit underwhelming at first, but as it got closer to eight, the pub began to fill up. Most people were there to see Bilge Rat.

As the band set up their equipment, people crowded into the area near the fireplace. Eight o'clock came and went, and the band wasn't ready. Jacob considered this a good thing because now customers would have to pay for their beers while they waited. He and Cora sold at least ten as Tadrick helped the band prepare. The man who had taken full advantage of the free beer promotion left when the beer stopped being free.

Jacob met Tadrick's partner, Darian, who played steel drums, but it was a quick passing greeting.

The singer of the band was engaged in an animated discussion with a tall woman just outside the big new doors. The rest of the band was ready to play, but they were waiting on the singer. The crowd seemed mildly impatient, but they kept buying beers, and most seemed happy to be there.

The tall woman yelled, "You've had enough chances to get your priorities straight," to the singer, loud enough to be heard over the hubbub of the crowd. She turned away from him and stormed off into town, calling, "Goodbye forever," as she left.

The singer glanced at the waiting crowd, a pained expression on his face, then took off after the woman.

"Shit," Tadrick said. "Darian was wondering when that," he pointed toward the commotion, "was finally going to blow up." He covered his eyes with his hand. "Perfect timing. Right on our most important night."

The crowd grew anxious. People no longer seemed happy to be there, and they all but stopped buying beer. The band looked a mix between nervous and embarrassed, talking to each other in a small circle in front of their instruments.

"Let's go see if there's anything we can do," Jacob said to Tadrick. He didn't have a clue what that *anything* could be, but something needed to happen if they were going to avoid disaster.

Jacob hurried to the band and Tadrick followed.

"...maybe that would appease them," Darian was saying.

"What do you plan to do?" Jacob said as he stuck his head into the circle.

"Darian thinks we should just play the songs without the words," one of the band members, an older ciguapa man holding a stand-up bass, said. "Instrumental like."

"I don't like it," another band member said.

"Well, what other option do we have?"

"What if someone else sang," Jacob offered.

"Who?"

Jacob looked to Tadrick. "Do you know their songs?"

Tadrick looked mortified. "No...not all the words."

For a moment, Jacob pictured himself singing with the band. It sent a thrill through his chest, but he didn't know any words to any sea shanties, and probably wouldn't have the nerve if he did.

"What if someone here can do it?" Jacob asked.

Tadrick and the band looked at him with blank expressions.

"Well, shit," Darian finally said. "It's as good an idea as any."

Darian broke from the circle, faced the crowd, and raised his arms.

"Alright, alright, can I say something really quick?" he called.

Slowly, the crowd quieted.

"So…it seems we don't have our singer tonight."

Someone in the back booed.

"We were planning on opening with *Starboard Nights*. Does anyone here know that song?"

Most of the crowd affirmed they did.

"Would someone like to get up here and sing it with us?"

At first, no one moved, other than looking down or away. But, tentatively, a man in the middle of the audience raised his hand.

"Great." Darian waved him forward. "Come on up here."

After some goading by those around him, the man pushed his way through the crowd up to the front.

"Here you go." Darian handed him a golden wand with a black leather grip. "This will make your voice louder. You sing into the end of it." He took the man's hand and positioned the golden end of the wand in front of his mouth. "Not too close, not too far away. Give it a try."

"Hello," the man said into the wand. His voice was amplified so loudly that everyone in the pub cringed and covered their ears.

"Little bit further away than that." Darian flashed him a nervous smile.

"Hello?" This time, the man's voice was louder than normal, but not ear-splitting.

"Perfect." Darian slapped the man on the back. "You'll do fine."

The band started to play a song. The music sounded great. They were a five-piece, with steel drums, regular drums, a bass, and a guitar accompanying the scared-looking volunteer.

When the music reached the right place, the man began to sing. His voice wasn't bad, but he could barely be heard over the music.

"Little closer," Darian said as he played.

The wand seemed to be the proper distance away, but the man was mumbling the lyrics.

"Go ahead, son," an older woman said from the front row, stepping forward and giving the would-be singer's shoulder a firm grip. "Belt it out for us."

Infused with confidence by the crowd's encouragement, he sang louder. He built up slowly, but once the chorus hit, he was really going for it. His voice was surprisingly good once he stopped holding back. Before long, the crowd danced about as if the original singer was there. Jacob had never heard the band before, but this version of it sounded pretty damn good.

When the song was over, a big cheer went up. The man's face was a deep red but had a wide smile across it as he handed the wand back to Darian.

"Do you know *Over the Gunwale*?" Darian asked.

"Uh...no. Sorry."

Darian shrugged and looked at the audience. "Does anyone want to give *Over the Gunwale* a try?"

This time, several hands were raised.

Darian pointed to a woman on the right side and she came up and took the wand. After a quick test to gauge the volume of her voice, the band went right into another song.

The woman's voice was even better than the first guy's, and the crowd was absolutely eating it up.

When her song was finished, another singer was brought up, and the process kept repeating. Some singers were much better than others, but even when the bad singers gave it a try, it was still a fun time for all involved.

Jacob was standing at the bar, pouring a beer while bobbing his head to the music when a group of young human men showed up at the pub, demanding their free beers. They were loud and obnoxious from the moment they came in.

"The free beer thing was only from seven until eight, guys," Jacob said. "Sorry about that."

"So, we were a little late." The young man in the front flashed a sardonic smile. "We still want our beers." He tapped the bar three times with his pointer finger.

"Just half a copper each," Cora said with a big, fake grin. "Still not too bad, although the beer isn't the best I've ever tasted." She forced a little chuckle.

"We're not laughing." The man's tone was much more serious, although he was still smiling.

Jacob's heart raced. He wanted nothing more than for these guys to just go away.

"Here." The young man reached behind the bar and snatched an empty mug. "We'll even pour 'em ourselves to save you the trouble." He positioned the mug under the tap and poured a beer that was almost entirely froth.

He handed the mug to his friend on his right, then reached for another.

"Stop!" Cora shouted, laying her hand on the mug he was trying to take.

"Or what?" He pulled the mug out from under Cora's hand with little effort and began pouring another beer. The entire time, he stared at Jacob, who couldn't meet his gaze directly.

Jacob wanted to do something. He knew he should do something, but his body wasn't responding. He stood, frozen in fear, while the man distributed poorly-filled mugs to his friends.

He glanced at Cora, who scowled at the man, her hands rolling into fists.

"There," the man said. "Was that so hard?" His expression and tone changed as if nothing of note had taken place. "I mean, the sign did say free beer. And it's the only reason we came in."

Jacob did nothing. As the loud group chugged and carried on, Jacob didn't move an inch.

"I'm weak," he said to himself, so quietly that he couldn't even hear the words. Cyrus had told him that his kindness wasn't weakness, and maybe that was true. But it didn't change the fact that he was, at his core, a weak person. He dug his fingernails into his palms and tightened his jaw, trying to hold off the beginnings of tears.

Tadrick, who had been standing near the band and helping with singer transitions, must have noticed the commotion because he quickly pushed through the crowd to get to the bar.

"What's going on?" he asked.

When Cora filled him in, Tadrick rounded the bar and stood directly in front of the group's leader. "The constable is just across the creek right now." He pointed toward the big double doors. "We told him we anticipated a busy night, so he's sitting at the next pub over having a leg of mutton and a glass of red wine. He told us to run and fetch him if we had any trouble."

The man looked down at him with a grin and took a swig of beer.

"You can either set those mugs down and leave right now, or I can head right over there."

The man didn't move, staring defiantly into Tadrick's eyes.

"Alright, then." Tadrick spun and marched toward the front door.

"Okay, okay." The man held up both hands, fingers splayed. "This place is boring, anyway. Beer is horrible, too." He looked at the group. "Let's get out of this dump."

Reluctantly, the men set down their beers and filed out, muttering curses as they went.

"Pricks!" Cora's face was still bunched into a scowl. But when she turned and saw Jacob, her expression softened. "Oh, don't give them a second thought," she said, trying her best to play it off. "There's always got to be a few assholes, but they're gone, now." She made a gesture toward the door that must have been something vulgar in ciguapa culture. "Good riddance!"

Jacob forced a smile.

"Nice story." Cora patted Tadrick on the back. "I wish I would have thought of something like that."

"I'm just glad it worked." He wiped his brow with his sleeve.

"The leg of mutton and red wine was a nice touch. Had me convinced."

Tadrick smiled. "I better get back and help with the band."

When Tadrick left, Cora patted Jacob on the back, too, then went to round up the empty mugs.

The next singer Tadrick signed up for the *you sing Bilge Rat's songs* thing was so bad Jacob couldn't help but cheer up a bit. A genuine smile popped up on his face, but only for an instant.

He took a deep breath. Everything was going great. He couldn't let a couple of bad apples ruin this amazing night. Through force of will, he pushed his feelings of inadequacy away and listened to the horrible singer.

Before the singer was done, Yandro entered the pub, giving Jacob another welcomed distraction.

"Hello, Jacob," Yandro said, his eyes already searching for Cora.

"Hello, Yandro. Would you like a beer?"

"Um…sure. Thank you." He had located Cora, who was busy taking an order from a table of patrons.

When Yandro was taking his first drink, Jacob noticed that Cora had now noticed Yandro, and was looking in his direction. As soon as the drink was down, Yandro looked to Cora, who quickly looked away to talk to someone else.

A customer called for Jacob, so he went to see what they wanted. As he took their beer order, he glanced back at Yandro. A human rushed into the pub and was very animated while talking with Yandro. After several looks in Cora's direction, Yandro got up and hurried outside with the human.

Cora, it seemed, missed the entire interaction.

When Jacob finally got the beer orders taken care of, he met Cora back behind the bar.

"I can't believe he didn't even say *hi*," Cora said, fuming. "Or goodbye!"

"I think his boss or someone pulled him away," Jacob offered.

"He still could have said *hello*. This isn't the biggest pub in New Dawn."

Again, Jacob said nothing.

"Hmm." Cora stormed off holding two beers for people at the far table.

A half-hour later, when the lively mood around the place had Jacob feeling much better, a big, burly man entered the pub with a woman under his arm. He looked familiar, and it only took Jacob a moment to realize where he knew him from. It was Cyrus, the captain of the ship he'd taken to New Dawn. He had cleaned up quite a bit—a haircut, a beard trim, and clean new clothes.

"Two beers, please," Cyrus boomed.

He stopped short and raised an eyebrow. Then his eyes opened wide. "It's you!" he said. He ran a hand over his beard. "What was it, Bright? Something Bright, am I right?"

"Yes, sir!" Jacob straightened to his full height. "Jacob Bright. It's good to see you again."

"Good to see you too, young man." He looked down at his woman friend. "Met this fella on the trip over. Had nothing but a few coins to his name." He turned back to Jacob. "This here is Jenny, the gal I told you about on the ship."

Jacob and Jenny waved to each other.

"Already found a job, I see." Cyrus scanned the pub, head subtly nodding.

"Well…I actually own this place. Me and my business partners, anyway."

"Oh! Even better." Cyrus gripped Jacob's shoulder over the bar. "A few days in a new town and you're already doing big things. I told you, didn't I?" He gestured toward Jenny. "Tell her what I said."

"Yeah. He did tell me I was going to hit it big."

"I just knew he was. Not sure how I know these things, but I saw a sparkle in his eye. Great judge of character, I am."

Jenny gave him a patronizing smile.

Jacob handed the beers across the bar. "These two are on the house," he said, feeling pretty important. He'd wanted to say that ever since he had a house to put anything on.

"Oh no." Cyrus held his big hands up in front of him. "You're just starting out, here, son."

"I insist," Jacob looked him in the eye and projected as much authority as he could. "You were an immense help to me. Your kind words steered me in the right direction when I was absolutely rudderless. You didn't have to help me, but you did anyway. It's the very least I could do for you, sir." It was true. The big man had been wrong about Jacob not being weak, but he had given Jacob a great gift with his other advice.

Cyrus said nothing. He seemed somewhat touched by Jacob's words.

Instead, he raised his glass, nodded, and took a swig.

CHAPTER 11

Bad News

The band played for almost two hours, continuing to cycle new singers through. When they were done, most of the customers left with them. A few stayed behind and kept drinking, though. Several asked for food. All but one rejected the block of cheese.

Eventually, all the customers went home, and the three business owners were left alone.

"Successful night," Cora said as she wiped down the bar.

"It really was." Tadrick seemed relieved.

Cora opened her mouth to speak but stopped herself before any words came out. Jacob assumed she was going to bring up the guys who stole beer from them.

"That whole... 'you sing our songs' thing really worked out." Jacob tried to steer the conversation as he set an armful of glasses into the sink.

"People loved that," Cora agreed. "Hell, I wanted to give it a try."

"I wonder if it was enough, though," Tadrick said. "Will they come back even when the band isn't here?"

"Do you think people would want to do that singing thing again?" Jacob added.

"Who knows?" Cora threw up her hands. "But we can ponder such things later. Tonight was a victory. Let's revel in that a little bit."

"You're right. It went better than we could have hoped." Jacob grinned. "A victory indeed."

But when Cora and Tadrick left for home, and Jacob lay in bed trying to fall asleep, his mind couldn't get away from the men who had taken the beer. He imagined a dozen different ways he should have handled the situation, none of them as weak and pathetic as what he'd done. He should have stood up to them, especially when they disrespected Cora. He should have done *anything*. Anything would have been better than the absolute nothing he did.

His thoughts drifted back to a time, only a year or so ago when his father was berating a kid at one of their shipyards. The kid couldn't have been more than twelve or thirteen and worked as a runner for the family business. He had let a note from a customer blow away in the wind, and this had enraged Jacob's father.

"The one thing you're paid to do is hold onto notes," his father had said as the kid cowered in front of him. "But apparently that's far too difficult for you?"

The kid was obviously trying to hold back tears as he looked up at the imposing man.

"Answer me!" Jacob's father shouted.

Both Jacob and the kid cringed.

"It's not too difficult, sir. I just...there was a gust I wasn't ready for."

With jerky, exaggerated movements, Jacob's father thrust a hand into his pocket and pulled out an envelope. "I know this is a tough concept," he said as he pinched the envelope between thumb and forefinger, "but just bear with me." He threw his hand into the air and the envelope fluttered violently in the wind.

"I..."

"You what? You realize that any idiot off the street could manage to keep a piece of paper held in their hand?"

The kid didn't answer. He continued to look up, terrified, as tears pooled in his eyes.

"Maybe you should crawl back to the cesspool you came from? I'm sure we could find someone else who could handle such a difficult task."

Jacob took a step forward, meaning to intervene somehow. His heart went out to the kid. He wanted to step in and admonish his father for mistreating someone so young.

Before he could say a word, his father turned his head sharply to face him, envelope still aloft. The look he gave Jacob seemed to dare him to speak up. He wanted Jacob to try and save this boy from his ire so he could put Jacob further into his place.

The two of them locked eyes for a moment, but the anger on his father's face made Jacob look down and away.

His father turned back and ratcheted up the intensity on the terrified kid. He raged on until tears were streaming down the kid's cheeks and blowing away in the wind.

The entire time, Jacob stood and said nothing.

Jacob had told himself then that he would never again stand silently by and allow injustices to happen in his presence. But apparently, that oath was meaningless. Again, he had watched when he should have acted, frozen in paralyzing, pathetic fear.

Eventually, his mind slowed down enough for him to fall asleep, although it was not very restful.

～

The next morning, the pub smelled of stale beer. It was a sign of a successful night. Jacob, feeling better in daylight than he had in bed the night before, opened the big doors to let in some fresh air and began sweeping the floor.

When he got to the area behind the bar, he noticed Mrs. Covington and Arthur lounging on their four-poster bed. He propped the broom against the bar and crouched down near them. Tentatively, he reached out a hand to pet Mrs. Covington's head, unsure if it would be welcome. She leaned into his hand, rubbing the side of her face along his fingers.

Arthur jumped off the bed and shuffled over to Jacob's other hand. Jacob was thrilled to be petting both of them at once. They really started to nuzzle up to him, seeming to enjoy every pet and scratch he could give.

"I'm going to have to get you two some nice bananas or something," he said, rubbing under their chins.

Eventually, he was able to pull himself away from the capybaras and continue cleaning. As he swept, he heard muffled voices coming from Juniper's place.

"I should probably go apologize for all the noise last night," he muttered to himself. "I hope we didn't keep the kids up."

Once outside, he saw Juniper and the town's constable coming out her front door. The constable turned and they carried on a conversation in the doorway. Juniper looked distressed.

Jacob found himself shrinking away. He didn't want the constable to see him and to know where he lived and worked after the whole botched capybara heist debacle. He retreated around the corner of the pub and peeked out from there.

The conversation was calm, but Juniper seemed as if she might cry. The constable stood with arms crossed and spoke in short sentences. With a slight breeze and the bustle of the town, Jacob couldn't hear a word of what they were saying.

He was about to head inside and mind his own business when the constable tipped his hat and marched away. Jacob ducked into the pub through the big doors and waited for the constable to cross the bridge. Then he hurried to Juniper's restaurant. She was still standing in the doorway, wiping tears from her cheeks with the hem of her apron.

"Is everything alright?" Jacob asked as he approached.

Juniper startled at his voice, then forced a smile when she saw him.

"I don't know."

"What was he here about?" Jacob pointed in the direction the constable had gone.

"He was here on behalf of Lowell Bank. I owe them money, and apparently, they're done waiting for it. They want to repossess the restaurant."

"What?" Jacob didn't know what else to say.

"I've asked for an extension, but they don't want to hear it. If I don't pay the full amount in two weeks, they'll take the building back so they can find another tenant."

"How much is it? If you don't mind me asking."

"Four gold, three silver, and nine copper."

Jacob felt for her, but there was nothing he could do to help. After last night's slice of success, they still only had three silver and seven copper to their names—woefully short of what Juniper needed.

She must have seen something in Jacob's eyes, because she said, "I don't want to take any of your money. You three are just starting out on your own. You'll need every copper if you're going to stay out of a predicament like the one I'm in."

"But—"

"I can always go back to the fish line if I need to. It's not ideal, but we'll get by with the money I make there."

"What about the kids? Who will take care of them while you're at work?"

"I'll have to get someone to watch over them on Solisdays. The fish plant only allows people off every other Solisday."

Most people in the League of Islands worked a three-day week—Iniday, Mediday, and Finiday, with the fourth day, Solisday, usually taken as a day off before the cycle started over again. Jacob's father had never taken a Solisday off as far as Jacob could remember. Work was his life, and could bear no interruptions. It had been the same for his employees if they wanted to keep their jobs for very long.

The thought brought up a point he hadn't pondered yet. Would the pub be open every day for the rest of time? He felt pretty strongly that they should probably close it one day per week. Maybe Iniday would be best?

He shook off the intruding thoughts and focused back on Juniper.

"Are you sure you won't consider taking help from us? We've got three silver and seven—"

"I'm sure. I appreciate the sentiment more than you could know, but it wouldn't be enough anyway."

Jacob stared down at the ground, wracking his brain for anything useful. It wasn't fair that this was happening to such a good person. The fish line was no job for a single mother with young children. The hours were long and the work exhausting. He had toured several fish processing plants with his father. Those were not fond memories. In particular, he remembered when he and a boy his age locked eyes across a table full of gutted fish. The look the kid gave him practically screamed that he would have given anything to trade places with Jacob.

"What if I were to get a loan?" Jacob asked. "Maybe that could cover the costs?"

"Mr. Lowell put a freeze on all loans last year. There had been too many cases of people getting money and disappearing off island. But I couldn't let you do something like that, anyway."

Jacob pinched his chin between his thumb and forefinger. If only there was a way to get a lot of money quickly. Of course, that probably wasn't the most original thought. He wasn't the first to want—

"The treasure!"

"Huh?"

"Have you heard of the Fenton Treasure?"

"I think I've heard those words once or twice, but I'm not sure what it is."

"It's a treasure that was hidden on this island years ago by this wealthy old woman. She wrote a poem that doubled as a clue to the treasure's location. No one has been able to figure it out, yet. But maybe we can."

Juniper didn't seem very heartened.

"Why don't you come over and check out the copy of the poem I bought from Mr. Davies? Maybe we could figure it out together."

Juniper sighed. "Sure. But could you bring it over to my place instead? The kids are off of school today and they're inside."

"Of course. Let me go grab it."

Suddenly, Juniper brightened a bit. "Oh. I almost forgot. Bring over a block of cheese, too. I think I have an idea."

Jacob cocked his head to the side, confused by her request. "Alright...I'll bring a block of cheese, too."

CHAPTER 12

Innovation

Cora was at the pub cleaning up when Jacob got back. He explained to her what was going on with Juniper as he hurried to his office to retrieve the poem.

"Oh, no," Cora said. "I'll come with you. It's too early for any customers anyway."

The two of them locked up and headed to Juniper's. Jacob felt somewhat silly as he awkwardly carried a block of cheese as big as his head in public, but no one gave him a second look.

"Hello, Cora." Juniper ushered them inside. "So, I was thinking about something Yandro said the other day, and wondered if I could try something with your cheese."

Cora perked up at the mention of Yandro but tried to play it off. Juniper still seemed troubled but was somewhat invigorated by whatever this idea was.

"Sure." Jacob handed her the block.

Juniper led them through the restaurant area to her kitchen.

The kids came out from another room and waved at them. Cora and Jacob waved back.

While Juniper rummaged through her cupboards, Jacob had an idea. He motioned for the kids, who were still peeking around the corner at them, to come over to the kitchen. Tentatively, they came out from around the corner and wandered closer. They both stared at the burn scar on his face, but he was used to kids doing that.

"Hello, Aspen. Hello, Ceda. Have you ever folded paper to look like animals before?"

They both shook their heads.

Jacob held up the Fenton Treasure Poem. "What animal would you like to see?" He didn't think it likely the poem would fade from his memory any time soon, but he made a mental note to write it down on a receipt later.

The kids looked at each other, seemingly goading each other to answer. Finally, Aspen said, "A capybara?"

"Perfect." Jacob began to fold the parchment on the kitchen counter. In no time at all, he held up the finished product—a tiny paper capybara.

"God in the trees!" Ceda said. "That looks just like one."

"How did you learn to do that?" Aspen asked.

"Well, I was an only child. I spent a lot of time entertaining myself when I was your age. A teacher at school taught me the basics. I just kept practicing from there."

Juniper had found what she was looking for—a strange metal instrument shaped like a pyramid—but she didn't interrupt the interaction between Jacob and the kids.

"Could you teach us?" Ceda asked.

"Absolutely. I have some old receipts I could bring over, and we can work on it any time you'd like."

Both kids lit up with adorable smiles.

"What do you say?" Juniper asked them.

"Thank you," they said in unison.

"No problem at all."

Juniper held up the metal instrument and had just started to speak when Ceda interrupted.

"What happened?" she asked, pointing to her own right cheek.

"Ceda!" Juniper scolded. "That's not a nice thing to ask someone."

"No, no, it's fine," Jacob said. "I don't mind at all." He gave both Ceda and Juniper reassuring smiles. "I don't usually tell people this, but I actually got this scar while battling a dragon."

The kids looked at him, wide-eyed and open-mouthed.

Jacob tried to keep a straight face, but it didn't last more than a few seconds. "Alright, it wasn't a dragon. What really happened was just an accident with some black powder on a ship. I was in the wrong place at the wrong time; simple as that."

"Does it hurt?"

"Not anymore. When it happened, it was the worst pain I've ever felt. You two need to be very careful around fire, or anything that can burn you, because I wouldn't want either of you to ever have to go through something like that. But no, it doesn't hurt at all anymore." He gave himself a light slap on the cheek as a demonstration.

"I'm sorry that happened to you," Aspen offered.

"That is so kind of you to say." Jacob was genuinely touched.

"I am, too." Ceda didn't want to be left out.

"Thank you. Both of you kids are so nice."

Their faces reddened a bit.

Jacob held the paper capybara out to them, and Ceda took it from his hand.

"You can keep that."

After several thank yous, the kids scurried back to their room.

Juniper cut a large corner off of the block and pressed it to the metal instrument on the counter. "This is a grater." She moved the hunk of cheese up and down against the grater and the hunk got steadily smaller, eventually disappearing completely. Juniper lifted the grater to reveal a pile of shredded cheese underneath.

"Alright. So, Yandro said something like, 'If only you had something to do with the cheese.' And it got me thinking; what if we shredded it and put it on some of my corn chips?"

Jacob shrugged, intrigued.

Juniper scooped a handful of corn chips from a ceramic container and spread them out on a plate. Then she sprinkled the cheese more or less evenly over the chips.

"And then..." She took the plate across the kitchen to an oven that was already lit. She slid the plate into the oven and closed the door. "Shouldn't be but a minute or two."

After a minute, she cracked open the oven door and peeked inside. "Almost," she said. Thirty seconds later, she took another peek. "Perfect." She slid an oven mitt over her hand and took out the hot plate.

Her creation looked appetizing but strange. The cheese had completely melted over the corn chips, covering most of them.

"Well," Juniper said. "Who wants to try one first?"

"You invented them," Cora said. "You should get the first one."

Juniper didn't argue. She took a chip by its corner and lifted it from the plate. The other chips around it, connected by melted cheese, were lifted too, but Juniper pulled them apart until she had one cheesy corn chip in her hand.

When she bit into it, she made a contented sound. For several wordless seconds, the only noise in the kitchen was the crunching of the chip as she chewed.

"I think we may have something, here." She grabbed another chip. "Try it."

Jacob took a chip from the plate and popped it into his mouth. The flavor explosion was unexpected and wonderful. The crunch and saltiness of the chip mingled perfectly with the warm melted cheese to create a taste he'd never experienced before.

"This is fantastic," Cora said with her mouth full.

No more words were spoken until the last chip was gone.

"We fauns don't use a lot of cheese in our dishes, but this is..."

"It's genius is what it is," Cora said.

Juniper blushed as she picked up a stray shred of cheese that had melted on the plate.

Jacob shot a finger into the air. "I have an idea."

"Yes?" Juniper popped the nibble of melted cheese in her mouth.

"You know the chicken in your pies? What if you took the chicken —just the meat, not the beets—and put that on top of the cheese?"

Juniper and Cora looked interested but unsure.

"Or is that a stupid idea?"

"No, not stupid at all. Let's try it." Juniper seemed to have forgotten about her troubles, wrapped up in cooking innovation, which was obviously a passion of hers.

The results of the meat experiment went over nearly as well as the initial discovery. The seasoned chicken complemented the other ingredients unbelievably well.

"Anything else?" Juniper said. "I mean, this is going to be tough to beat, but we can try."

"I don't know." Cora placed her hand over her mouth, deep in thought.

"Oh!" Juniper lifted a finger into the air. "I've got a few tomatoes, a few onions, and some olives. We fauns add those ingredients to a lot of dishes. I think it might just work here."

"Sounds good?" Cora seemed unsure of herself.

"Worth a shot." Juniper began chopping the onion.

Aspen and Ceda ran out from the back room and stood quietly in the entryway of the kitchen until Juniper acknowledged them. Jacob couldn't be sure, but he thought he saw a hint of annoyance on Juniper's face when they appeared.

"Do we have any paper we could fold?" Ceda asked.

"I don't know. Did you check your desk?" There was definitely annoyance in her voice, but it was hidden well.

"Oh, yeah." The kids ran off giggling.

Juniper let out a nearly undetectable sigh as she moved on to chopping tomatoes.

When she finished chopping up all the vegetables, they sprinkled each one of them over the top of the chips, melted cheese, and meat.

"Even better!" Juniper exclaimed after trying a chip with everything on it. The annoyance had seemingly disappeared.

Cora and Jacob tried the newest creation and agreed.

"How about fruit?" Jacob felt stupid about the suggestion as soon as he made it.

"I don't know," Juniper said. "I mean, I have a pineapple. It sounds weird, but we might as well give it a try."

Another plate was warmed up and covered with all the previous toppings, as well as diced pineapple.

"Okay, I think that was too far." Jacob resisted the urge to spit out his food and gulped it down with effort.

"Yeah." Cora frowned. "That one didn't work at all, did it?"

Juniper grimaced. "But all the rest..."

They all stood quietly, content and full.

"Hey!" Jacob said. "What if we sold this at the pub? You could cook it and bring it over when a customer orders it. And you would, obviously, keep the profits."

"Hmm." Juniper rubbed one of her horns in contemplation.

"Great idea." Cora nodded enthusiastically. "How much do you think we could charge for a plate of those?"

"Well, people were willing to pay half a copper to slice cheese from the block. So..." Jacob aimed his eyes at the ceiling while he thought. "I'd say at least two coppers."

"Maybe two and a half," Juniper said.

"I think once people taste this, they'll pay that gladly." Cora picked a chunk of pineapple from one of the chips, then ate the chip. "Maybe more."

"Look!" Aspen and Ceda called from the entryway.

They both held up paper that had been folded to resemble flowers. The work was unconventional, and the paper had been roughly bunched up in places, but the finished result was, at the very least, recognizable.

"Wow." Jacob gave them a thumbs-up. "Those are great."

Juniper's smile and nod were genuine, but Jacob still sensed an undercurrent of annoyance.

"Thank you!" they said in unison before hurrying away.

"Maybe we could raise enough money with these to pay the bank?" Jacob said when they were gone.

"I hate to contradict your positivity, but I doubt that." Juniper deflated just a bit. "We'd have to sell over two-hundred plates of these things. And that's not even taking the costs of the ingredients into account. Probably not going to happen in two weeks."

"Oh." Jacob wished he had something better to say.

The kitchen was silent for an awkward stretch of time.

Cora finally broke the silence. "What should we call these things?"

"Uh...corn chip delight?" Jacob offered.

"Or what about crunchies?" Cora shrugged.

"Crunchy delight?"

"Or melties."

"Melty delight?"

"Or flavor explosions."

"Exploding delight?"

"Really?" Cora looked disappointed in him.

"Yeah, that was bad. I do like crunchy delight, though."

They all looked at each other in silence while they thought.

"What's your full name?" Jacob asked Juniper.

"Juniper Flo'ri Nacia. Why?"

"I don't know. Just wondering if we could name them after you somehow."

"Flories?" Cora seemed unsure.

"Nacias?" Jacob offered.

Juniper pondered the idea with a hand over her mouth and her eyes narrowed.

"I really like nacias," Cora said.

"I think I do, too." Juniper nodded several times.

"I think we've got it," Jacob said. "Right?"

Cora and Jacob looked to Juniper for final approval.

She closed her eyes. "One order of nacias, please," she said as if testing how it sounded out loud. "I'll bring those nacias right out." She opened her eyes. "Nacia is my husband's surname. I've always loved the sound of it." She flashed a wistful smile. "He always supported me—my dream of owning my own restaurant. I think he'd be honored." Her smile grew bigger. "Nacias, it is!"

"Nacias are about to take this town by storm." Cora held up a hand to Jacob and a hand to Juniper. Jacob slapped her hand on the first try this time. Juniper looked confused, but slapped Cora's hand, too.

"We gotta get Tadrick to try these." Cora's eyes were wide.

"I'll make up another plate, minus the pineapple." Juniper got to work.

Jacob's face hurt from smiling so much. He rubbed his jaw muscles with both hands.

As Juniper worked, she said, "So what were you talking about earlier? About some poem?"

"Oh yeah." Jacob started to reach for the parchment but remembered he'd made it into a capybara and given it to Juniper's kids. He didn't need it anyway. He cleared his throat and recited it aloud:

> *"Hail to all explorers with adventure in their hearts.*
> *Let me regale you of the place where this adventure starts.*
> *It's easy if you work together, what I say is true.*
> *Just boat a creek on rainy main to all afloat for two."*

"Hmm," Juniper said. "Why is the last part in the faun tongue?"

"What?"

"That last line. That's the faun tongue, right?"

"Why do you say that?"

"Say it again." Juniper stopped fixing up the nacias to concentrate.

"Just boat a creek on rainy main to all afloat for two," Jacob repeated.

"Bo ta'cree con rai nemane to'a laflo ta'fo ortu, right?"

"What does that mean?"

"Twenty paces north from the big tree on the hill."

Jacob's heart threatened to bound out of his chest.

CHAPTER 13

The Big Tree on the Hill

"Are you telling me that this whole time, all someone had to do was recite the poem to a faun and they would have had it?"

"I'm not telling you anything." Juniper held her hands up in front of her.

"But that's it. That's what the wealthy woman, Mrs. Fenton, meant by working together. If someone would have simply chatted with a faun about the treasure, it would have been solved already."

"The big tree on the hill is so obvious," Cora said. "It has to be referring to the giant Ceiba tree on the hill to the north."

"But isn't that on Mr. Lowell's land?" Juniper said.

"Yeah. It is."

Jacob tried to picture the big tree to the north but came up blank.

"Do you remember the Smithe brothers?" Juniper asked.

"No." Cora looked up as she thought. "I don't think so."

"The two kids who were caught hunting on Mr. Lowell's land."

"Oh yeah. What ended up happening to them?"

"Their parents were fined some extravagant amount. And they spent time in the constable's jail. I think it was at least a month. And they were just teenagers!"

Jacob gulped. Two things he absolutely wanted to avoid were fines and jail time. The idea of either was terrifying. But on the other hand, if they didn't trespass on Mr. Lowell's land, the treasure would remain in the ground, and Juniper would lose her restaurant.

Jacob had let fear stop him far too many times in his life. This was an opportunity to push past it, to do something meaningful for a friend. As scary as it was, he found that his fear wasn't strong enough to stop him.

"Well, shit," Jacob said. "We already messed up one...not exactly legal adventure about as bad as anyone could. There's no way we'll mess up that bad again, right?"

"Are you saying you want to sneak onto Mr. Lowell's land?" Cora looked surprised.

Jacob gulped again. "Do we have a choice? I mean, the alternative is letting the treasure sit there undiscovered. I don't think I could live myself if we did that. Do you?"

"No. You're right. We have to try."

As night fell, a thick cloud cover rolled in and a light rain began to fall.

When Tadrick showed up at the pub, they filled him in on all the recent developments. He unreservedly agreed that they needed to find the big tree on the hill as soon as possible. No one wanted to wait, so they decided to go as soon as it got a bit darker. The pub only had one customer. They debated leaving someone behind, but there were no volunteers. Juniper had to stay behind with her kids, but the others decided to close the pub and give the last customer a free beer as a consolation. He seemed more than happy with the deal.

In the twilight, Tadrick hurried home to retrieve three well-worn hooded cloaks and a shovel. He returned as the last light of the day faded into darkness.

Getting to the tree would be difficult. None of them were familiar with the terrain on Mr. Lowell's land. There was an obvious hill with a big tree from their current vantage point, but once near Mr. Lowell's property, it was going to be a dense jungle with an unbroken canopy above. Juniper offered to create a will-o'-the-wisp using faun magic as a beacon of sorts, but they wondered if that would draw unwanted attention.

"No one's gonna be out in the rain at night," Tadrick said. "I think it might be better than getting lost in the dark on Mr. Lowell's land. We should get in and out of there as quick as we can."

"But if there is anyone who even peeks outside, they're going to notice a flickering blue flame on the hill," Juniper said.

"True."

Juniper rubbed a horn, narrowing her eyes in thought. "I could make it small. It would float just above the ground, and always be, say, thirty feet ahead of you."

"And it would lead us to the hill?" Jacob asked.

"Yes. If I could get a bearing from here." She focused her attention on the north. The tree and hill were barely visible in the dulled Ringlight. "Yes. I could do that if you wanted me to."

The three pub owners consulted each other with looks and all nodded.

"Alright." Juniper looked up and down the street. When no one was seen, she began to whisper and make circular motions with her hands.

An aquamarine fire, about as big as a capybara, appeared up the road about thirty feet. It was perfectly positioned between them and the tree. Juniper reached up and touched Cora gently on the shoulder.

"It will stay this exact distance from you, now," Juniper told Cora. "Always between you and the tree. When you want it to stop, brush off your shoulder as if trying to brush away dirt."

"Thank you." Cora seemed touched that Juniper had chosen her.

"Well." Tadrick looked around the area nervously. "We should probably get going before anyone wonders what we're doing with a magical blue fire out here."

Juniper wished them well as they rushed off behind the ghostly flame.

It wasn't long before they were off the road and into the jungle. The rain had picked up in intensity on the short journey, so the canopy was a welcomed reprieve from the brunt of it, even though it was extremely dark.

Even with the will-o'-the-wisp's guidance, it was tough to navigate through the dense vegetation at night. Everything they wore was getting wetter, and their progress was painfully slow.

"You didn't happen to grab a lantern, did you?" Tadrick asked both Jacob and Cora.

"No." Jacob was disappointed in himself. "But that would have been a good idea."

"Should we go back?" Cora said.

"Don't you have light magic?" Tadrick asked her.

"Yes. But it might draw attention, as well."

"Maybe just a little?"

"Sure." Cora pulled her cloak down from her right shoulder, revealing one of her silver rune tattoos. She traced it with a finger and said a single word Jacob didn't understand. A soft light began to glow from the palms of her hands.

Jacob had so little experience with magic that the will-o'-the-wisp and Cora's lighted hands would have absolutely amazed him if he hadn't been so focused on getting to the treasure without being caught. Those marvels were still endlessly fascinating, but he couldn't help but categorize them as simply means to an end at this moment. He would love to learn more about them later, though.

Cora's light made traversing the jungle easier, but it was still no stroll on the beach. The rain above the canopy was ever-increasing, creating a cacophony of percussive sound. And enough broke through to thoroughly soak them, now.

"I'm sure we're on Mr. Lowell's property, already," Tadrick said.

Just the thought was unsettling. Jacob didn't know much about Mr. Lowell, but from the few things he did know, he seemed like a very powerful and unpleasant man.

The ground began to climb under their feet. The steady incline made progress even harder.

"The jungle should end soon," Cora said. "I think we're actually on the hill now."

Her prediction was accurate. The vegetation came to an abrupt halt after another five minutes of trudging. The hill rose in front of them, nothing but short grass covering it aside from the giant tree on top. It seemed as if the jungle on the hill had been purposefully cleared away long ago.

"It's been like this since I was a kid." Cora pointed to the grass. "I heard that Mrs. Fenton loved this ceiba tree and used to spend her days leaning against it and reading when she was young."

"Seems like a good time to me," Tadrick said as he followed Cora up the hill.

"Ceiba trees are sacred to the ciguapa people," Cora continued. "Mrs. Fenton would often allow ciguapa weddings to be held on this hill. She said that the tree and all her land truly belonged to everyone and refused to enforce any legal rights in regard to trespassing. I remember hearing my parents talk about Mrs. Fenton several times when I was growing up. They always had nice things to say about her. There was mutual respect there. Even as a kid, I understood that."

"Too bad Mr. Lowell isn't as welcoming as she was," Jacob said.

"Yeah. When he came into possession of her land, Mr. Lowell made it immediately clear that the shared use of the hill would no longer continue. He put up signs all along the border back then. Most of them are gone, now, but I remember they made some pretty intimidating threats."

No one said anything for several steps as they climbed the hill. Jacob's thighs were burning and he was having a tough time catching his breath.

"Human and ciguapa relations took a real hit the day Mrs. Fenton died," Cora said. "We ciguapa were made to feel unwelcome on our own damn island. I remember my parents being so angry, but also so sad. I didn't fully understand at the time, but I knew something had changed for the worse."

"That's...not good." Jacob knew his words sounded stupid, but couldn't think of anything better to say.

"Yeah."

As they reached the top of the hill, the sky really opened up. A cloudburst relentlessly poured down on them, making vision and communication difficult. Lightning flashed to the north, illuminating everything in a flare of purple light.

"Well, we should probably hurry and get out of here," Tadrick called over the din. "I'll march off twenty paces."

He put his back to the northern aspect of the massive tree, then began to march. When he stopped, he thrust the shovel into the grass and began digging. After several minutes, he paused to rest, leaning against the shovel and panting. Cora offered to take over the dig, but Jacob took the shovel first, reminding her that they still needed the magical light from her palms.

Lightning struck again, much closer this time. The sky rumbled as if the gods were crumbling it to pieces.

Jacob sunk the shovel into the soil and tossed it into a pile that Tadrick had started. As the rain continued to hammer down, the pile of dirt was reduced to a stream of mud flowing down the hill to the north. Jacob dug with a singular focus. Scoop the soil, toss, and repeat. The work was soothing in a way. All else fell away as he moved dirt from one place to another.

After an unknown interval of time, Tadrick put his hand on Jacob's shoulder. Jacob thought he meant to take the shovel back, but instead, Tadrick shushed him.

"What's that on the skyline?" Tadrick pointed to the east. "I thought I saw it move."

Jacob saw nothing at first, but as he squinted into the rain, he saw what Tadrick had seen. There was a shape silhouetted against the muted glow of the Ring through the clouds on top of a rounded hill.

Cora brushed off her shoulder and said another ciguapa word. Both the light from her hands and the will-o'-the-wisp vanished, leaving them in darkness.

Jacob had looked away when Cora spoke. When he focused back on the silhouette, it was moving. A hooded figure progressed along the ridge, then disappeared.

"Who could that be?" Jacob asked.

"I don't know," Tadrick replied. "One of Mr. Lowell's people?"

"Hopefully it's nothing." Cora didn't seem as bothered as Jacob was, although she didn't relight her palms.

"No way they could tell who we are from there," Tadrick said. "But we should hurry up and get out of here." He looked at Jacob. "Here, I can take over for a bit."

"Can I get a few more scoops?"

It was hard to tell in the dark, but Tadrick seemed to give him a *go-ahead* gesture.

Jacob pushed the shovel into the dirt, but it struck something much more solid. He felt as if a caged animal was thrashing about in his chest. Probing the solid object with the point of the shovel, he carefully dug around it. When it seemed like the object might be loose enough to pull up with his hands, he fell to his knees, reached down, and gripped it.

The object was still lodged, but violent shaking tore it free.

As Jacob pulled it from the hole, he could make out its shape in the dull Ringlight. It was a small treasure chest, about the size of the block of cheese at the pub. He thought it was small for a chest that was supposed to hold vast riches, but maybe it was filled with precious gems. It didn't take many of those to add up to serious wealth.

Lightning crashed nearby with an ear-shattering crack.

As the rain continued to pour, Jacob held the treasure chest aloft over his head, triumphantly shaking it up and down and cheering something incoherent. He was sure his actions would be seen as overdramatic, but he didn't care at the moment. He could be embarrassed later, but right now, this was everything he hoped his new life could be. The pure adventure of it was joyous. And the knowledge that Juniper's troubles were going to be over because of what they had done filled him with a warm pride that pushed away the cold of the soaking rain.

The chest was full of something that clattered noisily as he shook it. He would have loved to open it right there, but the figure on the horizon pulled him back to reality.

"Alright," said Cora, slapping his back and laughing. "Let's get going."

Jacob tucked the chest under his arm and followed Cora back down the hill. Once under the canopy again, Cora made her light reappear.

The journey back was so much easier. They had already found the easiest route on the way up, and the incline was slightly downhill. Although the real reason for the ease of the trip

was that Jacob's mind churned with the possibilities this treasure would bring. Would there be enough to save Juniper's business, help the young orcs, and still have enough to maybe...buy his own ship and fill it with a crew including Cora, Tadrick, and Yandro if they wanted to go with him? It was a silly thought, but one that made him happy.

They came out from the jungle onto the dirt road that led to Mrs. Covington's. Cora cut the light and hurried down the familiar road.

Lightning flashed again, further west.

In no time, they were back at the pub.

Just before he stepped inside, Jacob glanced back the way they came.

He could have sworn there was a hooded figure barely visible where the road touched the skyline. With a whispered curse, he jumped inside and slammed the door behind him.

CHAPTER 14

The Treasure Chest

"I'll start a fire." Jacob tossed his soaking cloak on the nearest table. He grabbed wood from a small pile around the corner from the bar. Inside, he was dying to open the chest, but a warm fire was going to be so nice for him and the others. They were dripping all over the floor and shivering in the cool air of the pub.

Jacob's hands were shaking as he struck flint to steel. He did his best not to wet the tinder, keeping his dripping shirt as far away as possible. The first several strikes produced nothing, but eventually, a spark landed in the perfect spot and began smoking. Carefully, Jacob blew on the emergent flame until all the tinder was ablaze. Jacob held his breath and hoped he wouldn't have to repeat the process. Luckily, the kindling caught fast, and soon, an orange, not-magical fire crackled in the fireplace.

The three of them huddled close around its warmth. It may not have been formed with magic, but the relief the fire brought to Jacob's frigid hands was magic enough. They all stood silently as warmth worked its way into their bones.

"Alright." Jacob rubbed his rewarmed hands together. "Let's see what's inside."

Cora and Tadrick were clearly champing at the bit to open the chest, too. The entire time they were huddled around the fire, they couldn't keep their eyes off of it.

Jacob squatted to get a closer look at the chest. It must have been beautifully stained and well-polished at some point. Even though it had awaited discovery for years in wet soil, it seemed as if a quick rinsing might have it shining in no time. The latch and hinges showed the most wear—what was once gleaming brass had been tarnished to a greenish patina by the elements.

"Go ahead and do the honors." Cora held her open palms out toward the chest.

"Are you sure?" Jacob asked.

"You're the one who pulled it out of the ground. You should open it. Right, Tad?"

Tadrick nodded in agreement.

Jacob grinned and fiddled with the latch on the front. The latch clicked open and his heart skipped a beat.

Slowly, he opened the lid, revealing a single rolled sheet of well-battered parchment tied with a red ribbon sitting on a pile of small river rocks.

"What?" he said, not able to grasp what he was seeing yet.

The three of them stood, staring into the chest for the span of several breaths.

"Well, let's see what it says," Tadrick finally said as he picked up the parchment.

He untied the ribbon, then rolled it out so everyone could read it. The parchment was filled with wonderful calligraphy, the same script as the original Fenton Poem. It read:

Congratulations!
You've discovered the second clue!

You have worked together, combining the common and faun tongues to find what many have sought. I hope that my little adventure has helped expand your minds, and I hope the word gets out that such a collaboration was necessary. I believe that the only way forward in our great League of Islands is through working together. Only when all the races learn to realize our

"Another clue?" Jacob hung his head. He should have known this would be nothing more than a clue. The poem mentioned this being the place where the adventure *starts*. It seemed painfully obvious, now. He felt stupid for expecting anything else.

They all stood and stared at the ground.

"How many are there going to be?" Tadrick broke the silence.

"Who knows?" Jacob said. "It literally took years for anyone to figure out the first clue. How can we expect to find the treasure in two weeks?"

"Maybe the second won't be as hard?" Cora said, hopefully. "I mean, now we know what Mrs. Fenton was trying to do with this whole thing; fostering cooperation between the different races on the islands."

"Well, let's take a look." Tadrick shrugged. "You never know."

The three of them crowded around the parchment, which Cora had laid out on a table with empty beer mugs holding down the corners.

"Does that look like any language you're familiar with?" Jacob asked Cora.

"No. But I only know the ciguapa and human tongues."

"Doesn't look familiar to me, either," Tadrick added.

"Hmm."

"What do you think the big three means?" Cora tapped the number.

The other two shrugged and shook their heads.

The fire popped in the fireplace, drawing their attention.

"You know what?" Cora said. "We can think about this tomorrow. I'm going back by the fire for a bit."

"Good idea." Tadrick followed her to the floor in front of the fireplace, where they both sat down.

Jacob stared at the parchment for a few more minutes, gears turning, but not engaging anything resembling rational thought.

Returning to the fire sounded really nice.

Tadrick scooted over as Jacob slid in next to him, and the three of them imbued themselves with warmth in silence. The only sounds were the crackle of the fire and the pit-a-pat of the subsiding rain.

THE MELON PATCH

Mrs. Covington shuffled out through her door, Arthur following close behind. Once outside, she sniffed the morning air before leaping gracefully into the pond. She submerged her head, then let herself float to the surface, just high enough to breathe.

There was...something in the air. It was a familiar scent, but she still couldn't place exactly what it was. A glance behind her showed that Arthur had noticed it, too. He hadn't even jumped in the water yet, too busy following his nose around the grassy side of the pool.

Mrs. Covington dunked her head one more time, then climbed out of the pond. The morning sun had risen just high enough to reach her, so she stood and soaked it in as she dripped water onto the grass. The feeling was pleasant, but her stomach rumbled as she caught the scent again.

Arthur had already made it to the base of the hill that rose up alongside the creek to the north. His nose was high in the air, moving up and down as he tried to pinpoint the scent's location. As Mrs. Covington came up beside him, they exchanged a series of chattering sounds.

Mrs. Covington ducked her head and pushed in through the underbrush at the bottom of the hill. She kept her eyes closed until she made it through to a clearing of sorts built into the hillside. Someone had dug out a flat area and put a wooden picket fence around it. The fence was just a bit taller than Arthur, who had come out from the underbrush just behind her. Without delay, he hopped his front feet onto the fence and tried to peer over it.

Mrs. Covington stood next to the fence and positioned an eye so she could see through one of the slits between boards. Inside, the fenced area was teeming with just-ripened cantaloupes. One of them had been smashed, and there was a bare spot where several had been picked. Her mouth watered as she inspected the fence for any entrances, finding none.

Arthur moved his body backward and forward with his front feet on the fence, trying to knock it over. The fence was much too strong to break, though, so he eventually gave up the effort.

The two capybaras circumnavigated the fenced area twice, but there were no obvious weaknesses to exploit.

Mrs. Covington searched the immediate area for anything that might be of use. The only thing she found was a large rock several steps uphill. It was lodged into the ground, but most of it was sticking out. Mrs. Covington circled to the uphill side of the rock and began pushing on it with her front feet. The rock became much looser in the dirt, but wouldn't budge enough to roll out from it.

Arthur watched her from near the fence as she worked on dislodging the rock. He looked at her, the rock, and the fence several times. He scratched an itch on his right side with his back foot, sniffed the air again, then trudged uphill to join Mrs. Covington. The rock was wide enough for both of the capybaras to fit their feet on. Arthur sidled up to her, placed his front feet on the rock, and began to bounce up and down, mimicking Mrs. Covington's rhythm.

The rock was loose after only a few of these bounces. It started to tip precariously to the downhill side. Both capybaras kept up the pressure, keeping time with each other as the rock inched its way out of its place.

The soil on the downhill side gave way, and the rock rolled out of the hole. Arthur was not quick enough to right himself as the rock moved out from under his feet, and his momentum caused him to tumble forward. He rolled down the hill behind the rock but was able to regain his footing, somewhat gracefully, after only one rotation.

The rock picked up speed as it plummeted toward the melon patch. It struck another rock on its way down, causing it to spin into the air. With a clamorous crash, it careened into the fence, breaking away the top halves of two of the wooden pickets. The rock landed on a cantaloupe, smashing it to pulp, then came to rest against the pickets on the other side of the fence.

Without delay, Mrs. Covington hurried down the hill and leaped into the newly-accessible patch. Arthur, who seemed no worse for wear after his tumble, followed her in over the broken part of the fence.

Mrs. Covington bit into a chunk of the burst cantaloupe. The flavor was sweet and wonderful. It may have been the best thing she had ever tasted. Using her front feet to hold the pieces in place, and her front teeth to scrape the melon from the rind, she made quick work of the remaining bits.

The two of them continued their feeding frenzy until they were beyond satiated. They stood motionless in the melon patch, basking in gastronomic glory for several minutes. Then, slowly, they wandered over to the opening in the fence. With bellies full, it was harder to crawl over the broken pickets, but they were able to just make it over.

Mrs. Covington traversed the downhill climb, pushed back through the underbrush, and slid into the pool, where she did nothing but float for the rest of the morning.

CHAPTER 15

You Sing

Jacob awoke with the clue on his mind. He felt that the big number three was the most significant part, but didn't know why. After laying in bed, pondering its meaning, he got up and wandered out back. Mrs. Covington and Arthur were floating contentedly in the pond behind the pub. Jacob took a chair from the outdoor covered area and set it near the creek. He spent most of the morning watching it go by while he contemplated the clue. The combination of the babbling water and the happy capybaras made for a relaxing start to a day.

At around noon, Jacob meandered back inside to find three men waiting for him at the bar. A human in expensive-looking clothes was flanked by a tall ciguapa with slicked-back hair and a large, muscular human. The ciguapa and large human both straightened as Jacob entered.

"Pardon our intrusion," the man in the fancy suit said. "I was feeling quite thirsty, and hoped to get a drink in your fine establishment."

"Oh, no intrusion at all," Jacob replied. "I let time get away from me out back. I really should have been in here waiting for potential customers."

The entire time Jacob had been in his presence, the tall ciguapa man studied his every move.

"One beer, please." The rich man held a finger up.

"Just one?"

"They're working." He looked Jacob dead in the eye without a hint of warmth in his expression.

"Alright, then." Jacob poured the beer, a vague unease taking residence in his chest.

He slid the beer across the bar to the man, who picked it up and took a tiny sip.

"If you don't already know, I am Mr. Lowell," the man said importantly. "Commissioner of the New Dawn City Council and owner of a significant portion of this island."

"I didn't recognize you. But I have heard of you." Jacob couldn't stop his eyes from going to the clue, which was rolled up at the end of the bar. The ciguapa man followed his glance, eyes narrowed.

"Most people have," Mr. Lowell said. "Most people know that I own the hill with the giant Ceiba tree on it, too. Did you know that?"

Jacob's heart dropped into his stomach. "No...I didn't know that." He poured every bit of concentration into keeping a straight face.

"You're new to this island, aren't you? I heard that Mr. Davies sold you this...charming little pub only days ago. Is that right?"

"Yes, sir. I am the new owner."

"So, as the owner, you would have full knowledge of the comings and goings from this place, day or night, rain or shine, correct?"

"Well...yeah. Of course." Jacob gulped. "Why do you ask?"

"I just wanted to make sure you were staying safe." Mr. Lowell's smile did not even come close to reaching his eyes. "You see, my property was trespassed upon very recently. I think it's important for those of us who own land and buildings to remain vigilant at all times. I wouldn't want you to have anything stolen from you, as it seems has happened to me."

"Thank you. But I don't have much to worry about in that sense. I don't have much here that anyone would want to steal." Jacob did his best to remain calm and guarded. Mr. Lowell knew something about the events of last night, but how much he knew was still a question.

"Yes, I can see that." Mr. Lowell looked around the pub, unimpressed. "I, on the other hand, have much to lose. Have you heard about the Fenton Treasure?"

Jacob suppressed a gulp. "I have. Not much, though."

"The worth of that treasure is something I do not take lightly. And it is widely believed that the treasure is hidden somewhere on what used to be Mrs. Fenton's land. Which is now my land."

"Oh yeah?"

"Yeah." Mr. Lowell looked him in the eyes for the span of several breaths, never blinking. The ciguapa was still staring daggers into him, too. "So, I figure, we, as neighbors, should look out for each other. Don't you agree?"

"Of course."

"Good. So, then you would tell me if you knew anything about the trespass on my property last night, right?"

"Of course."

"Of course. And I, in turn, will let you know about any threats to you or your business partners. There are powerful people on this island who could, say, have this pub reduced to rubble with the stroke of a pen. We absolutely wouldn't want something like that to happen."

"No." Jacob couldn't force out anything else.

"Well." Mr. Lowell took another sip of beer. "I feel like this conversation is far from over, but I will take my leave of it for now. I'm intrigued about where it will lead us next, and I wouldn't miss it for the world." Mr. Lowell nodded, and the big human slapped a copper coin on the bar. "It was nice to make your acquaintance. I look forward to the next time we speak."

Jacob nodded and scooped the copper from the bar as the three men stood to leave.

Before taking a step, the ciguapa man leaned across the bar and snatched the rolled parchment, never taking his eyes off of Jacob. His ever-watchful stare dared Jacob to object, but it was a dare he couldn't accept. Instead, he stood frozen as they exited the pub.

Cora and Tadrick showed up together not long after Mr. Lowell and his henchmen left. Jacob told them about the encounter, trying his best to remember every word that was spoken.

"So that cloaked figure we thought we saw on the skyline was real, then," Tadrick said.

"Yeah." Jacob blinked. "And I saw the same figure down the road just before we entered the pub. I didn't say anything because... Well, I should have told you."

"The important thing is that we all get on the same page," Cora said.

"The clue!" Tadrick blurted. "Does anyone remember what it said?"

Cora nodded. "Get me some paper and I'll write it down." She pointed to her head. "It's all up here. I couldn't think about much else last night."

Jacob retrieved a sheet of paper from his desk—thankful for Cora's memory—and Cora rewrote the clue.

"So, what should we do about Mr. Lowell?" Jacob asked. "Even if we solve this clue, we'll have to contend with them."

"We'll be careful." Cora shrugged. "If and when we find the treasure, we'll have to be a bit more discreet about spending the money."

Cora had such a carefree outlook on life. Jacob envied her.

"We'll be more careful." Tadrick was less worried than he should have been, too.

Jacob didn't see much success in trying to get his business partners to take Mr. Lowell more seriously, so he studied the clue Cora had written down instead.

Olwwoh Eurwlhu

3

"I'm gonna go ask Juniper if it makes any sense to her," Jacob said, taking the clue.

Next door, he found Juniper serving food to a small faun family. He waited for her to finish, standing in the doorway and reading the clue again.

When she had set all the plates down and spoken to the customers in the faun tongue, she walked over to Jacob.

"Can I get you some nacias?" she said with a smile.

"Well, yeah. I'm not going to turn those down."

"Come with me." She motioned for him to follow her into the

kitchen. He waved to the faun family as he passed them, and the kids waved back.

"What happened last night?" Juniper asked as soon as they were alone. "I would have come by earlier but I slept in late."

Jacob told her about everything, including Mr. Lowell's visit. As she pondered a response, Jacob handed her the paper.

"Does this make any sense to you?"

Juniper looked down at the paper, narrowing her eyes. She tried to sound out the words in many different ways, furrowing her brow when she was done.

"I have no idea," she finally said.

"Do you know any orcish?"

"I'm afraid I don't. Never seen it written, anyway."

"Damn. Alright, we'll keep working on it."

Juniper made him a plate of nacias. "Bring this back to share," she said as she handed it to him. "Hold it by the little towel. The plate is hot."

She balked when Jacob tried to pay her for them, but he insisted and ultimately won. After leaving three coppers on the kitchen counter he whisked the nacias away to his friends.

On his way back to the pub, he saw Yandro making a delivery to the mercantile store across the creek from Mrs. Covington's. Jacob called to him, inviting him to come by and try their new invention. Yandro held up a finger, indicating he would swing by when he was done.

Cora was pleasantly surprised by the nacias, letting out a little squeal of excitement when Jacob backed in through the front door.

"Save some for Yandro," Jacob said as he set them on the bar. "I invited him over to give them a try."

Cora flushed, and her jaw subtly tightened.

Moments later, Yandro burst in, looking handsome as ever.

"Come here and try these before they get too cold." Jacob waved him over.

Yandro greeted everyone, but only Jacob and Tadrick responded to him.

With an eye on Cora, Yandro bit into a cheesy chip.

"Wow." He closed his eyes and chewed. "This is really good."

"They're called nacias," Jacob said, proud despite having almost nothing to do with their creation.

"You figured out something good to do with the cheese." Yandro flashed Cora a smile, but she didn't return it. After eating another, Yandro said, "You were really busy the other night," to Cora.

"Yep." Her delivery was deadpan.

"That's good...right? I haven't seen the place that full...well, ever before."

Cora crunched into a chip, looking toward the fireplace.

Jacob felt the awkwardness and wanted to help alleviate it. "Yeah. It was a great night. Cora really made it look nice in here. I think the atmosphere was perfect...and stuff."

Cora shot him a look that cut him short from whatever small talk he was about to engage in next.

"Yeah, it does look great." Yandro's hopeful smile was all but gone. "I would have stayed longer, but my boss had something urgent for me. So..." He stopped himself mid-sentence and frowned.

Cora said nothing.

"So," Yandro continued, "I guess I'll see you guys later. Thank you for the chip things. I think you got something there."

Jacob and Tadrick said their goodbyes while Cora rubbed a rag over a spot on the bar. When Yandro was gone, Jacob wanted to ask Cora about the cold shoulder but also didn't want to stick his nose where it didn't belong.

~

Around dinner time, a couple who had been at the pub for the grand reopening came in.

"Are you guys planning on doing that singing thing again?" the woman asked. "The *you sing* thing, where the band plays and people from the audience can sing with them?"

"Well..." Jacob gave inquisitive looks to his partners. "We meant to gauge interest in the idea. But we kinda got distracted.".

"The singer left for good," Tadrick said. "I could ask Darian if they'd be interested in doing that again. We'd have to pay them, though."

Jacob looked to Cora, who nodded her approval.

"Yeah, ask them if they'll do it again. Maybe we could have them come every Finiday night?"

"Sounds good to me," Cora said. "People seemed to like it."

Tadrick jumped up from his stool. "I'll go ask right now."

As Tadrick exited, Jacob asked the couple if they would like to try a new food creation, free of charge. When they agreed, he hurried over to Juniper's place.

She was clearing the table where the family had eaten when he entered.

"We've got our first order of nacias!" Jacob said. "If you don't mind giving a plate away for free."

"I don't mind," Juniper said. "Gotta get the word out somehow."

She carried a stack of dirty dishes back to the kitchen and came out five minutes later with a hot plate of nacias.

Jacob thanked her, then brought the plate to the couple, who had ordered two beers while they waited. As he watched them take their first bites, Jacob held his breath, hoping they would like them as much as he did. He let it out when both of them perked up with eyes widened. They didn't even wait long enough to swallow before they started praising the tastes.

"Will you have these here, to order?" the man said between chews.

"Yes. In partnership with the wonderful restaurant next door, we'll be serving these now. They're called nacias."

The couple made short work of the plate, devouring every chip and going through two beers each in the process. Jacob did his best not to be awkward and stare as they ate, but he was excited. Coins were jingling in his ears as he imagined the word about nacias spreading like wildfire through the town. He pictured the pub full to capacity, everybody crunching away to their hearts' content.

Tadrick came back with a line of sweat on his brow. He waved Jacob and Cora toward the big doors, out of earshot of the customers. "The band said they'll do it."

"Great." Jacob put two thumbs in the air.

"They want fifty coppers a night, though."

"That sounds reasonable...right?" Jacob had started confident but faded to unsure by the third word.

"I think so." Cora's eyes were aimed at the ceiling. "We could make that back in nacias and beer sales in no time if the crowd is anything like it was last time."

"I think it's worth a try," Tadrick said. "We have to take some bold risks if we're going to give this thing a chance to work." His expression changed from excited to much more serious. "But I don't think I should be part of the decision, because I have interest on both sides with Darian."

"I've known you a long time," Cora said. "You're not gonna do something stupid and put the pub in danger just so you and Darian can swindle money from this place. Your input is just as valid as ours."

"Yeah," Jacob added. "And if this works out, it could be mutually beneficial for a while to come."

"So, you'll have that *you sing* thing here, then?" the woman called from the bar. "I don't mean to be impatient, but we have to get going."

"Yes, ma'am," Tadrick said. "We will."

"Every Finiday night?"

"Every Finiday night." Cora looked confident. "Tell your friends and family."

"And you'll have these chip things here?" the man asked.

"Absolutely," Jacob said. "All the nacias you can eat."

CHAPTER 16

Deciphering

Tadrick said he'd be right back, then left the pub again. When he returned about an hour later, he carried a flat piece of wood and some paint.

"I'm going to make a sign for tomorrow's festivities," he said as he got to work on the floor near the fireplace.

Jacob served beer to a lone customer while Tadrick painted. The man was tall, stout, and had a fencing sword in a sheath attached to his belt.

"Hello, sir," Jacob said to the man. "My name is Jacob."

"I'm Micheal." The man nodded.

"You're a sword fighter?"

"Not exactly a fighter, but I do like fencing for sport."

"I'd love to do that someday." Jacob had always been fascinated with the idea of learning how to use a sword. He wondered why he'd never acted on it.

"You should, then." Micheal nodded again.

"You know, I really should." Jacob's eyes pointed unfocused at the floor.

The man sipped his beer, seemingly lost in thought himself.

Mrs. Covington jumped down from her bed and waddled over to where Tadrick was painting, apparently fascinated by his work.

The fencing man left before his beer was even finished. When he was gone, Jacob rounded the bar and peered over Tadrick's shoulder. The sign looked fantastic. Each letter was perfect, like the print in a book.

"Oh!" Tadrick pulled his brush from the board. "I almost wrote *macias* instead of nacias. Not quite used to that word yet."

Tadrick got back to painting. When he finished, the sign read:

TONIGHT!
YOU SING
with Bilge Rat!
And Try the Taste Sensation
Sweeping New Dawn
NACIAS!

Next to the word *nacias,* he painted a realistic plate full of delicious-looking nacias. He was an impressive artist.

Mrs. Covington tried to take a step onto the board as he painted, but Tadrick gently held her back with his left hand while painting with his right.

When the plate was complete, Tadrick stopped and dropped the brush into a jar of murky water. "Holy shit." He stared at the sign.

"What?" Cora leaned over the bar, trying to see.

"I might actually have it."

"Have what?" Jacob asked.

"The clue."

"What?" Cora swung around the bar and joined the other two in gaping at the sign.

"It's..." Tadrick took a moment to collect his thoughts. "When we were kids, my older brother and I used to write things in code to each other. The code was super easy, but none of our friends could ever figure it out without us telling them how it worked."

"And?" Cora spun her hand in a circle, urging him on.

"And the code was done by moving each letter forward or back one place in the alphabet. I was just reminded of it when I almost wrote macias. It was like what we used to do. An *n* would sometimes be an *m* in our code."

"So, the three might mean how many spots to move over in the alphabet," Cora said, obviously much faster to catch on than Jacob was.

"Exactly!"

"Let's try it." Cora rushed to the bar, grabbed the paper with the clue, and returned to the floor by the sign. "If we move forward three, the first letter is *r.*" She wrote an R under the O, then continued to work wordlessly until she was done. Under the strange words of the clue, she had written:

Olwwoh Eurwlhu
Rozzrk Hxuzokx

"Well that doesn't make any sense, either," Tadrick said. "Try going back three letters."

Cora nodded and went back to work. This time when she finished, it read:

Olwwoh Eurwlhu
~~**_Rozzrk Hxuzokx_**~~
Little Brother

"Little brother!" Jacob had no idea what it meant, but they were getting somewhere.

"I know what that means!" Cora was giddy as she stood.

"What?"

"In the ciguapa tongue, little brother is *poqu harro,* which is what we call the smaller of the two islands on the lake."

"The lake?" Jacob was unfamiliar.

"There's a lake about an hour's walk to the west from New Dawn. There are two islands out in the middle of it—Big Sister and Little Brother."

"So, we...or you two just figured it out, then?" Jacob's eyes were wide.

"I think we did." Cora shot Tadrick an inquisitive look. He shrugged and nodded back at her.

"It's only Mediday," Tadrick said. "We've got our big night, hopefully, tomorrow. But should we close down and go check this out now?"

"I want to," Cora said, resolute.

They both looked to Jacob. While considering the impulsive idea, he noticed Mrs. Covington standing on the freshly-painted sign. When he gently shooed her off of it, she left paint footprints across the top left corner. It looked as if it was done on purpose.

"Nice." Tadrick focused back on Jacob, awaiting an answer.

Jacob thought about Mr. Lowell, and whether or not he'd have people watching them tonight. He wondered if this night would be any different than any other night. If he was being honest with himself, he couldn't wait to get out to discover the next part of this treasure hunt. They could be extra careful. There really wasn't a good reason not to go right then.

"Let's do it," he said, eliciting cheers from Cora and Tadrick.

A few customers wandered in before they could close. One of them even asked for nacias. But as soon as the pub was clear, they locked up and left. The sun was low on the western horizon, the sky already beginning to darken. Jacob thought it would have been nice to search for this clue in daylight, but closing the pub with patrons still drinking wasn't easy for him.

No will-o'-the-wisp was needed for this expedition. Cora was very familiar with the journey because her family lived in a village not far past the lake.

When they left, they tried a bit of misdirection, just in case they were being followed. Cora took them on a dirt road that led through a dense patch of jungle, but about halfway through, she led them down an embankment, around a giant tree, and onto a small hidden path. Eventually, the path split in three directions, allowing them to go back the way they had come. Jacob kept looking over his shoulder but never saw a trace of anyone.

Feeling clever and relatively safe, the three of them made the hour-long trek across rugged terrain without many words. At one point, there were two humans with muskets strapped to their backs and several ducks in their hands about a hundred yards to the north, but besides them, the area seemed free from people.

When Jacob was just starting to feel his thighs burn from the hike, a dog with golden yellow fur burst out of the underbrush, eliciting an embarrassing little shriek as Jacob instinctively recoiled. The dog, however, was anything but scary. His tongue hung out the left side of his mouth and his tail wagged furiously.

"Oh! I'm sorry," came a woman's voice just before she emerged from the tree line. "Tripp, stop bothering him."

"He's okay." Jacob tried to play it off like he hadn't just shrieked. He bent forward and scratched Tripp behind an ear.

"Hey, I'm Adriana," the woman said. "You've met Tripp." She turned as a man came out from the trees just behind her. "And this is my husband, Steven."

Jacob and Steven waved at each other. "Nice to meet you," Jacob said.

Cora and Tadrick backtracked from where they'd been hiking out ahead. They exchanged pleasantries with the hiking couple and petted the very enthusiastic dog.

"You headed to the lake?" Adriana asked.

"We sure are," said Cora.

"Oh, nice. We're just coming back from there."

"Was anyone else down that way?" Cora asked.

"Nope. Not a soul."

"Good," Cora said. "I mean…"

"I get it," Adriana said with a smile. "That's why we come out here, too. To be alone out in the wilderness."

"Yeah. That's what I meant," Cora said, recovering well.

"Well, have a nice hike," Adriana said.

"Thanks. You, too." Jacob gave the dog a final scratch behind the ear before continuing on their journey.

It didn't take long before Jacob's chest was expanding and contracting in giant breaths as he did all he could to keep up with Cora's pace. When they finally reached the edge of the lake, he found a fallen log and collapsed onto it. Tadrick bent forward with his hands on his knees.

"Now we just have to swim." Cora was barely breathing hard.

"Seriously?" Jacob went limp and let himself roll to the ground.

Cora laughed. "No. But we'll have to find a boat. Shouldn't be too hard. A lot of ciguapa fish this lake from boats."

"And we're going to take one?" Jacob asked.

"Yeah. Ciguapa are much more communal than humans. The boats don't belong to any one person. As long as we return it where we found it, and don't cause any damage, we're welcome to any boat we find."

"Hmm." Jacob didn't understand how that could possibly work but didn't have the energy to pursue it any further.

"I'll let you two rest a minute." She smirked as she headed down the bank to the left.

"You good?" Tadrick asked Jacob between breaths.

"Yeah. Are you?"

"I think so."

Jacob tried to laugh but found it difficult.

"Found one," Cora called as she jogged back to them. "It even has a sail." She pulled some grass and tossed it into the air. Jacob could just make out in the Ringlight that the breeze took the grass out into the lake. "And a favorable wind."

"But how will we get back?" Jacob wished he didn't have to ask.

"For someone who wants to be a sailor, you sure don't know much about sailing, do you?"

"I…"

"I'm sorry." Cora placed a hand on Jacob's shoulder. "That was rude. We all have to start somewhere." She turned and headed for the boat, motioning for him to follow. "I'll do my best to teach you how to tack on the way back."

The boat Cora had found was barely big enough to hold the three of them, but she swore it would make the journey.

"Alright, Jacob," Cora said. "You're about to get a crash course in sailing. At night. From an amateur at best."

"Could you not call it a crash course?" Tadrick was looking pale.

"Oh, don't worry so much."

"You know I can't swim."

Cora seemed to force her expression to be more serious. "I promise I'll keep this vessel upright. No swimming necessary on this voyage."

Tadrick nodded. He didn't look very reassured, but he awkwardly climbed into the boat, keeping a wide stance as it rocked with his weight.

Cora had Jacob help her push the boat into the water while Tadrick sat at the bow. They pushed until they were waist-high in the lake, then jumped up on either side of the stern. Jacob did his best to focus on Cora's sailing instruction instead of thinking about the walk back to the pub in soggy boots.

Luckily, Cora was a patient teacher. She took her time showing him each step while naming every line, yard, and sail. The boat only had one sail, so that was easy, but learning about the mechanics of sailing was fascinating. He forgot about the soggy trip back in minutes, enthralled with the idea of becoming a real sailor.

By the time they neared Little Brother, Jacob controlled both the sail and the rudder with confidence, although Cora did have to take over to avoid crashing into the beach too fast.

Feeling the pride of learning a new skill, Jacob bounded to the beach like he wasn't completely exhausted.

"Now what?" Tadrick asked.

No one had an answer.

The night was clear, allowing Ringlight to bathe the tiny island in a silvery blue glow. Besides the small patch of beach where Cora had landed, the terrain was mostly rock. There was very little, if any, vegetation to be seen. The island's only feature seemed to be a ten-foot-tall rocky prominence near its center.

"Let's search the island." Jacob shrugged. "It's not gonna take too long."

Cora went left, Tadrick went right, and Jacob made his way directly across to the rocky spur.

When Jacob arrived at the rock, he methodically inspected it, walking around it widdershins because he loved the word *widdershins.* He started as low as he could reasonably see, crouching as he examined the rock as closely as possible. He stood a little higher and made his way around the rock again. He continued around and around the natural monument one level at a time. Eventually, he made it to a place higher than his eye level. He had to find footholds and boost himself up to inspect the rock properly. Before he knew it, he was several feet from the ground, sweat beading on his forehead and saturating his hair.

With a grunt and a final upward lunge, his eyes crested the somewhat pointy top.

There was something carved into the rock at the tip. It looked like one of the magic runes ciguapa people wore as tattoos. This one was a vague representation of...a garment of some type. Maybe a cloak.

"Cora," Jacob called. "I found something."

Both Cora and Tadrick ran to where Jacob clung to the rock.

"What did you find?"

"It looks like a carving of one of your tattoos.... I think."

"What does it look like?"

"A cloak? Or a—"

"Veil?"

"Yeah! A veil. That's what it is."

"Alright. You can come down from there."

Jacob tried to gracefully climb down, but his foot slipped and he slid down the face of the rock, skinning both palms in the process.

"Are you okay?" Tadrick asked, rushing to him.

"Yeah." Jacob looked at his hands. His fingertips and the bottoms of his palms were skinned, but not to the point of bleeding. They hurt, but the excitement of clue-hunting dulled the pain. "I'm fine. Thanks."

"It's a rune I have," Cora said after hearing Jacob wasn't hurt. "One of the first ones we get. It's called *rinym* in our language, which is something like *reveal* in the human tongue."

Without much of a pause, Cora pulled up a sleeve and traced the tattoo on her shoulder, murmuring, "Rinym," when finished.

A violet light sprang to life on the ground. It seemed like a giant had taken bioluminescent algae from Cora's glass ball lights, only purple, and used it to write words on the island like Tadrick painting his sign. Nearly the entire east side of the island was lit up in a violet glow.

"It says something." Tadrick backed up toward the water.

Jacob looked down to find himself between a *d* and a *v*. He followed Tadrick to the edge of the island.

It was hard to see the complete message, but as far as Jacob could tell, it read:

. . .

Iroorz Nlex
  Dv idu dv srvvldoh
  Zlwerxw jhwwlqj brxu iggw zhw

"More nonsense," he said.

"Apply the code." Tadrick whipped out a small notebook and began writing. After about a minute, he turned the notebook around to show Cora and Jacob. It now read:

Follow Kibu
  As far as possible
  Without getting your feet wet

Cora retraced her tattoo and said another word. The purple words vanished in an instant

"Does *Kibu* mean anything to either of you?" Jacob felt like he knew their answers before they spoke. When they both answered in the negative, he said, "I figured that'd be the case. It'd be way too easy if *Kibu* was common knowledge."

"Let's get out of here," Cora said. "We still have a long way to go to get home."

They were about to push off when Cora held up a hand. "Look," she whispered, pointing across the lake to where they had come from.

Jacob squinted, and could just make out the forms of two people in the Ringlight.

"It's Mr. Lowell's henchmen." Cora's eyesight must have been way better than Jacob's.

"So, they figured it out, too." Tadrick kept his voice low.

"Either that or followed us here," Jacob whispered.

"Quick, let's pull the boat around to the other side of the island." Cora was knee-deep in the water, pulling a rope tied to the bow before Jacob could even process what she said. He waded into the water as quietly as possible and helped by pushing the boat's stern. Tadrick followed his lead.

"You think they saw us?" Jacob asked as they rounded the small island, now out of sight from the henchmen. "They had to have seen that glow at least."

"If they did, they did." Cora shrugged. "Not much we can do about it. This isn't Mr. Lowell's land, so we've got just as much right to be here as they do, anyway."

Jacob nodded, although he was much less nonchalant about the whole thing. His worries were twofold: he was afraid of what Mr. Lowell could do if provoked, and he was afraid of someone else finding the treasure before they did.

"I'll have to give you the tacking-into-the-wind lesson later. We'll sail *with* the wind to the other shore and circle back from there. It'll only add another hour or so to the trip."

Only? Jacob didn't give voice to his dismay, not wanting to sound like a complainer.

The trip to the opposite bank was quick. After securing the boat, the three of them started their hike around the north side of the lake. When they were more or less even with Little Brother, the island lit up in the familiar purple light. The glow out on the water was equal parts eerie and beautiful.

"They figured it out." Tadrick kicked a rock.

"Let's just hope they don't know what *Kibu* means," Jacob added.

"Maybe they haven't broken the code yet," Cora said as she hiked out ahead. "They might have just followed us here like you said."

The journey back was much more arduous than the journey to the lake. On several occasions, Jacob felt like curling up beside the trail and falling asleep, but Cora kept them moving until they were back within the safe confines of the pub.

Jacob pulled off his boots and flung them into his room. "I'll see you two in the morning." He said before following his boots and flopping onto his bed.

CHAPTER 17

Another Idea

The next day around lunch, three different groups came to the pub specifically for nacias. Altogether, they sold seven plates in the span of two hours. Word of mouth was spreading fast through town. Not nearly fast enough to save Juniper's restaurant, but much faster than Jacob could have realistically hoped.

Tadrick spruced up the capybara footprints on the sign to make them whole, then propped the sign up facing the bridge. When he came back in, Jacob found himself alone with Tadrick behind the bar. Cora was taking a nacia order from a young couple in the corner.

"How is your book going?" Jacob asked.

Tadrick was momentarily taken aback by Jacob's interest. "It's going really well." His eyes lit up. "I think going on these real-life adventures is inspiring me. I'm churning out words right now, and I think they actually might not be horrible."

"I doubt they're horrible."

"Well, they've been pretty bad before, but I feel like I'm improving as a writer. At least I hope I am. It's so hard to tell while you're doing it."

"I bet." Jacob felt the pull, somewhere inside, to be a storyteller himself. He had never thought about writing stories, but sometimes, while daydreaming, he would picture himself in front of a crowd, regaling them with some fanciful exploits he and his crew had undertaken.

"Do you ever read?" Tadrick asked. "Just for fun?"

"No. I don't. But that doesn't mean I don't intend to. My father was an avid reader, but he only read things that could get him ahead in business. He looked down on reading fiction, or anything fun, because he felt it was a tremendous waste of time." Jacob scratched his head. "One time he caught me with a copy of *Griffin the Unrivaled*. He took it away and sold it to a local bookstore. When he came home, he threw a copy of *An Annotated History of the East Paradise Company* on my bed. I tried to read it, but it bored me to sleep every time."

"That's awful." Tadrick's expression was one of utter pity. "I don't know what I would have done without books to escape into as a kid. Have you tried to get a copy of *Griffin the Unrivaled* as an adult?"

"No. I hadn't thought of that. But I should, shouldn't I?"

"Why not?"

Jacob paused a moment. "Is it any good?"

"It's a classic. Which, to me, means somewhat dry at times. And the hero worship can get a bit nauseating. But overall, I think you'd enjoy it."

"What's a classic?" Cora said as she rounded the bar to pour drinks.

"*Griffin the Unrivaled.*"

"Never heard of it." Cora finished pouring the beers, then hurried away.

"You need anything?" Jacob called as she went.

"You could go tell Juniper we need one order of nacias with just the corn chips and cheese."

"Got it." Jacob flew out the front door and jogged around to Juniper's place.

After passing on the order, he returned to find Tadrick looking at the door as if he was waiting for Jacob to get back.

"So," Tadrick said, "I brought up reading because..." He stopped himself and motioned for Cora to join them.

"Yeah?" Cora said, wiping spilled beer off her wrist with a rag.

"I was kinda hoping to ask you two about an idea I had."

"Okay." Cora tossed the rag in the sink.

"Um. I was wondering if you might think putting on a reading night every once in a while could be a good idea."

"A reading night?"

"It would be a really quiet night where people could come and read books, or maybe play games or something." He looked to Cora. "Could you make a light in the ceiling for reading? Like with magic?"

Cora gazed up at the ceiling, traced a tattoo on her arm, and spoke a word. An artificial light began to glow from the ceiling just over their heads.

"Yes. Just like that. Perfect."

Cora smiled.

"But would it take too much energy to do this for an extended time?"

"No. Not really. It would tire me out a bit, but most of the work is being done by the invisible energy that permeates everything. I could do it for a few hours a week with no problem at all."

"But...will there be people who shun the idea because it's ciguapa magic?" Jacob hoped his question wasn't stupid.

"Of course, there will," Tadrick said. "But I find that the kind of people who read for leisure often aren't the type to be bigoted."

"When would we do it?" Cora asked.

"I don't know. Maybe every other Mediday or something?"

"I think it's worth a try," Jacob said. "I mean, it couldn't hurt."

"I hope not, anyway," Tadrick replied.

"I've been meaning to ask you two about something, too," Jacob said. "I was wondering if we should close the pub on Inidays? It would be nice for all of us to have one day off per week, wouldn't it?"

"Yes." Tadrick and Cora spoke at nearly the same time.

"Great." Jacob was relieved the idea went over so well. "So, closed on Inidays, reading nights on Medidays, *You Sing* on Finidays, and...what on Solisdays?"

"We could do dancing." Cora performed a graceful spin. "Maybe to traditional ciguapa music?"

"That could work." Jacob considered doing a spin himself, but stopped short. "Do you think we could attract many ciguapa customers that way?"

"I'm not sure. But maybe." She shrugged. "My parents are actually planning on coming by tonight."

"Really?" Tadrick seemed genuinely shocked. "I've never met them the whole time I've known you."

"I know. They don't get out much." Cora pursed her lips to the side. "But I really should have taken you to see them at some point. You're like my best friend."

Tadrick looked touched. He started forward to hug Cora, but seemingly changed his mind at the last second and it ended up being a somewhat awkward overhead hand slap thing.

"I better go see if those nacias are ready." Cora spun and hurried out the door.

In preparation for the night's festivities, Tadrick and Jacob began moving tables to accommodate the band. As they were finishing up, the constable strolled into the bar.

Jacob's pulse sped up, and sweat immediately sprung from his palms.

"Hey!" the constable said when he saw Jacob's face. "It's you. From out by the farm in the middle of the night."

"Yeah." Jacob hoped he wouldn't be recognized, but at least the constable had a wide grin plastered to his face.

"It's not every day you wander straight into the middle of the world's worst capybara heist." The constable chuckled.

"How can we help you?" Tadrick asked. His tone all but wiped the grin from the constable's mouth.

"I have a couple of reasons for stopping by if you want to skip the small talk," the constable said. "The first of which is on behalf of Mr. Lowell."

Jacob's heart beat even faster.

"He asked if I could come in and give the place a once over. It seems he's concerned that there might be something of value here. Something that belongs to him." The constable rounded the bar, making no effort to hide the fact that he was looking underneath it. "You wouldn't have something like that here, would you? I mean, you weren't exactly the most competent capybara thieves I've ever met. You're not going to be able to pull one over on the richest man this side of the League of Islands, are you?"

"No. We don't have anything like that here." Tadrick looked the constable in the eye when he spoke.

"Good. Good." The constable poked his head into Jacob's room as he passed it. "Then I can move on to my second piece of business. It seems your neighbor, who lives in a house just upstream from you, believes you may have something to do with the destruction of a whole patch of melons up on the hill." The constable pointed in the direction of the hill behind the creek. "I'm guessing you don't know anything about that either."

"We don't." Jacob shook his head. "Honestly."

"You've got a couple of domesticated capybaras in here, right? Maybe it was them?"

"I suppose it's a possibility, but we don't know anything about it."

As if the gods were playing a prank on the pub owners, Mrs. Covington shuffled in through her little door with a cantaloupe rind in her mouth.

"Ha!" the constable said, mirth back in his expression. "Perfect timing if I've ever seen it. You have got to be the worst criminals I've ever met."

"We can pay for any damages," Jacob said, slightly panicked. "We didn't know they were getting into anything."

"Oh, take it down a notch. We're talking a patch of melons, not a priceless treasure or anything."

"So, we don't need to pay?"

"Now I didn't say that. Your neighbor would very much like to be compensated for the damages done. Says a silver should just about cover it."

"A silver?"

"Well, there's the cost of the melons, and the cost of the fence your capybaras destroyed. Sounded like a fair price to me. Or you could see him in court if you want to dispute the amount." The constable shrugged.

"No. We'll just pay it." Jacob looked to Tadrick. "Right?"

"I don't want to spend any time in court."

Jacob fished a silver from his coin purse and handed it to the constable.

"Thank you for making my job easy in this matter." The constable seemed genuine.

"While we have you here," Jacob found his mouth speaking words that he hadn't thoroughly considered yet, "I wanted to ask you about the faun restaurant next door."

"What about it?"

"You told Juniper that the restaurant would have to be shut down if she didn't pay an unreasonable sum of money in an unreasonable amount of time." Jacob couldn't believe he was being so bold with an officer of the law.

The constable sighed. "I know people think that all constables are bastards, but I try to do my best to not disrupt lives unless I have to. And in this case, I have to. I'm only here to keep the money flowing smoothly in the direction of people much more powerful than I am. They don't take disruptions of any kind well. I know that's not the answer you want to hear, but that's the answer I have for you."

"But what if we put our pub up as collateral or something? Could that buy her more time?"

"Listen. I could run it by Mr. Lowell, but I don't think he's going to be in a benevolent mood when it comes to the three of you. You've found yourselves on his bad side, which is a side most try to avoid."

"But don't you have power over him? You're the constable here."

The constable gave a solemn half-smile. "You're young," was all he said before leaving.

CHAPTER 18

Raise Up Your Beer

People began showing up at Mrs. Covington's around seven. Many of them asked for free beer, and some of those people left when told that had been a one-time promotion.

The band showed up around seven thirty. Tadrick helped them set up while Cora and Jacob took orders.

The number of people was a bit less than Jacob had hoped for, but not bad. All the stools at the bar, including the three-legged one, were filled, and three others milled around the stage area, possibly waiting to sing.

A woman wearing a red and black gown and a lacy black hat with a peacock feather protruding from the back strolled up to the bar and ordered a beer in a raspy, almost sultry voice.

"This wind is bound to bring in some unexpected people," she said while Jacob poured. "Should make for an interesting night."

Jacob cocked his head to listen to the gentle wind, which he hadn't noticed before. "It is a bit breezy out, isn't it?" He slid the beer to her with a smile. "Name's Jacob. I don't believe I've seen you in here before."

"I'm Kira." She held out a hand, which Jacob shook. "This is my first time here. Lovely place you've got."

"Thank you very much." Jacob meant to ask her about the cryptic thing she'd said about the wind, but she had nodded, smiled, and turned away before he could spit it out.

He looked outside through the big open doors to see palm trees swaying just a bit more than usual.

Jacob was pouring a beer for another, less interesting customer when two tall ciguapa people walked in with a child of about ten between them.

"My family." Cora's voice was part excited, part trepidatious. "That's my little brother, Calo."

Calo rushed to Cora and jumped into her arms. When she finally put him down, his face lit up as he saw Mrs. Covington and Arthur. He ran to them, fell to his knees, and scratched both of them under their chins.

"Hello, Cora," her dad said as he approached the bar. His accent was much thicker than his daughter's, but he was still easily under-standable.

Cora rounded the bar and wrapped her parents in a long, wordless embrace.

She stepped back from them and held a hand out toward Jacob. "Dad. Mom. This is Jacob, my business partner."

Cora's dad put a finger to his forehead, then brought it down to the center of his chest where he drew an imaginary circle. After the greeting was complete, he held out his hand. Jacob shook it, impressed by the strength of the man's hand.

"My name is Calo, the elder, and this is my wife, Mila," Cora's father said. "We appreciate your offer to make our Cora an equal partner here at the pub. We don't let the fact that it was likely just a smart busi-ness decision diminish our appreciation for what you have done for our daughter."

Being unsure how to take his words, Jacob smiled.

"She was in a rut," Mila said, shaking Jacob's hand. "But after becoming a partner here, she has really...come to life."

"Well, she is an absolute joy to work with and a huge part of any success we've had so far."

"We know you'll continue to treat her with the respect she deserves." Calo's stern look was intimidating.

"Of course...sir."

Mila flashed a warm smile. "It's so good to see Cora immersed in her work. It's teaching her responsibility."

Cora playfully rolled her eyes, then went and checked on a couple of waving customers.

"We love to have Cora around, but when she goes off to work, it gives me and my wife more intimate time together." Calo's face was completely serious. Jacob almost giggled nervously but stopped himself just in time.

"We'll often send her little brother to a friend's house," Calo continued, "so we can be as intimate as we please."

"It's true," Mila said, seemingly unfazed by her husband's words. "That's another benefit of Cora's newfound interest in the pub."

Calo put a hand on Mila's shoulder and looked into her eyes. "We could go somewhere right now?" he said as if Jacob wasn't there. "Cora could watch Calo the younger for an hour or so."

"That sounds wonderful, but we came here to support our daughter. We should probably stay."

"Of course. You're right, my love. But I look forward to getting you alone and—"

In a panic, Jacob tipped a beer over on the bar. "Whoops!" he said, grabbing a nearby towel and wiping up the mess.

Cora hurried back to the bar, her face at least a shade darker than usual.

"Hey, Mom and Dad." She pointed around the pub. "We're pretty busy right now and Jacob needs to help out with the customers."

"Of course." Calo nodded.

"It was so nice to meet you," Mila said as Cora whisked Jacob away.

"I'm sorry I left you alone with them," Cora whispered. "They didn't start talking...uh..."

"Yes," Jacob said, eyes wide.

Cora let loose an embarrassed groan. "They're so weird with that stuff. Sorry."

"It's fine." Jacob did his best to play it off like he hadn't just been mortified.

From the corner of the pub, Tadrick's voice resonated through the amplifying magic wand. "Welcome, everyone, to our second night of You Sing, featuring Bilge Rat!"

The audience, which had grown steadily since Cora's family arrived, cheered, many of them already raising their hands to sing.

"We've got a new system tonight," Tadrick continued. "There are little scraps of paper on each table, along with pencils. If you want to sing a song with the band, write your name and the name of the song you want to sing on one of the scraps and bring it to me at the bar."

Several patrons followed his instructions. One of them handed the paper to Tadrick as he stood in front of the band.

"Alright. We have our first request of the night. Lilly would like to sing *Basdrif, the Cat Pirate of Sunshine Cay.*" He looked to the band. "Is that okay?"

The band members discussed among themselves for at least a minute.

"That's one of the first songs we ever wrote," Darian said. "We might be a little rusty, but we can give it a shot."

Lilly, a young human woman with shoulder-length brown hair and glasses, stepped onto the stage holding a mug of beer. Tadrick handed her the wand as the band began to play. It only took a few notes before they were all on the same page.

Lilly was a fantastic singer, and the song was both fun and ambiguous. Jacob spent much of it trying to figure out if Basdrif was a person who pirated cats or an actual cat that happened to be a pirate.

The next singer was a faun woman named Cathy who sang *A Capy for Good Luck.* Her singing was possibly even better, and the song had a wonderful sing-along chorus.

But the next person to try, a human named Roger, was truly awful. There was a charm to his singing, though. It didn't seem to matter much if a person could sing or not. The thing that made or broke someone's You Sing attempt was the amount of fun they had with it. If a person was really going for it and working the crowd, the quality of their voice was a distant second.

The band played for well over an hour. During that time, many beers were quaffed, and many nacias devoured. When the band was done, almost all of the customers stayed this time.

At one point, while the band was still packing up their instruments, a drunk man stood on one of the barstools.

"Alright, you lot," he called over the din. "*Na na na nas* on this side." He pointed to the open-air side of the pub with both hands. "And *heys* on this side." He swung his pointer fingers around to the fireplace side of the pub.

Jacob had no idea what the man was saying, but everyone else, including Cora and Tadrick, seemed to know exactly what he meant. Surprisingly fast, the patrons separated themselves into two groups with a three-pace gap between them.

When everyone was in place, the man held his hands in the air, then brought them down and started singing. Everyone in the pub, aside from Jacob, sang along with him.

Raise up your beer
    Let's raise up a cheer
    Let the worries just melt away
    Good friends are near
    Hey! We're all friends here
    And we're making the most of this day

Raise up your beer
    Let's raise up a cheer
    There's no reason to start a fight
    Good friends are near
    Hey! We're all friends here
    And we're making the most of this night

The first time through, everyone sang in a normal singing voice. But the second time, they all brought it down to a whisper. It was a strange but wonderful sound—dozens of people all singing in whispers at once. When the whispered verses were done, the place absolutely exploded with sound as each person sang at the top of their lungs. The boisterous singing and joyous togetherness of the whole performance raised goose-bumps on Jacob's arms.

But the song wasn't quite done yet.

Next, people on the open-air side whispered, "Na na na na."

Then the people on the other side whispered, "Hey!"

This continued back and forth, each cycle building in volume and intensity until they were roaring again. Then, on some agreed-upon point, the fireplace side people sang, "Done!" instead of "Hey!"

The pub went completely silent, except for one drunk guy in the back who said, "Na na na oh..."

For the next ten seconds, no one made the tiniest peep. Every single person in the pub, every human, every ciguapa, and every faun had huge smiles on their faces. When about ten seconds were up, the whole group cheered and applauded themselves.

"What was that?" Jacob asked Cora when the noise died down

enough for him to be heard. He was still tingling. He'd never experienced anything like that before.

"It's a New Dawn thing," Cora said. "A tradition, but I don't know when or where it started."

"I love it."

"It's pretty great, right?"

Before Jacob could answer, he completely tensed up, the words he was about to say came out as a wheezing gasp.

"What?" Cora asked.

"My...father." Across the pub, Jacob's father had just entered through the main door. He was dressed in his most expensive, most formal attire and had a mild expression of disgust as he looked around the crowded pub. When he locked eyes with Jacob, he walked slowly to the bar.

"Hello, sir," Jacob said, still in shock.

"Have I heard correctly?" his father said, skipping greetings as per usual. "Are you the owner and proprietor of this establishment?"

"Yes. Well...my business partners and I." He pointed to Cora, then to Tadrick, who was bringing mugs to a table under the outdoor cover.

Jacob's father glanced at Cora for a fraction of a second, then focused on his son. The expression of mild disgust never relented. Cora raised a hand to wave but brought it back down when the man barely acknowledged her existence.

"It seems you have a potentially successful venture, here. Do you feel you've proven your point?"

"I do, actually." Jacob suppressed a smirk, not wanting to seem smug.

"So, now that the point is proven, and you've made me chase you down across islands, are you ready to come back and carry on the family business?"

The impulse to smirk vanished. Jacob fidgeted with the seam of his pant leg while his father stared unblinking. "I..." Jacob gulped. "No. I'm not. I want to stay here and see this out."

His father blinked and blew out a noisy breath. "But is this even sustainable? Have you written out a business plan?"

Cora was pulled away by customers trying to order nacias. She looked to Jacob's dad again, ready to greet him, but the man didn't favor her with so much as a glance as she left.

"I don't have a formal business plan, but things are going pretty good. Better than I expected, really."

"And do you think it's wise to take on business partners you barely know? A young kid who looks like a delinquent, and a ciguapa woman?" The look of disgust deepened.

For a fraction of a second, Jacob considered backing down. He would do what he always did when it came to his father—shut his mouth and meekly agree. But his father's harsh words about Tadrick and obvious prejudice against Cora awakened something new in him that wouldn't let that old habit come to the surface. He refused to allow his friends to be mistreated by this man.

Heart pounding, he stood up to his full height.

"Yes. I do think it's wise. In fact, bringing them into the business is the exact thing that has made it successful. Tadrick and Cora's innovations have turned this place from a dark, failing dive into the charming little spot you see here." He gestured from one side of the pub to the other. "The only thing I did, quite literally, was to bring the two of them on with me. That great decision led to any success we're having."

"But—"

"And Cora's unfiltered love for life has begun to change me as a person. She is an absolute treasure, and I wouldn't trade meeting her, or Tadrick, for all the success in the world."

"Fanciful and dramatic. Sometimes I forget how young you still are. You'll see that such romantic ideas are unsustainable eventually, but in the meantime, you need to ensure that you're doing what's right for your future. This simply can't compare to—"

"I am doing what's right for my future." His heart continued to pound, his chest tingling with a mixture of fear and pride and...relief. This confrontation hadn't reached a conclusion, but standing up this time, instead of running away like before, felt like a victory in itself. The release of tension manifested from his shoulders to his stomach. He had lived with the fear of this moment for far too long.

"But it's not—"

Cyrus and his lady friend materialized out of the *na na na na* side of the crowd. The big sea captain roared an unintelligible greeting, shook Jacob's hand, then pulled him into an awkward embrace over the bar.

"Yer place has just been blessed." His voice was gruff and loud as ever.

"Blessed?"

"Sure. A pub in New Dawn isn't really a pub until it's had that song bouncin' off its walls. I'm not the most religious person, but I'd daresay the gods just took notice of your little establishment."

"If they did, I hope they're pleased." Jacob did his best to make it seem like Cyrus hadn't just interrupted a life-altering event.

Cyrus's eyes flicked to Jacob's dad, then back to Jacob. Recognizing something in the air between them, he said, "You two know each other?"

"Father," Jacob said, "this is Cyrus, the captain who brought me to this island."

"Father. Of course!" Cyrus clapped Jacob's dad on the shoulder, staggering him. "You must be head over heels proud of your boy. Just look at what he's done. You shoulda seen this place before he owned it."

"Hmm." The sound Jacob's dad made could have been construed as agreement or dismissal.

"Hmm?" Cyrus said, mocking the ambiguous answer. "He deserves a bit more than that, doesn't he?" His tone walked the line between being playful and bitingly critical. "Shit, if I'd have ever had a son, I could only wish to be so lucky as to have him grow up to be the young man that Jacob is."

For a man who was rarely shaken, Jacob's dad looked extremely uncomfortable in Cyrus's presence. "It appears that he could have done much worse, here. That much is true."

Cyrus looked like he wanted to press the issue, but left it there.

"Anyway," the big man said, "just wanted to congratulate you on hosting that rousing rendition of *Raise Up Your Beer*. It's one of my favorite things about New Dawn, Jenny here bein' my absolute favorite." He smiled and tilted his head toward his friend.

"Thank you, Cyrus. It was quite a thing to experience. I'll have to learn it and sing along next time."

"To be sure." Cyrus gave him another firm handshake. "Not that you'll be wantin' to leave what you've built here, but, in my well-informed estimation, you're more than ready to join a ship's crew, now. You may not realize it, but you're carryin' yourself differently. You've gained a lot of confidence in a short time. If that means anything to you."

"It does. It means a lot." A warmth permeated Jacob's chest.

Cyrus turned and shook Jacob's father's hand. "Good to meet you." He put an arm around Jenny and blended back into the crowd.

For the span of several breaths, neither Jacob nor his father said a word. Jacob nearly dismissed himself to attend to customers but didn't quite have the nerve.

"It's late," his father finally said. "And the din is giving me a headache. I'll be returning home in the morning."

Jacob considered asking his father for a loan to save Juniper's restaurant, even though he knew it wasn't the right thing to do. If his father consented, Juniper would only be switching one set of grubby rich hands for another. The only difference would be that she and Jacob would both be under the same thumb. But even though he knew all of this, he still would have asked if he thought there was a chance, but it was hopeless. His father would never give money to help a stranger.

"Give my love to Mom," Jacob said, his expression betraying no emotion.

Jacob's father nodded. He looked as if he wanted to say something else, but cut himself short. He nodded again, then turned and left.

Jacob blew out a deep breath, feeling like he just rode out swells in a storm. He had run the gamut of emotions—feeling angry, sad, relieved, and elated all in one eventful evening. But now, even though the surprise interaction with his father was far from perfect, the warmth in his chest persisted. He found himself smiling and standing tall, buoyed by Cyrus's kind and encouraging words, and unable to resist feeling a bit of redemption in the way the big sea captain rebuked his father.

He looked around the pub for the woman who had said something about the wind bringing in interesting people but she had apparently gone. She had seemed a bit on the eccentric side, but her prediction had been spot on.

The party-like atmosphere continued until about midnight when the crowd finally started to disperse. Cora's family had gone not long after the encounter with Jacob's father. Calo the younger had a hard time saying goodbye to the capybaras, who had really taken to him, while Calo the elder had a hard time keeping his hands off of his wife. They all gave Cora long embraces while telling her how proud they were of her, and how much they loved her.

How wonderful that must be.

Comparing Cora's parents to the interaction with his father was inevitable. But Jacob found himself leaning toward being happy Cora had that support instead of feeling sorry for himself.

For the first time in as long as he could remember, Jacob had an inkling that he was a good person who was capable of damn near anything he put his mind to. He didn't need validation from anyone. He could feel his worth, as tangible as the warmth in his chest.

CHAPTER 19

Paper Fish

The next day, Jacob awoke at sun up. He hadn't had nearly enough sleep but felt energized and ready to face the day.

The pub was an absolute mess. Just about every table had beer mugs of varying degrees of emptiness on them. Nacia scraps were everywhere. The floor was littered with crunched-up corn chips.

Whistling the melody of the pirate cat song, Jacob took to cleaning. He started with the bar, toweling off stale, spilled beer and polishing it to a shine. Then he filled the wash basin with water from the creek. He added soap and washed every mug in the place. He dried them with a new towel and set them in perfect rows on the shelf behind the bar. The tables came next, followed by a thorough sweeping and mopping of the floor.

When he was finished, he stepped back to one of the walls and admired his work. The place looked brand new; as brand new as an old pub could look anyway. He had worked up quite a sweat without realizing it.

After tossing out the dishwater, he refilled the basin at the creek and gave himself a proper sponge bath behind the pub, hoping no one would come back there and see him in any degree of nakedness. Luckily, the only ones who saw him were Mrs. Covington and Arthur, who were contentedly floating near each other in the pond.

He washed his clothes and hung them on the line Mr. Davies had put up behind the pub.

Feeling fresh and clean with new clothes on, Jacob unlocked the front door and waited for customers to arrive. It was Solisday, the day most people were free from work, so he expected, or at least hoped, the day would bring a steady stream of business.

While he waited, he counted the money they had made the previous day. It was a good, possibly even great, amount. It was more than he would have guessed. Nearly five silver. If they had two months instead of two weeks, saving Juniper's business would have been much less of a problem.

While Jacob still had the money all laid out on the bar in stacks, the front door swung open, and the two shady-looking men from the first time Jacob had set foot in the pub came in. They went to their usual spot in the corner and called out that they would like two beers.

As quickly as possible, Jacob scooped the money off the bar and into his leather coin purse. The coins made a ridiculous amount of noise as they clanged together. As he slid one of the stacks, a few coins missed the purse and fell off the bar, clattering to the stone floor with all the subtlety of a sword fight.

The two men in the corner perked up, staring at Jacob as he stooped to pick the coins off the floor. As he shoved the coins into his purse, the men stood and approached the bar. One of them carried the crossbow-sized suitcase they always had with them. He unclasped the latch as he approached.

Jacob froze. He considered running out the back door, but his legs wouldn't cooperate.

As the man began to open the case, Juniper and her two kids came in through the front door.

"Hello," she called. "I brought you a traditional faun drink." She held up a bright orange concoction in a tall glass.

The men slowed to a stop. The man with the case closed it as they turned and meandered back to their seats.

"Perfect timing," Jacob said. "I'm dying of thirst."

Juniper handed him the drink and he tipped it back. The flavor was intense—an explosion of fruitiness. It was delicious.

"This is great." Jacob took another, longer pull.

"Yeah. I love it."

"Can we pet Mrs. Covington?" Aspen asked.

"Of course," Jacob said. "She'd love that."

The kids hurried to the little four-poster bed behind the bar where both capybaras were now lounging.

"I hope things weren't too loud over here for them last night," Jacob said between drinks.

"Not at all. Those kids could fall asleep in the middle of a cannonade."

"Good."

Jacob poured two beers for the men and brought them to their table, avoiding eye contact as much as possible. When he got back to the bar, he waved Juniper closer and spoke in a low voice. "We found the next clue."

"You did?" Juniper kept her voice quiet, too. "That's great. What did it say?"

Jacob glanced at the men, who were conversing with each other as they drank. "Follow Kibu as far as possible without getting your feet wet." Jacob paused. "That mean anything to you?"

"Kibu?"

"Yes. K-I-B-U."

"No. I'm afraid I've never heard that word."

"Hmm."

"The first clue involved the faun language, and the second clue used the ciguapa language," Juniper said. "Maybe this one references the orcish language."

"Of course." Jacob felt stupid for not thinking of that already.

"Maybe we could ask Shelu and Korga what it means?"

"You're brilliant."

"I don't know about all that." Juniper blushed just a bit.

"Mr. Jacob," Aspen said. "Could you teach us how to make paper animals, please?"

"Let me grab some paper and we'll start right away." Jacob hurried to his room and brought back a small stack of old invoices. He took a seat at one of the tables, and the kids sat across from him.

"When I was a kid, the first thing I learned to make was a fish. Do you want to try that?"

Both kids nodded, holding a sheet of paper in their hands.

"Alright, so the first step is to fold the paper exactly in half, from this corner to that corner."

Jacob was instantly immersed in teaching. The kids were excellent listeners and picked it up quickly. The whole process brought him back to his school days. He looked back on the teacher who had taught him to fold paper animals, Mrs. Bonny, with a warm reverence.

When the paper fishes were complete, Jacob looked up to find that the shady guys had gone, and Cora and Tadrick were at the pub. He congratulated the kids on a job well done and told them they'd try a turtle next time. The kids thanked him and went back to petting the capybaras.

As Jacob, Juniper, Cora, and Tadrick were discussing who would go to see the orcs, a large group came in and asked if they could sit out under the cover and have seven orders of nacias. Juniper needed to stay and cook, and Cora said she didn't feel like walking at the moment, so Tadrick and Jacob volunteered to go see Shelu and Korga.

There was no good reason to wait since they were in a race against Mr. Lowell's men for the treasure, so they took off as soon as the beers were poured for the big group.

On the way to the cave, Jacob asked how Darian was doing.

"Pretty good," Tadrick responded.

Jacob thought he might elaborate, but Tadrick just kept walking in silence.

"He's pretty private, isn't he?" Jacob felt as if he was treading a line he should consider leaving alone, but kept on in hopes he wasn't crossing it.

"He is." Again, Tadrick left his answer short. Jacob was ready to move on when Tadrick started again. "He had a real tough time growing up. He's not as ready as I am to be so open about...us."

"Oh." Jacob had no idea how to respond.

"He's getting more comfortable. Slowly. But until he's there, I'm not pushing it."

"Yeah. Just be supportive, right?"

"Exactly. I like supporting his music stuff because he's the most alive when he's playing with the band." Tadrick smiled. "It's funny to watch him playing in front of people. He's hardly recognizable compared to the usual, reserved, quiet Darian. Like when he started calling for people to come sing with the band! I don't know if you noticed, but my jaw was just about on the floor." Tadrick's face shone with a happiness Jacob hadn't seen in him yet. "I love to see that confident side come out."

"That was pretty great." Jacob nodded, smiling.

"Maybe someday he'll be ready to be seen with me in public as we really are." Tadrick shrugged.

"Yeah, maybe." Jacob stopped there, figuring he'd pried enough.

For quite a while, no one spoke. Tadrick still had the remnants of a wistful smile on his lips. Jacob was dying to ask him about something else, but he waited for the smile to completely fade away.

"How long have Cora and Yandro been...carrying on as they do?" Jacob finally asked.

"What? The thing where they both obviously like each other but neither one will come out and say it?"

"Yes. That."

Tadrick looked to the sky, thinking. "Probably since about a month before you bought the pub."

"Have you ever asked her about it?"

"Not directly. I drop little hints and things sometimes, but that's about it."

"Hmm." Jacob didn't know what else to say on the topic.

"She was hurt pretty bad by her last...suitor. I won't get into details, but the way he left her was cruel and unnecessary. So since then, she's been pretty guarded, and I completely understand that." Tadrick cleared his throat. "I mean, I have those issues myself, to be honest. It can be tough to put yourself out there, even a little bit." He looked to Jacob. "What about you? Do you find...such things any easier?"

"Not at all." Jacob chuckled nervously. "I have very little experience with romantic relationships. I let the only girl I ever loved slip through my fingers, if I'm being honest."

"What happened?"

"Well, I was too caught up in my old life, I think. I chose the family business over her." Jacob rubbed the back of his neck, looking down as they walked. "It was the worst mistake of my life. And I only did it because I wasn't being true to who I really was." He closed his eyes and let out a deep breath. "I swore to myself then that I would never let that happen again."

"Being yourself can be tough," Tadrick said.

Jacob nodded.

They walked in silence for a while but eventually started discussing the treasure. They talked about the latest clue until they arrived at the orcs' cave.

Once there, they called for Shelu and Korga from the beach outside the cave. When no one answered, they searched the immediate area but found no sign that they were there.

"Well shit," Jacob said.

"Do you want to look around town for them?" Tadrick asked. "They might be working somewhere in town, and we need to get this figured out."

CHAPTER 20

Guided Tour

Jacob and Tadrick entered the town on 1st Street, which ran parallel to the bay. The dirt road turned to cobblestone as it passed over the creek, just like 3rd Street did in front of Mrs. Covington's.

One of the first stops Tadrick wanted to make was to a book store on 1st called Tome Sweet Tome. Even though he wasn't the biggest reader, Jacob found the place to be wonderful; a quaint, cozy little shop on the corner, bursting with character.

"Hey, maybe you'll have your book in here someday," Jacob said before they entered.

"That's the dream." Tadrick's voice was hopeful, but his expression betrayed doubts.

As they entered, the scent of old books with just a trace of something like cinnamon greeted them. Jacob was taken aback by the chaos of overflowing bookshelves haphazardly arranged in non-symmetrical rows throughout. With the shelves packed full, books were stacked up on top of them, some of the stacks damn near reaching the ceiling. A spiral staircase in the back corner seemed to lead nowhere, while a smaller staircase on the opposite wall led to a seemingly functioning door that only a small child could walk through.

"Welcome," an older woman in glasses said from a stool behind a counter.

"We were wondering if we could ask you about something." Tadrick kept his voice down, as there were other customers inside perusing the shelves.

"What do you got for me?" the woman replied.

"Have you ever heard the word *Kibu*?"

"Yes, I have. Just this morning when someone else asked me the same question."

"Really?" Jacob's muscles tensed.

"Yes. Not more than an hour ago. A tall ciguapa man who was kind of intimidating."

"So, do—"

"Not that I have anything against ciguapa people in general," the woman clarified, sitting up taller on her stool. "Just...this man, in particular, was...not very nice."

Jacob hadn't taken her comment as bigoted in any way. He had met that particular ciguapa man, and he was, in fact, intimidating as shit.

"Did you tell him what the word meant?"

"I would have if I'd known myself. But I don't have the foggiest idea what it means." She held up the book she was reading. The title was *The Orcish Tongue on the Continent.* "After he left, I had an inkling that the word may have been orcish in origin. I've been trying to run it down out of sheer curiosity, but not having any luck so far."

"Thank you, ma'am." Tadrick turned to leave.

"What would an author need to do to have his or her book sold in your store?" Jacob asked.

Tadrick's face was instantly red.

"Write it," the woman said with a smile.

"That's it?"

"That's it on my end. But he or she would have to get it published first, of course. There's a publisher here in town he or she could give it to. I would tell him or her that it's definitely worth a shot."

"Okay, I will. Thank you for the information."

Outside, Tadrick shot Jacob an annoyed glance. Jacob thought it best to stay silent.

"I want to be mad at you for that," Tadrick said. "It was embarrassing, even though she didn't necessarily know you were talking about me."

"I'm sorry." Jacob wished he'd kept his big mouth shut.

"I was saying that I wanted to be mad, but I'm not. You only did that to help me. You've been nothing but supportive when it comes to my...writing stuff. So, thank you for that."

"You're welcome. But I don't think I've done much besides ask you about it once or twice."

"Yeah, and that's what I appreciate. Most people seem like they don't want to be bothered by it. Darian cares because he kind of has to, but no one in my family seems to care at all."

"I'm sorry about that, too."

"Oh, it's fine. I really shouldn't whine about it. I'm just happy that you're taking an interest."

"Do you think I could read it when you're done?"

Tadrick's face reddened again. "I don't know if it would be your thing."

"I don't know. A story about a dragon sounds pretty interesting to me."

Tadrick let a smile break through.

"Well, back to our mission," he said. "Maybe we should check a pub for the orcs. There's only one in New Dawn, besides ours of course, that allows orcs. The Dripping Bucket."

Jacob remembered seeing that pub on his first day in town. It had seemed pretty rough.

"Alright," Jacob said. "Lead the way."

They headed in the direction of Mrs. Covington's but took a left instead of a right on 3rd Street. Outside The Dripping Bucket, a man lay in the middle of the road, a stray dog sniffing at his feet. His position suggested that he'd been thrown out the front door recently. He stared at his skinned palms and moaned drunkenly.

When they entered, a lively argument between two human men was taking place in front of the bar. Jacob would have spun around and left as soon as he saw there weren't any orcs in the pub, but he saw Yandro at the far side of the bar talking with someone who worked there. Yandro noticed him, too, and waved him over. Jacob gulped, then slunk over to where Yandro was, giving the arguing men a wide berth.

"Hey," Yandro said. "I'm just delivering a keg here, and your place is coming up..." He looked at a crumpled piece of paper he pulled from his pocket. "Well, I've got two other deliveries, and then Mrs. Covington's. Is Cora working today?"

"Yes. She'll be there."

"Okay, great. Maybe I'll see you guys there, too?"

"Maybe. We're looking for Shelu and Korga. Haven't seen them around town, have you?"

"Nope. Haven't seen any orcs today."

One of the arguing humans took a swing at the other, knocking him backward. The man who was hit stumbled and would have fallen on his butt, but Yandro caught him under the arms and lifted him back to his feet. The man Yandro had helped charged forward and tackled the other man to the hard-stone floor.

Chaos broke out in the pub. As if they had been waiting for some kind of cue, just about everyone inside started fighting each other. Glasses were smashed and people were sent crashing through tables.

Yandro shrugged. "Happens all the time. We should probably get going."

Jacob would have been way ahead of him, but a giant of a human stood in their way, staring at them with obvious ill intent and holding a broken chair leg in his massive hand.

With amazing swiftness, Yandro stepped in front of Jacob and Tadrick.

"Excuse us, sir." He pointed at the door. "Just trying to get out of here."

The man said nothing, instead swinging the chair leg at Yandro's head.

With little apparent effort, Yandro ducked under the makeshift weapon, grabbed Jacob by the sleeve, and pulled him forward, saying, "Go!"

Jacob sprinted past the man. At the front door, he turned to wait for Tadrick.

The big man recovered quickly. He lifted the chair leg above his head and drove it down at Yandro. Again, the handsome ciguapa dodged the blow, stepping to his left as the chair leg whizzed by him. He grabbed Tadrick and pushed him past the man.

Now furious, the big man charged at Yandro, meaning to tackle him. Smiling, Yandro jumped toward the wall with one foot, then used the wall to launch himself over the man with the other. The human's momentum carried him forward until he crashed to the floor in a heap.

Yandro didn't even look back. He put an arm around both Jacob and Tadrick and led them out the front door. Outside, he rushed them into a nearby alley.

"He probably won't find us here." Yandro continued to guide them through the alley.

"That was amazing!" Jacob looked over his shoulder but saw no one.

"I didn't know you could do...all that," Tadrick said.

"Yeah. I dabble a little bit in herima, a ciguapa self-defense art. It translates, more or less, to *let them beat themselves.* Not a fighting style, per se."

"You were brilliant at it," Jacob said. "Thank you."

"No problem at all. Glad I could help." He stopped at the other end of the alley. "I gotta circle around and get my supplies from the back of that pub. Hopefully, I'll see you at Mrs. Covington's in a bit."

"Are you sure you should go back there?" Jacob asked.

"Yeah. I need my supplies. I have a lot of ingredients for those nacias to deliver to you." He flashed a carefree smile.

"Thank you." Tadrick slapped him on the back. "See you later."

"Wow," Jacob said as Yandro jogged away.

"That was crazy."

"Yeah." Jacob's heart was just now starting to slow a bit.

The two looked around, unsure of what to do or say after all the excitement. Jacob was relieved that the big man was still nowhere to be seen.

"Hey, we're pretty close to my place," Tadrick said. "Do you want to see it?"

"Sure!"

"I mean, it's not much, but I figure since we're so close..."

"Yeah. Let's do it."

Tadrick led Jacob through another alley, then took a left on a street without a sign.

"There it is." Tadrick pointed to a small house painted a vibrant sky blue. Ferns lined the walkway to the front door, which was painted bright green. "Darian's at work, and there's not much to see inside besides instruments and art supplies."

"It's a charming place," Jacob said. "I love it."

"I do, too. But we better get looking for Shelu and Korga."

The next place they decided to look was the docks. As they approached through the busiest part of town, Jacob couldn't keep his eyes off the massive galleon anchored at the bay. Its masts were as tall as the Ceiba tree on the hill. The sails were furled, but each one still looked like it could cover Mrs. Covington's. A topless mermaid smiled out from the bow.

He could never place a finger on why, exactly, but Jacob had always longed to be on a ship like that. As they made their way around the area, searching for the orcs, he tried to narrow down the reasons for his desire to be on a ship's crew.

Was it the freedom of the sea? That likely had a lot to do with it, but those feelings had been much stronger when he was still at home, still feeling trapped in the family business.

Was it the camaraderie he imagined on board? That was probably another big part, although he had found a wellspring of camaraderie at the pub, now.

It wasn't the sea itself, since just the idea of bobbing up and down on ocean swells made him slightly green around the gills.

Whatever it was, he found that upon reflection, the desire was fading a bit. He still felt a strong pull out to sea, but Mrs. Covington's, and the people he met there, were a comforting anchor, keeping him on land for the foreseeable future.

As he pondered these things, an extremely rough-looking crew from one of the ships at the docks swaggered past him and Tadrick. Jacob kept his head held high, feeling only slightly intimidated. They did smell pretty awful, though. Holding his breath, he gave them a nod and a smile, which they all ignored as they passed by.

"We could try the market?" Tadrick offered.

"Sure. Whatever you say, boss."

Tadrick rolled his eyes. "Alright. This way."

Jacob followed him toward the First Church in the center of town.

The church was a colossal structure. Thirty-seven blue spires, one for each of the human gods, shot up from the roof of the white stone building. Jacob had seen impressive churches before, but this one had an older, more numinous quality than any he'd seen.

Stretched out in front of the church was a sprawling market in the town's main square. Jacob could hardly believe that he hadn't seen this before. It was a sight to behold. The whole place bustled with activity, creating a dull roar that echoed around the square. There were people selling everything from trinkets to golden magic wands. One edge of the square was dedicated entirely to live animals, and the opposite side was home to myriad food stands.

"You ever have ciguapa corn on the cob?" Tadrick asked.

"No."

"You've got to try it." Tadrick led Jacob to one of the food vendors. He held up two fingers and said a word Jacob couldn't place. The young, beautiful ciguapa girl behind the table nodded, then turned to retrieve his order.

Jacob pulled out his coin purse, but Tadrick stopped him. "It's on me."

"I should be buying you something after the guided tour of New Dawn you've just given me."

Tadrick waved the comment away as the girl brought back two large cobs of corn covered in several substances Jacob couldn't identify. He thanked the girl, paid her, then handed one of the cobs to Jacob.

"I know it looks scary, but trust me." Tadrick bit into his corn with a moan of pleasure that was embarrassingly loud. No one in the market gave him a second glance.

"Alright." The corn did look scary, but Jacob was all about trying new things.

He took a bite, stood, and chewed, trying to identify any of the flavors he was experiencing. Sweet, savory, and spicy all at once, it was unlike anything he'd ever eaten before. Giving up on figuring out what the tastes were, he let himself enjoy the mouthful of strange but delicious food.

"Wow!" he said when he was done chewing.

"Told you. I have to get one every time I come through the market."

"I think I just started a new tradition, too."

The two of them stood near a palm tree, trying to stay out of the way of foot traffic as they contentedly chomped away on their corn.

"We almost ended up in there." Tadrick pointed to a building on the corner, then took another bite.

The building was constructed with white stone, just like every building surrounding the town square, but this one was much more utilitarian. The word *CONSTABLE* was chiseled above the main door. And *JAIL* was written over a smaller door on the right. A shiver shook through Jacob as he imagined being locked inside, so close to the excitement of the market, but unable to partake. It really could have happened, too, if the constable was less forgiving for what he had called, "The world's worst capybara heist." Jacob wondered if anyone was sulking in a cell right now, just a few paces away.

"Why don't you check out the market a bit?" Tadrick said when he was done eating. "I'll search around the square for the orcs and I'll meet you where we came in. How about an hour? That work?"

"That would be great." Jacob was eager to see what else the market had to offer.

Over the next hour, Jacob purchased things from three stalls. The first was a clothes seller, where Jacob bought two pairs of black pants, two shirts—one blue, and one purple—and a black tricorn hat. The clothing was much less fancy than anything he'd worn in his old life, and much more vibrant. It had a bit of a sailor feel to it, which Jacob liked a lot.

The second stall he shopped at was an artist selling paintings. He bought a wonderful painting of New Dawn from a bird's eye view—if the bird flew high enough to see both the docks and the market, but not so high that it looked more like a map than a decoration. Mrs. Covington's was represented on the right edge of the picture—a quarter of it, anyway.

The third thing he bought was a watermelon to give to Mrs. Covington and Arthur. He thought they'd love it, plus it might keep them from straying into someone else's garden again.

When he made his way to the meeting place, Tadrick was already waiting for him. He held a much smaller canvas with a painting of a mermaid on it.

"No luck with Shelu and Korga."

"Should we be worried about them?" Jacob asked.

"I don't think so. This island is bigger than you'd think. They could be anywhere."

"Okay. I guess we'll have to try again later."

"For now, let's get these new decorations up." Tadrick held up the painting with a grin.

CHAPTER 21

Yandro

Mrs. Covington's was fairly busy when Jacob and Tadrick returned. The barstools were full, and three tables had people sitting and eating nacias around them.

"Any luck?" Cora asked while pouring a beer.

"Nope." Tadrick held up his painting again. "But we did get some new paintings."

"How have things been going here?" Jacob wasn't used to leaving the pub for long stretches during business hours. If he was being honest, it had been nice to get away today.

"Good. Pretty steady all day. Juniper has been here most of the time you were gone. She's just gone back to fix up two more plates of nacias."

While Cora was talking, Jacob took a knife from behind the bar and cut the watermelon in half. He backed up to the door in the rear of the pub, still listening, and set the halves down just outside.

Cora followed Jacob to the back door, signaling for Tadrick to come with her. "So, what's the plan for finding the orcs, then?"

"I don't know," Jacob said. "Maybe we can go back tonight, or tomorrow morning?"

"I guess we can see how it goes." Cora shrugged.

Jacob was about to speak when Cora started again.

"Oh, I wanted to run something past you two. I've been brainstorming about the whole ciguapa dance thing we talked about possibly doing on Solisdays. I have a tentative plan that we can put into action next week if you guys are okay with that?"

"Of course," Jacob said.

"Come on." Tadrick shook his head. "You don't get to make plans or decisions around here."

Cora playfully rolled her eyes. "Good. So, I was thinking I could get my cousin and her friends to play the music. They're still in school, but they're not too bad. And we could pay them next to nothing." Jacob must have reacted noticeably, because Cora said, "What? We wouldn't be taking advantage of them or anything. They just want the opportunity to play in front of people. They'd be more than happy to take payment in nacias, trust me."

"Sounds good."

"I figure we could make some flyers again. Maybe this time focus on neighborhoods with more ciguapa people. We could clear out a good-sized dance floor pretty easily by moving a few tables around."

"Perfect," Jacob said. "Maybe you could—" He stopped himself short, remembering what Tadrick had said about her past relationship.

"What?"

"Nothing."

Cora narrowed her eyes and stared at Jacob.

"It was nothing," Jacob said. "Really."

"Were you going to say something about Yandro?"

"Yandro? Why would I say anything about Yandro?" Jacob thought he played it off fairly well.

Cora's eyes opened wide; her face took on an expression of absolute embarrassment.

"I..." Jacob had never seen her so mortified. "I was just kidding around."

"Yeah. Of course." Jacob wanted to help alleviate some of her devastation. "I was going to say that maybe you could invite your parents." He figured the small lie didn't hurt anything.

"I don't know about that."

As Jacob looked at Cora, he had an idea. It wasn't a particularly good idea, but it was something. He started talking before he could properly consider it. "You know what I picked up from the short time I was around you and your family?"

"What?"

"Well, I just loved the way you and your parents showed love and communicated with each other. It was night and day with the way my family and I communicate. And your dad definitely isn't shy about communicating with your mom."

They all laughed.

"I think all relationships should be like that. Well, not like *that* exactly, but..."

More laughter.

"If we didn't hold back so much for fear of what other people might think, the bonds we form with people would be so much...more real." Feeling like he was on a track and unable to stop, he continued. "I'm learning that being true to myself is the only way I'm ever going to have a meaningful connection with anyone. You know what I mean?"

"Yeah..."

Both Cora and Tadrick seemed as shocked as he was about his sudden loquaciousness.

He may have added to his soliloquy, but, as if ordained by the god of love herself, Yandro burst in with a fresh keg.

"Hello!" he said, all smiles. "Been a long time since I've seen you two." He pointed to Jacob and Tadrick.

"Have you saved any other lives since we last saw you?" Tadrick asked.

"Oh, no." Now Yandro looked embarrassed. "Just delivered a few kegs."

Cora looked confused.

"Yandro pretty much saved our lives at The Dripping Bucket," Tadrick told her.

"Oh yeah?" Cora's interest was piqued.

"I don't know about that." Yandro's eyes pointed to the floor. "Just used a little herima to get out of a tight spot."

Cora perked up even more. "Oh, nice. I wish I would have learned more of that in the village when I was younger."

"You still could," Yandro said. "I think you'd be great at it. You're smart and passionate and so full of confidence. Plus, you've got a really great...er...athletic...uh...build." He had started off full of energy but ended with his face in his hands. "I mean.... It's important to be strong in herima."

Cora suppressed a giggle.

Whatever was going on here was great. Even though Yandro was temporarily embarrassed, Cora was opening up and standing tall, radiating confidence. Jacob was riveted. He found himself really hoping for a breakthrough.

"So, I'm putting on an event here pretty soon," Cora said.

"Oh yeah?" Yandro brightened, seeming happy to be moving on so quickly. "What kind of event?"

"Something with traditional ciguapa music and dancing." Cora ran her fingers through her long blue hair, eyes flicking from Yandro to the corner of the ceiling.

"Dancing?"

"Yeah. You know; moving in time to music." Cora's too-literal awkwardness was overcome by an upturn on the corner of her mouth. She looked directly into Yandro's eyes.

"Oh, that." Yandro's smile was wide. His ability to play along so quickly made Cora light up with a smile to match it.

"Would you like to move in time to music with me?" Cora asked.

Jacob clenched his fists in celebration but gave no other outward indication that he cared about their interaction.

"Yes!" Yandro said, smile as bright as a sunbeam. "I would love to do that."

Jacob grinned, alive with joy. As he watched Cora break through whatever had been holding her back, he realized just how much he cared for her. He really wanted her to be happy.

"Finally!" Tadrick said, hands out to his sides and a wide grin across his face.

Cora kicked him in the shin.

CHAPTER 22

Orcs and Clues

The night got busier, so eventually, the decision was made to try and find the orcs again in the morning.

Juniper came over bright and early after dropping her kids off at the schoolhouse, ready to go.

"Cora and Tadrick said that we could go without them if we wanted." Jacob rubbed the sleep from his eyes. "I don't get the idea that they're early risers."

"Well, that's alright." Juniper's energy level was much higher than Jacob thought possible at this time of the morning.

Jacob stretched his arms into the air and yawned. "Let me change clothes and I'll be right out." He trudged back to his room and put on his new pants and new blue shirt. They were comfortable and, as far as he could tell, looked good on him. He put on his tricorn hat as he entered the main pub.

"What do you think?" he asked Juniper as he slid out of his room with a flourish, suddenly energized.

"I love it!"

Jacob had a distinct but strange feeling that he had just unlocked something within himself. It was only clothing, but something about dressing this way made him feel more alive.

He took his hat off and bowed to Juniper. "Shall we go, then?"

"We shall."

They took off down the road on a bright, cloudless day. The Ring above shone silver in a sky that seemed particularly deep blue. There was a slight breeze out of the south, and the temperature was perfect. Jacob and Juniper enjoyed the day wordlessly for a while as they walked.

When they came to the mines, Juniper stopped and faced them. She bowed her head, eyes closed, and whispered to herself. Jacob kept his distance and didn't stare, figuring this must be about her husband.

Juniper kissed two of her fingers, knelt, and touched them to the ground.

"Sorry about that," she called to Jacob as she hurried to catch up. She didn't seem upset at all.

"No problem." Jacob was unsure if he should say anything else.

"Sometimes I can't believe it's already been five years since he passed," Juniper said.

"I'm sorry."

Juniper nodded and flashed him a thankful smile.

"Why do bad things happen to good people?" The question was rhetorical, and Jacob immediately wished he'd kept his mouth shut.

"He was a good man. That's for sure."

"You, too," Jacob said. "You're the good person I was talking about."

"You might not say that if you spent any time in here." Juniper held a finger to the side of her head.

"What do you mean?"

"Well..." She seemed to struggle with whether or not to say something. "I'm selfish, for one."

"I'm not sure if I've met a less selfish person, to tell the truth."

"It might seem that way, but I know myself. All day, all I can think about is getting away."

"That's natural. Especially for someone with so much on her plate."

Juniper stopped and faced Jacob; her face much more serious. "You really don't understand, though." She looked like she might cry. "I can sit there at home and have one of those beautiful, innocent little kids tell me about their day, and all I can think about is being alone on a beach somewhere, or out doing just about anything else. If that's not selfish, I don't know what is."

"But you're not alone on the beach. You stay with them, and you're a great mother to them."

"That's not the point. I would never leave them. I love them more than anything. But my selfish mind is never satisfied."

Jacob wished he was better with words. He wanted to tell her how good of a person he thought she was, but couldn't find a better, more relevant way to say it.

"You're overwhelmed," he finally said. "You're a mother on her own trying to raise two school-age children and run a business at the same time. By yourself. You're a faun, which is a tiny minority in the League of Islands, so I'm sure that can't be easy. You find yourself subject to a cruel, rich human and you've got no one to fall back on. And then, if you lose your restaurant, the prospect of working long hours on the fish lines or wherever is probably stressful, too." Jacob had let the words tumble out as they formed.

Juniper stood across him, an arm's length away, fighting off tears.

"I'm sorry. That was cru—"

Juniper rushed forward, gushing tears, and wrapped her arms around him, gently laying the side of her horn on his chest. Jacob enfolded her in an embrace and let her cry. He wasn't sure how many minutes passed as she sobbed into his shirt, but he would have stood there all day if necessary.

When she was done, she stepped back and used the sleeve of her shirt to dry her eyes.

"Oh, God in the Trees." She chuckled to herself and shook her head. "That was unexpected." She looked up at Jacob, her eyes red, but integrated into her genuine smile. "Thank you."

"I'm not sure I did anything."

"You let me hear it from an adult perspective that wasn't inside my own head. Then you let me get it out."

"Oh." Jacob had stumbled blindly into helping her. He figured he should probably just leave it there.

"I love those kids," Juniper said. "And I have a lot of reasons to count myself as blessed, but I've just been feeling like my life has one note, lately. It's a wonderful note, but it's on its own."

"I get that." Jacob nodded. "That very thing is the reason I quit my family business and moved here. I just never heard it put so simply and profound....ly, if that's a word?" The corner of his mouth turned up. "Hard to make a danceable song with one note."

Juniper nodded and smiled, still wiping away the remnants of tears from her cheeks.

"Well, shit," she said. Jacob had never heard her curse before. "I suppose we should get going, again."

Jacob agreed, and they started back down the road.

Juniper had hidden her frustrations well. Jacob had only ever noticed her being annoyed with the kids one time. He didn't think she looked upset before, but he could see a slight change in her, now, from the way she walked to the tightness of her facial features. She seemed a bit lighter, like Jacob did after one beer on an empty stomach.

When they reached the secluded bay that was home to Shelu and Korga's cave, the two orcs were fishing from the beach.

"Hello!" Juniper called.

When Shelu turned and saw Juniper, her face lit up in a tusky smile. "Hello, Juniper!"

The orcs set down their poles and hurried over to greet Juniper. They greeted Jacob, too, but were particularly excited to see the faun woman. Jacob wondered what the history of orc and faun relations was like, disappointed in himself for knowing nothing about it. Korga was much more cordial this time, much less distrusting now that he knew Jacob meant them no harm.

"So, Juniper and Justjacob, why you come to see us?" Shelu asked.

Jacob stood silent, hoping Juniper would take the lead.

"We have a question for you," Juniper said. "Do you know the word *Kibu*?"

"Kibu?"

"Yes."

"Of course, we know Kibu." Korga nodded. "It's one of most important words for orcs."

"What does it mean?"

"It is name of...brightest star in sky. First star to...appear." He pointed to the sky, not much higher than the horizon to the north. "There."

"Thank you very much," Juniper said.

"Why you need to know Kibu?" Shelu asked.

Jacob wished they had discussed whether or not they would tell the orcs about the clue and the treasure. He would respect Juniper's decision either way, but he was hoping she would artfully withhold the truth from them. He didn't want the orcs to suffer any unintended consequences from the race to the treasure with Mr. Lowell and his men.

"We saw it written, and were curious." Juniper left it simple, and not exactly a lie.

The orcs seemed slightly confused by her answer, but neither of them pressed her.

"How has work been?" Juniper asked. "Any progress on getting enough money to sail home?"

Shelu blinked. "Jobs here and there. But still long time before we can go home."

Korga's shoulders slumped. Juniper reached up as high as she could and rubbed one of them. It was the first time Jacob had seen anyone touch the young male orc.

"I will try again to find work for you," Juniper said.

"We thank you, again."

"And we thank you for the help with our word."

After goodbyes, Jacob and Juniper started back home.

When they were off the beach and back on the road, Juniper said, "I hate to lie to them, but I just figured it would be better for them to not get caught up in the whole thing if something goes wrong. I wouldn't want Mr. Lowell's men questioning the orcs and trying to have them punished or anything like that."

"That's exactly what I was thinking." Jacob flashed her a smile. "We're on the same page."

"Yeah, we are."

"Just to make sure, I wanted to see if we were on the same page about something else."

"Okay."

"If we do find the treasure, we'll give them enough money to go home, right?"

"Of course!"

"Okay. Good."

They walked without speaking for a spell.

"So, we come back tonight?" Jacob said. "And follow Kibu as far as we can?"

"Absolutely."

～

On the way back, a hooded figure stood in the middle of the road near the mines. As Jacob and Juniper got closer, it was obvious that it was Mr. Lowell's ciguapa henchman.

"You have been to see the orcs, Shelu and Korga, at their cave," he said as they approached.

"Is that a question?" Juniper held her hands out to her sides.

"It's a fact." The man pulled back his hood, revealing his handsome, but somehow unnerving face, and slicked back hair. "I don't think we've been properly introduced. My name is Mali. You are Juniper, owner of a faun restaurant for a few more days, and you are Jacob, thorn in my side."

Juniper showed no indication of backing down from the man. Jacob tried to mimic her stoicism.

"What did the orcs tell you?"

"Nothing." Juniper's face betrayed no emotion.

"What does Kibu mean?"

"We don't know. We went to see Shelu and Korga because we thought Kibu might be an orcish word, but they said they'd never heard of it." Her ability to lie with a straight face was impressive.

"That is untrue. I have often heard orcs using the word on Mr. Lowell's estate. They won't tell me its meaning because I am close to Mr. Lowell."

"Why are you close to Mr. Lowell?" Juniper asked. "Doesn't that make you feel like...I don't know, a traitor?"

"A traitor to whom?" Mali said, his expression unchanging. Then, before Juniper could answer, he said, "Your answer doesn't matter. He pays me well."

Juniper gave a derisive snort. Jacob wished she would stop taunting him.

"We've determined that Kibu is, in fact, an orcish word. We also know you visited the orcs, who are your friends. So, the assertion that you don't know its meaning is laughable."

"Who said we were friends with them? They did some work for us. That doesn't automatically make us friends." Juniper's confidence in this situation was something to behold. "You work for Mr. Lowell. Do you think he considers you a friend?"

Mali didn't react to the question, but Jacob thought he saw his jaw clench.

"This is a waste of my time." Mali frowned. "Tell me the word's meaning, or we will keep eyes on you until we have found out."

"Why don't you keep eyes on this?" To Jacob's utter astonishment, Juniper turned around, bent over, and slapped her own ass so hard the sound echoed off the hills.

Wordlessly, Mali pulled his hood back onto his head, turned, and strode away.

Juniper stood and turned back around. Before Jacob could even attempt to make sense of what he'd seen, Juniper burst out laughing. Her laugh was loud and wonderful and catching. In a matter of seconds, Jacob was bent over with laughter alongside her. The two of them carried on for long enough to make Jacob's face and stomach muscles ache.

"That kinda hurt!" Juniper said between giggles.

"I bet!"

"I don't know what came over me. I damn near showed him my bare ass and tail!" She breathed a few times with her eyes closed, regaining her composure. "It's just...I have no time for someone like that. A rich person's lackey."

"Yeah." Jacob couldn't find any other words.

"One thing I can say, though. Today had some unexpected new notes, didn't it? Some lows and some highs."

"And some notes I would have never guessed existed."

CHAPTER 23

Kibu

It was an Iniday, so there was nothing for Jacob to do when they got back but wait. Juniper would have normally opened her restaurant for lunch, but she left to try and find someone to watch Aspen and Ceda overnight. She was friendly with several parents of kids from school and hoped one of them might be able to take them. Cora and Tadrick hadn't shown up at the pub yet, but Jacob imagined they would come in at some point to find out if he'd contacted the orcs.

While he waited, Jacob took a chair out back and sat beside the creek. The soothing sound of rushing water helped wash away the tension he was holding. The two capybaras lounging in the pond made for an even more relaxing scene.

Eyes focused on nothing in particular, Jacob became lost in thought.

An image of a treasure chest dug up from the beach flashed in his mind. Then an image of his first love smiling at him—the dimple on her left cheek. He thought about a giant frog he caught in a creek similar to this one when he was seven. Then a two-masted ship with himself at the helm, barking orders to his loyal crew.

"Wakey, wakey," Tadrick said, squeezing Jacob's shoulder.

Jacob startled awake and shot to his feet.

"Whoa there!" Cora jumped back playfully. "Any luck with Shelu and Korga?"

Jacob oriented himself to the land of the waking, then told them what the orcs had said.

"I know that star," Tadrick said. "The North Star. It's the only star that remains fixed in the night sky. It's always north of us. Well, magnetic north, which is actually slightly northeast." He blinked. "Sorry. My dad's a sailor."

"So...we just follow it until our feet get wet?" Cora looked back and forth from Jacob to Tadrick.

"That's what it said," Jacob replied.

"So tonight, then?"

"That's what Juniper and I were thinking."

"I can't wait!" Cora had a sparkle in her eyes and a grin on her lips.

Juniper found someone who could watch the kids. She came over to the pub dressed in what she called her gardening clothes, which were plain and slightly dirty. She carried a spade and a cloth bundle full of corn chips.

"I figured this might be an all-nighter, and we'll want some snacks."

"Good idea," said Jacob.

"I have an idea, too." Cora raised her hand as if in school. "Since Mali, or whoever, said that Mr. Lowell's men were watching us, I had an idea to throw them off. I could create an illusion that looks like the four of us and send it off in a different direction."

"You could?" Jacob knew she could create illusions, but wasn't aware she could do something quite so elaborate as that. "Do you think it would fool them?"

"For a little while. Hopefully long enough for us to get going while they're distracted."

"Would it take much energy?" Tadrick asked.

"Yeah. It will take a lot to make the illusion good enough. I'll be tired, but I think it'll be worth it."

"Alright." Jacob poked his head out the front door, looking northeast to the horizon. The sun had just set, and Kibu was barely visible in the sky. "It's time to go," he told them as he closed the door behind himself.

Cora took a deep breath, then traced one of her rune tattoos while saying a ciguapa word. A multicolored mist began to swirl in the pub. The swirl diverged into four separate swirls, which began to take the rough forms of people.

At first, the figures were fuzzy, but soon began to coalesce as four distinct people. Jacob resisted the urge to reach out and touch the misty apparitions as they became more solid, less see-through. In a matter of heartbeats, the figures took on the appearance of their exact doppelgängers. Jacob felt strange seeing a version of himself looking back at him. The other him did look great in those new clothes, but he needed to work on his posture.

He looked to Cora, whose face was serene, but her hands were clenched into tight fists. The concentration it must have taken to create something like that was incredible.

The only thing off about the doppelgängers was their complete lack of expression or movement. It was as if they were frozen in time, staring at nothing.

Wasting no time, Cora sent the crew of look-a-likes out the door and to the southeast. Their movements were clunky, but not completely unnatural. Jacob wanted to watch them go but knew it would be giving up the whole illusion if he was seen.

Now Cora closed her eyes and pressed her lips together until they blanched. Jacob imagined she must be making the illusions go through town by memory. He was sure he couldn't have done the same.

"Okay," Cora said after another two minutes or so, a little out of breath. "Let's hurry."

Jacob poked his head out the door again, looking both ways for any sign of Mr. Lowell's henchmen and seeing none. He waved the others forward as he exited the pub.

The group ran down the road to the north, then turned right at the first possible chance. They zig-zagged through the more rural section of town until they reached the beach. Staying amid cover whenever possible, they hiked northward in the fading light.

Before long, all the light had bled from the horizon, leaving only Ringlight to travel by. Kibu twinkled from the northeast, a beacon guiding them through the night.

They passed the orcs' cave quietly, still not wanting to get them involved in case of trouble. Another thirty minutes and they ran into giant signs on the beach that read:

PROPERTY OF MR. LOWELL
  NO TRESPASSING
  VIOLATORS WILL BE PROSECUTED
  TO THE UTMOST DEGREE OF THE LAW

Between each of the dozen or more signs was a length of rope that connected them, creating a line from the sea to the rocky outcroppings beyond the beach.

They all stopped at the rope.

"There's only one question." Tadrick's voice and face showed no emotion.

"And that is?" Jacob said.

"Do we go over, or under?"

Jacob laughed, thankful for the moment of levity. The thought of setting foot on Mr. Lowell's land again made his chest tighten and his palms sweaty.

"Under." Cora pointed down. "Less chance of tripping."

"But we'll get all sandy that way." Juniper played along perfectly. "I say over."

"She brought the snacks." Tadrick pointed a thumb at Juniper. "I'm voting with her."

They all turned to Jacob.

"We could go around." He pointed toward the sea.

"And get our feet wet?" Cora said.

"Alright, over, then."

Cora made a show of being upset while gracefully jumping over the rope. The others followed.

Not far from the signs, the beach took a turn to the right. If they were going to follow Kibu as far as possible, they would have to continue that way along the beach.

The terrain changed quickly; the sand gave way to more and more rocks. It became clear that they were traveling toward the end of a peninsula that came to an eastward point. By the time they made it to the end of the peninsula, the ground was nothing but jagged rocks.

One rock formation towered above the others. It rose up at least fifteen feet from the edge of the water. A lone pine tree grew out from the side of the rock in an impressive display of resiliency. The rock was strange looking, almost unnatural. It was cylindrical, with a flat top.

"Well," Cora said, searching the ground, "this is as close as we can get to Kibu without getting our feet wet, right?"

"Seems that way." Juniper stood on the tip of the peninsula, looking both ways.

After a thorough search of the area, they discovered nothing unusual.

"Maybe it's up there?" Tadrick pointed to the top of the rock formation.

"It's gotta be." Cora ran her hands along the rock face, searching for handholds. "It's way too smooth to climb, though," she said after feeling all the way around it.

Jacob gauged its height again. "What if someone stood on my shoulders?"

Cora was at his side in a flash. "I'll do it."

It was much harder in practice than it was in his mind. Cora was relatively light, but it was still awkward to get her up to her feet on Jacob's shoulders. At first, he bent forward with his hands on his knees and had her try to climb up his back. Cora had enough balance to do it, but Jacob moved too much under her feet. Through trial and error, they eventually had Jacob face the rock and squat on his haunches. Juniper and Tadrick helped lift Cora to Jacob's shoulders, then did their best to help as Jacob tried to stand to his full height. He strained and pushed up with everything he had, letting out an embarrassing grunt of maximal effort as his legs finally straightened. Juniper and Tadrick stood on either side of him, helping him stay steady.

"I think I can climb from here," Cora said.

She moved to the right, unbalancing the tentative equilibrium they had found. Jacob engaged every muscle in his body in an attempt to stay still. Just as he thought they were going to tip over, Cora's weight was gone.

A rock the size of a copper coin struck Jacob in the forehead as he looked up.

Cora had found a foothold about three feet up from the top of his head. Along with a handhold near the top of the formation, she had managed to pull herself high enough so she could see what was up there.

In a skillful show of agility, she threw her right leg up at the same time she lifted with her left hand. As her body went perpendicular to where it was a moment before, she rolled to her right and disappeared on top of the formation.

A second later, her head poked out over the side. "That was fun," she said, grinning.

Her head disappeared again. Jacob backed up until he could see her standing up on top. She traced one of her rune tattoos and light burst from her hands again.

"I don't see anything up here," she said after a minute or two. "Just a bunch of loose rocks." She looked down over the side. "Could you toss me up that spade?"

Juniper nodded, then launched the spade up toward Cora's outstretched hand.

"Thank you," Cora said as she caught it.

The sounds of metal clashing with rock came from above. Then the thuds and crashes of rocks falling on the other side of the rock tower.

This went on for quite some time. Jacob wondered if Cora had been the best person to choose for this job. She had already been drained of energy by her illusion.

"There's definitely something under here!" Cora called, her voice giddy.

A shock of excitement coursed through Jacob's body.

"It's a door," she said after more digging. "I...just a minute."

The rocks continued to plummet off the far side at an even faster rate. Jacob fought the urge to ask for updates, letting her work.

"I'm going to try and open it," she called.

There was a screeching sound of metal on metal, accompanied by more tumbling rocks.

"It's a hole," Cora called. "Or, like, a mine shaft. There's a ladder, and I can't see the bottom of it."

She moved to her right and crouched out of view.

"I think I have an idea." She grunted as if lifting something. "Yeah. I think it's gonna work."

In another minute, she looked down at them over the edge. "Back up."

When they all complied, Cora kicked something, and a rope ladder unrolled over the side, ending almost perfectly at ground level.

"Come on up," she said.

CHAPTER 24

Down the Mine Shaft

Climbing the ladder was relatively easy. Juniper's hooves slipped a few times on the way up, but she recovered well and kept moving. Jacob followed, then Tadrick. Once everyone was up, Cora pulled up the rope ladder, rolling it into a bundle, then pushed it back down into the pitch-black mine shaft.

"I'll go first," Cora said. "Since I've got the light magic."

"Aren't you getting tired?" Jacob asked. She looked exhausted.

"Yes. But I'm way too excited to stop now."

"Have some chips first." Juniper untied her bundle and offered it to Cora, who ravenously tore into them. "I brought water, too." Juniper let Cora hold the bundle while she ate, then took a strap off from around her shoulder that Jacob hadn't noticed. Attached to the leather strap was a flagon of water.

Cora took the water, chugged several gulps, then passed it to Tadrick. He took a quick pull and handed it to Jacob, who was very thirsty but followed Tadrick's example before passing it back to Juniper. Cora offered the chips to everyone, and they all took a few.

"Alright," Cora said after they'd passed the water around again, "I feel much better now. I promise."

She sat at the edge of the shaft, dangling her legs inside. Carefully, she grasped the top rung and lowered herself down. Her magical light bounced around the shaft as she descended.

"I'm at the bottom." Her voice echoed strangely through the shaft. "Come dow—"

Cora and the entire shaft were suddenly bathed in bright blue light.

Jacob's heart jumped into his throat as he imagined Cora burning in magical fire.

"Wow!" Cora called from below. "You guys gotta see this."

Tadrick mounted the ladder and hurried down. Jacob gestured toward the hole, indicating that Juniper could go next. When she did, he followed her down; claustrophobic, a little scared, and giddy with excitement.

When he got to the bottom, Jacob turned to see a spacious cavern that opened up from the shaft. Although, upon consideration, it was more of a chamber than a cavern. The walls were flat and symmetrical, forming a perfectly-squared room about thirty feet by thirty feet. The blue light came from glowing blue writing along the walls, ceiling, and floor. Jacob didn't recognize the language.

"It's faun sigaldry." Juniper traced some of the writing with a finger. "But way beyond my level of expertise."

"Look." Tadrick pointed to the middle of the far wall. "The human tongue."

Several lines in the human tongue were written at approximately eye level. Underneath them were two glowing handprints, one above the other.

The magical blue writing on the wall read:

A Choice:

Top Hand- A third of the treasure for you, and two-thirds to two random people in <u>serious</u> need who you do not know.

Bottom Hand- All the treasure for you.
  You have sixty seconds to decide.

. . .

The floor under their feet lit up. A line of blue light traveled from their feet, across the floor, and up the wall to stop next to the two hands. The line turned into the number 60. Then 59. 58.

"The top, right?" Cora had a hint of panic in her voice.

"Yes." Juniper was a bit more resolute.

Tadrick hesitated until the wall got to 53, then said, "Of course."

They all looked to Jacob.

"You got us here, boss," Tadrick said. "I know you don't like that title, but without you buying Mrs. Covington's, I'd still be bored and depressed, handing out knives for the block of cheese in an artless room right now."

42.

41.

Jacob's instinct was to pick the top hand, but he wanted to think it through.

If they took the whole treasure, they'd be able to do whatever they wanted with it, and they would absolutely help people in serious need. For one, they would help Juniper keep her business, which would allow her to be a better mother to Aspen and Ceda. For another, they would help Shelu and Korga get home to their parents.

34.

33.

But what about a ship? He had dreamed for a long time now of owning his own ship. Of being the captain of a crew. He would pick people like those here with him in the chamber. Like Yandro, or even Shelu and Korga if they were interested. He pictured the masts, the sails, the figurehead.

25.

24.

He could be richer than his dad. He could prove to him that he was a worthy son. That he wasn't stupid, or lazy. Just different.

16.

15.

But money wasn't the measure of worth. That knowledge had always lived inside him, but now he knew, at his core, that it was true.

10.

The others were looking extremely anxious, but why should Jacob be the one to decide this, anyway? In truth, he aspired to be more like each of the other people in the room with him, but they were looking to him in this moment. He didn't understand.

6.

5.

Jacob relaxed his shoulders. He was sure a third of the treasure would be enough to help Juniper and the orcs. And if they could change the lives of two other people in serious need as well, they would do it. That was what his friends had chosen. He would follow their lead.

He stepped forward and placed his hand on the top print. It flashed a brilliant blue, then darkened into nothing.

The room was silent. Everyone stared at the place where the hand-prints had just been.

Nothing happened.

"Uh..." Cora furrowed her brow.

Seconds ticked by, and still nothing. Jacob started to wonder if they'd made the wrong choice. Then he started to panic. Was this entire thing some kind of strange joke? Did someone get here before them? Was it realistic to be standing here expecting a life-changing treasure to just pop out of nowhere so they could all live happily from then to never, as the storybooks always ended? He was—

A grinding sound erupted from the floor. One of the stones moved down, then over, creating a perfectly square hole.

Something began to emerge from the opening. At first, it was unrec-ognizable, but as soon as it crested the surface of the floor, it became clear.

"A treasure chest!" Cora roared.

The chest continued up until the stone it sat on was level with the floor.

They all stared at it. Jacob's heart performed feats it had never dared before. He had a spell of dizziness but managed to keep his feet under him.

"May I?" Tadrick asked the group.

Jacob and the others simply nodded to him, mouths agape.

Slowly, Tadrick pulled the golden latch on the front of the chest. It snapped open with a loud click that echoed around the chamber. He looked to his friends, then lifted the lid.

Inside was exactly what Jacob imagined it would be. It was filled with gold coins that shined unlike any he'd ever seen. On top of the coins was a sprinkling of gems of every color and four golden chalices, inlaid with gems of their own.

A rolled sheet of parchment tied with a red ribbon sat on top.

Jacob, feeling quite out of his body, noticed himself taking and unrolling the parchment.

It read:

Congratulations!

The treasure is yours! All of it. That was just a little test I thought up. I figured I'd add one little hiccup to weed out any greedy treasure hunters.

Anyway, my greatest wish is that you decide to use your newfound wealth to make our world a better place. And it seems like you're the type to do just that!

That is what I set out to do with this treasure hunt. I wanted to create a call to adventure, a spectacle that could help unite people in common cause. I know these goals are grandiose at best, but I hope I achieved them in some small way.

Through no great deeds of my own, I have more money than I could ever use in a hundred lifetimes. This wealth has been passed down in my family for generations. For one person to have as much money as I do when others are struggling is unjust. I intend to remedy this situation, and this treasure hunt is just the beginning. I believe my purpose is to help others, and I hope I can realize that purpose with what little time I have left in this world.

I urge you to exercise empathy.

I urge you to be kind.

Cora dug her hands into the treasure and scooped it up, allowing coins and gems to fall through her fingers. All the others, not being able to help themselves, did the same.

~

Getting the treasure chest out of the chamber was going to be a problem. It wasn't quite big enough to hold Mrs. Covington, but it looked heavy and was sure to be awkward to carry. The note had said that faun magic would help them get the treasure home, but they couldn't find any indication of that.

Cora and Tadrick grabbed golden handles on either side of the chest, saying they were going to test its weight. After a countdown from three, they lifted it off the ground.

Blue light flared out from the bottom of the chest. Both Cora and Tadrick, who had been straining against its weight, now seemed free from it.

Tentatively, they both let go of the handles.

The chest didn't fall. It floated in the air exactly where they'd dropped it.

Cora grasped a handle again and pulled the chest in her direction. It glided through the air toward her.

She lifted the handle upward, and the chest rose to eye level.

Juniper peered underneath the chest. "It's more sigaldry," she said. "The most powerful I've ever seen by far."

"Thank you, Ashby." Cora pushed the chest so it floated halfway across the room. "This is great."

With the chest being floated by faun magic, getting it out of the chamber was easy. It was only when they got it outside and down from the rock formation that they realized another potential problem.

"What are we going to do, just waltz back into town with a floating magical treasure chest glowing blue from the bottom?" Cora said.

"Well," Juniper said, "let's get going back home. Hopefully, we can think of something on the way."

The *something* Juniper thought of before they were even off the rocky peninsula was brilliant, in Jacob's opinion.

Once they had reached the edge of the sandy beach, where there were trees and other vegetation, Juniper searched for fallen coconuts, finding two. Using the spade, she cut each coconut in half.

She asked the others to search for coconuts and sticks of any size and to toss them into a pile near the chest. While supplies were collected, she pulled several blades of tall grass and sat near the floating chest.

Jacob marveled as Juniper got to work. In no time at all, she was done, and the treasure chest had undergone a complete transformation.

The halved coconuts were made to look like wagon wheels with sticks for axles. They were secured to the chest by tying long strands of tall grass. The sides of the chest were concealed by sticks. A long stick handle was attached to one side of the chest. A palm frond was tied underneath to conceal the glow as much as possible.

The treasure chest now looked like a homemade wagon.

The rest of the coconuts that had been collected were placed on top of the chest. So, to anyone who passed by them on their way into town, it seemed as if they had been out collecting coconuts at night. It wasn't the most plausible story, but it was a great deal better than a floating chest.

Juniper pushed the chest down until the wheels were nearly touching the ground. She grasped the handle and pulled the chest as if it was a normal, pull-behind wagon. The effect was not the most convincing reproduction of a rolling wagon, but it would pass as good enough in the dark.

On the way into town, they only passed one person, who barely even glanced at them.

When Juniper pulled the treasure chest into the pub and the door was closed behind it, Jacob gave an exaggerated but heartfelt sigh.

CHAPTER 25

Celebration

The four of them looked at each other just inside the door of the pub. No one seemed to know how to react. Jacob saw joy, excitement, anxiety, and confusion on all their faces.

Tadrick broke the staring standoff by rounding the bar and grabbing something from underneath. He lifted a full bottle of rum over his head and said, "Let's celebrate!"

The anxiety and confusion were gone from Cora's and Juniper's expressions—only joy and excitement remained. Jacob found himself grinning as he joined the others near the chest.

"I've been keeping this bottle down here, waiting for the right occasion. And if this isn't it, I don't know what would be." He set the bottle on a table by the chest and began taking coconuts off the makeshift wagon. When it was cleared enough, he opened the chest, took out the four bejeweled chalices, and poured rum into them. He handed a chalice to everyone, raised his skyward, and said, "Here's to us. We did it!"

The crew clinked their golden cups together and drank. The rum, which Jacob had never tried before, was strong, but not as overpowering as he thought it would be. He only winced a bit as it went down.

When the bottle of rum was emptied, they moved on to beer.

"That'll be half a copper, sir," Tadrick said to Jacob as he filled his chalice at the tap.

Jacob took a gold coin from the chest and dropped it on the bar. "I'd like to start a tab, please," he said with a grin.

"Alright." Tadrick's eyes pointed to the ceiling as he did some mental math. "You've got nine hundred and ninety-nine beers left. But no more after that!"

"I'd like to buy a round for the entire pub."

Both Tadrick and Jacob lapsed into giggles, too tipsy to keep up their little scene.

"Look," Cora said, crouching down in front of Mrs. Covington. "She's fancy, now." She had clasped some kind of necklace around the capybara's neck.

"I feel pretty fancy, too." Juniper struck a few poses, drawing attention to her ears, which were adorned with giant emerald earrings.

"Nice!" Cora said.

"Do you want to learn *Raise Your Beer*?" Tadrick asked Jacob. "I feel like singing it right now."

"Of course."

"I'd like to learn, too." Juniper was all smiles.

"I gotta pee." Cora stumbled toward the door, but then, seemingly sidetracked, made her way to the treasure chest and took two handfuls of coins, letting them fall through her fingers back into the chest. "That's so satisfying," she said to herself with a giggle.

Jacob was proud of how quickly he picked up the song. The three of them sang it while Cora spent a considerable time out behind the pub. Jacob thought about going out and finding her, but she appeared back at the door, leaning on the frame.

Juniper, who had been drinking and laughing along with everyone from the start, stood, her face suddenly serious.

"I don't want to kill the mood, here," she said. "But before we go too far, there are a few things we need to discuss."

Jacob was immediately ashamed for letting the celebration get away with him. Of course, there was a lot to figure out.

"I think the first thing we need to do is find a place to hide the treasure," Juniper said. "For all we know, Mr. Lowell and his men could come calling this morning."

"Good idea." Jacob nodded. "I was thinking of putting it up on the roof. Is that...good?"

"Not bad." Juniper rubbed one of her horns, deep in thought. "But it would be tough to hide it well up there with the pitch and everything."

"We could sink it into Mrs. Covington's pool," Cora offered, still leaning on the door frame.

"That's good!" Jacob said.

"We could bury it, pirate-style," Tadrick offered.

Everyone considered the options. Jacob liked the idea of burying it the best but didn't want to step on Cora's toes.

"I like Cora's idea," Juniper said, "but I think burial is the best option."

"Yeah. I agree." Cora took a swig of her from her chalice. "Mrs. Covington's pool is pretty clear. Might be able to see it down there on a sunny day."

"Let's get digging, then," Tadrick said.

They took Juniper's spade out back and searched for the best place to dig, deciding on a spot just in front of a little cover that Mr. Davies had built for storing firewood. Everyone took their turn digging. Cora and Tadrick kept drinking between their shifts, but Jacob switched to water, already feeling like he may have overdone it.

When the hole was dug, they put the coins, jewels, and chalices back in the chest, lowered the chest into the ground, and covered it back up. Juniper smoothed out the dirt over the dig, making it look as natural as she could. They took debris from the yard and spread it evenly over the ground.

During the celebration, something had been gnawing at the back of Jacob's mind, but now that they had bought themselves some time to think, the relief was palpable.

"We'll have to discuss how we're going to discreetly use the money at some point, but I don't think now is the time." Juniper brushed some dirt from her pants.

"Sounds good." Cora and Tadrick thudded their mugs together and took long drinks.

"What are we going to do tomorrow?" Jacob asked the group.

"It's going to be reading night," Tadrick said. "I already made a sign for it and everything. I even told the..." He covered his mouth and burped. "...the bookseller, and she said she would help spread the word."

"Good," Juniper said. "It'll be best if we act natural, like nothing has changed. I think focusing on a successful reading night will be perfect."

Cora and Tadrick knocked their mugs together again and finished their beers.

"I'm going home and going to bed." Juniper yawned. "You all have a good rest of the night."

"I'm going to bed, too," Jacob added. "You two have fun."

Cora and Tadrick gave them fake, exaggerated sad faces.

"I guess we should probably call it a night, too," Tadrick agreed.

Once everyone had left, Jacob lay down in bed with clothes and boots still on. He fell asleep about as soon as his head touched his pillow.

THE FLEDGLING

Mrs. Covington was tired and hungry. The only thing that seemed to motivate her to get up from lying down or come out from floating in the pool these days was food. The hay the humans put out was never enough, all the water plants in the pond had already been eaten, and the melon patch had a sturdy new fence around it.

She was thinking about getting up from an afternoon nap to scrounge for food when something crashed into the middle of the pool.

Whatever it was thrashed and splashed around in a colorful frenzy.

Mrs. Covington stood to get a better look. Arthur was still sound asleep in the grass.

The thing in the middle of the pond continued its hysterics, squawking like mad as it twisted and turned.

In ephemeral moments of calm, it was clear that the thing in the pool was a fledgling parrot. It was bright blue with vibrant yellow markings.

It seemed to be getting tired.

Mrs. Covington slipped into the pond. The water was nice and cool, refreshing on a hot day. She dipped her head under the water and brought it back up.

The parrot was still struggling on the water's surface.

Mrs. Covington paddled out to the middle of the pond. She submerged herself underwater and came up beneath the little fledgling.

It gripped the fur on her back with enough strength to hurt her a bit. The bird continued to squawk and carry on until it realized it was no longer in danger of drowning.

The capybara swam back to shore and climbed out of the pond. She lay down on her belly to allow the parrot to more easily get off her back, but the bird maintained its unabating grip.

Mrs. Covington munched on some nearby grass. She looked at Arthur, who was still sleeping. A dog barked from somewhere far enough away to not be worrisome. She changed the angle of her ears to make sure.

After a while, Mrs. Covington stood and meandered around the area. She made a big half-circle around the pond, pausing here and there to take a nibble of grass. The parrot moved around on her back, changing its grip, digging its claws in deeper.

Mrs. Covington made another slow half-circumnavigation of the pool.

The bird stood up and flapped its wings, but didn't go anywhere. Mrs. Covington stopped while it fussed and flapped around. When it ceased, she made her way to a particularly tall tuft of grass on the far side of the yard.

The fledgling flapped its wings again. Its squawking triggered responses from other parrots up in the trees somewhere.

Mrs. Covington munched on the tall tuft of grass, then strolled across the length of the yard, always staying in the warm light of the sun.

An adult parrot landed near the pool and squawked. The fledgling squawked back. Then they both squawked together. The adult parrot was a brilliant blue, a striking contrast amidst the dirt and grass of the yard.

The older parrot leaped from the ground and flew to a branch overhead.

The fledgling flapped its wings furiously. It loosened its grip on Mrs. Covington's fur and lifted into the air, squawking the entire time.

Mrs. Covington watched as the fledgling flew away. It zipped across the yard, up the hill, and into the hollowed-out trunk of a tree. The adult parrot followed it.

Arthur stirred, lifting his head and looking around. Mrs. Covington took another bite of grass, and Arthur laid his head back down to sleep.

CHAPTER 26

Reading Night

Thankfully, nothing unusual happened the next morning. By noon, when customers started showing up for nacias, Jacob was much less anxious. The day moved slowly as a steady stream of hungry customers came in.

Tadrick brought in an armload of pillows in the afternoon. He arranged chairs sporadically around the fireplace, then placed a thin, square pillow on every seat. When he was finished, he put the sign he'd painted out front.

Jacob built a fire, very mindful of the treasure under his feet as he collected firewood from under the cover in the back. Cora lit the ceiling with magical reading light. The ambiance was perfect for a night of reading—quiet, warm, and cozy.

At around sundown, the first person with a book in hand showed up. He was on the shy side, so he had to be gently coaxed into buying a beer and finding a seat. In the first fifteen minutes, only two more people came in, one of whom was the bookseller. But as the night went on, several more meandered in.

It wasn't going to be a big night financially, but it was a nice change of pace from the cacophonous chaos of You Sing nights.

About two hours into a quiet reading night, the door crashed open and five loud men stomped into the pub. Jacob closed his eyes and gritted his teeth when he noticed who they were. It was the same group of guys from the grand reopening who had stolen beer.

"What in the thirty-seven hells is reading night?" the one who had poured the stolen beers said, scanning the pub. "Looks boring as shit."

The rest of the men laughed.

"Can we help you?" Cora stood to her full height, muscles tense.

"We heard you were giving out free beers again."

"You heard wrong."

Tadrick put down his book and stood. Jacob hadn't moved since they walked in.

"No." The man approached the bar. "I heard it from a pretty reliable source. I don't think they would have lied to me."

The man grabbed a mug from behind the bar, but Cora put her hand on top of it, gripping it tight.

"I appreciate your offer to pour it for me." The man ripped the mug from Cora's grasp in a violent heave. "But don't worry. I got it."

More laughter from his entourage.

As the man poured himself a beer, a feeling of resolution came over Jacob. He found himself suddenly unafraid. Anger pulsed through him, but it was more than that. He had a cold resolve to act. Jacob would simply no longer tolerate the mistreatment of his friends.

He lunged forward and slapped the beer from the man's hand mid-pour, sending the mug tumbling, and beer splashing to the floor. Before the man even realized what had happened, Jacob rounded the bar and stood directly in his face, staring into his eyes.

Something about pushing past his fear and actually doing something was absolutely thrilling. Jacob couldn't wipe the wide—and probably insane-looking—smile from his face.

"She said you heard wrong." Jacob's voice was steady, with just a hint of glee.

The man, who was taller than Jacob, stared down at him. Jacob returned the stare, unblinking, a smile still spread across his face.

Something in the man's eyes screamed insecurity. Behind the bravado and bullying was nothing but weakness.

"This guy's crazy." The man looked away to his friends. "But if I knock him out, they'll probably go running to the constable. I'm not doing time in jail for this lunatic." He backed away, smiling at his group. "Let's go somewhere less boring."

The group of men seemed dumbfounded. They furrowed their brows and frowned as their apparent leader rejoined their ranks. Without another word, they left the pub.

The reading customers, who had apparently all put their books down, applauded. Cora and Tadrick joined in.

Jacob soaked it in for about half a second, then turned away and grabbed a towel for the spilled beer. His hands were shaking as he knelt to pick up the pieces of the broken mug. He felt like he might cry, but he wasn't sad. He was proud of himself and extremely thankful the confrontation was over.

The Constable

Apart from the momentary intrusion, reading night was a success. Tadrick was pleased with the turnout, which ended up being seven people. He had told them beforehand he would be happy with three or more.

As the last customer went home, Jacob congratulated Tadrick on his idea.

"I think it might even grow." Tadrick pushed a chair back to its normal place.

"Even if it doesn't, it was nice, and I'd like to keep doing it," Jacob said as he wiped down one of the tables. "And when your book comes out, I'll join them."

Tadrick's face reddened, and he unsuccessfully suppressed a smile.

"Me, too," Cora said as the front door swung open. "We're just closing up," she called to the person who had walked in, without turning to look at them.

Jacob tried to act as normal as possible as the constable entered the pub, not flinching or changing his facial expression through force of will. The constable carried a strange leather pack on his back that was long and fairly skinny, like it might have held a musket.

"Good evening." The constable's voice was so loud it was startling.

"Good evening, constable." Jacob tipped his new hat.

"What brings you by, sir?" Tadrick asked, his voice artificially pleasant.

"You're never one to beat around the bush, are you," the constable said to Tadrick. "I suppose I gotta admire that about you."

"It's just...it's not every day the constable comes in here."

"Yeah, well I really shouldn't browbeat you too much. I am, in fact, here on official business. I don't think it's too hard to guess that I'm here again on behalf of Mr. Lowell."

"Oh yeah?" Jacob said, stupidly.

"It seems he had another case of trespassing on his land."

No one spoke or reacted.

Mrs. Covington and Arthur, likely annoyed with the constable's booming voice, got up and waddled outside.

"Only this time, it seems like they got up to a whole lot more mischief than before." The constable rounded the bar, casually looking underneath. "Now, I'd be lying if I told you I understood everything he told me. There were some unbelievable little tidbits he gave me. Something about a rock tower with a trap door on the top, then something about ancient faun magic or some such." He opened the door to Jacob's room and looked inside. "If I didn't know him to be an extremely competent man, I'd have thought there was something wrong with him."

Still, no one spoke. The constable fixed his gaze on Jacob.

"Any of this sound familiar?"

"I can assure you; I know almost nothing about faun magic."

"Well, I'm sorry, but that's a bit hard to believe, seeing as how you've taken to your neighbor, and that she has previously made a—what do you call them—a will-o'-the-wisp, for you. Isn't that faun magic?"

"The only thing she's made for us is nacias," Cora said. "Have you had a chance to try them yet?"

"You know, I haven't. Have heard a lot about them, though. You all have found yourself a little recognition around town, and that's not so easy to come by." Now he tipped *his* hat. "Congratulations on that." He seemed so genuine with his praise.

"Thank you." Cora remained stoic.

"Do you mind if I take a look out back? I hate to bother those capybaras when they were just trying to get away from all the racket, but I can be quiet out there."

Jacob figured he would probably go whether they gave him permission or not. Heart pounding, he said, "Sure."

The constable had to duck so the strange leather pack he wore would fit through the door. Once in the back, he pulled out a wand from a holster on his belt and made the tip light up, illuminating the area all the way to the capybaras in the pond.

"A golden wand, huh?" Jacob said, making nervous small talk.

"Yes, indeed. Working as a constable can be dangerous sometimes. Best to be protected, you know?"

Jacob nodded. He didn't remember the constable having a wand the last time they met, but he didn't pursue it.

The constable walked across the yard, then turned and walked to the other side. His steps were slow and even.

"You never got a crow," the constable said as he paced.

For a moment, Jacob didn't know what he meant, but then he remembered the capybara heist and his excuse for being alone outside in the middle of the night. "No. Never got one."

"Oh, I'm just kidding you. I think we figured out why you were really out there." He kept up his slow, methodical zig-zag across the yard without seeming to pay much attention to what he was doing. "How is your new capybara fitting in, here?"

"Well, I guess he lived here before, but Cora's former betrothed took him away." Jacob was somewhat put at ease by the constable's casual conversation. "He fit back in right away. Those two get along really well."

"I'd say so! The female seems to be pregnant."

"Really?"

Even Cora and Tadrick were shocked.

"I'm no expert, but I would say she's just about due."

"But we just got Arthur back like a week ago," Jacob said. "You were there."

"But I stopped seeing that guy about four months ago, so Arthur was around her until then," Cora explained.

"Well, there you have it." The constable continued his methodical pacing.

There was movement around the corner of the building. The constable held his wand in that direction, revealing Juniper with its light.

"I heard voices back here and wondered what was going on," she said, half-asleep.

To Jacob's great consternation, the constable had stopped directly over the treasure chest.

"Hello, ma'am." The constable tipped his hat again. "I almost hate to ask, but were you with this group last night?"

Juniper didn't say a word. She looked unsure how to answer.

"I'm not going to ask what you all were doing, just wondering if you were with them is all." The constable flashed her a comforting grin.

"Yes. I was with them."

The constable hung his head, but just for a second. "I'm sorry to hear that."

"Why?" Juniper asked.

"Well...let me show you." The constable took the leather pack off over his head and opened a few clasps at the top. He reached in and pulled out a shovel.

Jacob's knees wobbled, but he kept his feet.

"When someone buries something," the constable said as he drove the shovel into the dirt, "the ground over the top of it is going to be slightly different for a while." He tossed a shovel full of dirt to the side. "It'll be a bit spongy under your feet. Just a bit. Some might not even notice the difference."

Jacob considered running, or charging the constable, but knew he wasn't going to do either. Instead, he watched the man dig until his shovel struck the top of the chest. It didn't take him long.

Cora looked like she really wanted to run or fight, but Juniper gave her a subtle shake of her head, warning her not to do anything rash.

The constable grunted with the effort of pulling the chest from the ground. Apparently, the faun magic was no longer active. He turned and faced them, wiping sweat from his brow as they stared.

"Is that the Fenton Treasure?" Tadrick asked. "It was buried back here the whole time?"

"It is," the constable answered. "And it's only been buried back here for about a day."

CHAPTER 28

Questions

The constable brushed off his shovel and put it back into the leather case.

"So, let me tell you how this is going to go." His voice was authoritative but slightly dejected. "I'm not a complete prick. I don't want to arrest the lot of you. But I am required to have one of you to turn in to Mr. Lowell as the perpetrator. He's the most powerful person on this island, and he's demanding that someone be made an example of." He sighed. "So, we're going to go down to my office. Each of you will take turns giving me your story and we'll see how they match up. I've been doing this a while, and you've already proved yourselves to be the world's worst criminals, so just tell me the truth and we'll get this sorted the best we can."

"But we're hardly criminals," Jacob said. "The Fenton Treasure was hidden by Mrs. Fenton herself, with the express understanding that anyone was welcome to it if they could decipher the clues."

"True. But Mrs. Fenton is gone, and that treasure, legally, belongs to Mr. Lowell now. One or all of you also trespassed on his property, at least twice."

"Isn't possession four-fifths of the law or something like that?" Tadrick asked, pointing at the chest.

"In most instances, sure," the constable replied. "But this isn't most instances." He held his hands up. "I think it's best if you stop talking, now. The two things you've already said could easily be incriminating in court. Let's get to my office first. I'll hear your stories there."

"What about my kids?" Juniper's voice had a definite edge of panic to it.

"I'm assuming they're somewhere else for the night. Am I right?"

"Yes. But just until morning."

"I promise you we'll have this sorted before then."

"I—"

"It's time to come with me." The constable waved them forward as he started for the center of town.

The town's square was eerily empty. All the market stalls were closed, the vendors home and safe in bed. The only oil lamps still burning were in front of the constable's office, which doubled as the town's jail.

The constable had asked Jacob and Tadrick to carry the heavy chest through town. The entire way he kept a close watch to make sure no one was corroborating stories. Cora had tried to whisper something to Jacob, but he couldn't understand what she'd said.

While struggling to carry the chest, Jacob obsessed over what he was going to tell the constable. He didn't want to go to jail. The thought was terrifying. All of his success here would have been for nothing. What would happen to the pub, his co-owners, or Juniper?

The constable's office was plain. It consisted of a large desk strewn with files and papers, with one chair behind it and two chairs in front. There was an ornamental rug on the floor and a shiny sword, a cutlass, mounted on the wall. The brass nameplate on the desk was unreadable, covered by a roll of parchment.

There were two doors on the wall to the left and one on the right that must have led to the jail. A shiver shook through Jacob just thinking about it being so close.

"Set the chest there, please." The constable pointed to the side of his desk.

Jacob and Tadrick set it down. Jacob would have reveled in the relief of unburdening himself from the heavy chest, but his mind was far too burdened to care.

"You." The constable pointed at Jacob. "Take a seat at my desk, here."

Jacob complied, sitting at one of the two chairs in front of the desk.

"I'm going to have each of you ladies go into separate rooms over there, please." He pointed to the two doors.

Reluctantly, they did as they were told.

"And you." He pointed at Tadrick. "I'm sorry, but I'm going to have you wait in the jail until it's your turn to tell your story. There's no one in there right now, so you don't have to worry about that."

Tadrick opened the door to the jail area without a word, head held high, and closed the door behind himself. Jacob thanked the gods he didn't have to go in there. It may have broken him.

"Alright," the constable said to Jacob, "I'm going to start with you."

He rounded his desk and sat on his chair. The sword loomed menacingly over his head.

CHAPTER 29

Jacob's Story

"Like I said, Mr. Lowell wants someone to pin this on." The constable interlaced his fingers on the desk. "He doesn't much care for the truth, just so long as someone takes the blame. He's felt his grip on this island slipping for the last few years, and sees this as an opportunity to reestablish his position."

The constable looked into Jacob's eyes with a stare that made him shiver.

As he tried his best to hold the constable's eye contact, Jacob's mind raced. He imagined himself in a jail cell—alone, afraid, and depressed. How long would he have to stay there? Weeks, months, years? He was in the prime of his life. Things were really starting to look up for him. He hadn't exactly started from the bottom, but he had built a good life for himself in a very short time. He loved his life, now. The sea still called to him, but he had found a crew to belong to on dry land. His friends were everything to him. To be locked away from them for any amount of time would be unbearable.

His friends.

That was where this whole thing became agony. The thought of one of them sitting alone in a cell twisted his stomach into knots.

Cora was so young and full of potential. She wasn't much younger than Jacob, but her unabashed optimism made Jacob feel older in comparison. She was an absolute gift to the world—

vibrant, fun, kind, and compassionate. She would be devastated by isolation. And to be young and in love, or at the very least infatuated, with someone who it seemed had been made for her—someone who would treat her how she deserved to be treated. Jacob had known love like that once, and he had let it slip away. If the love between Cora and Yandro was thwarted, it would be a godsdamned tragedy.

Tadrick was more or less in the same boat. Young and bursting with creativity. He had more talent than Jacob could ever dream of, and he used it as a force of good. He had Darian, as well. Jacob had no one. No one to miss him at night if he was locked away.

Then there was Juniper, the strongest person he had ever met. She had endured a devastating loss and kept on with her head held high, with the kindness in her heart untarnished. She was a wonderful mother to two wonderful kids who had already lost their father. Juniper getting blamed for this was not an option.

"So?" The constable held his hands out to his sides.

Jacob cleared his throat. "It was me," he said, hanging his head.

"By yourself?" There was more than a hint of skepticism in the constable's voice.

"Yes."

"How did you get up on that rock tower?"

A shock coursed through Jacob's chest. He had forgotten the constable knew so much. He probably visited the site where the treasure was hidden. And with his talent for deductive reasoning, he would see through Jacob's lies easily.

Still, Jacob had started down this road, and he wasn't going to turn back.

"I had a rope."

"What did you secure it to?"

"I threw it up and over the rock formation, then secured it on the ground on the other side." Jacob shocked himself with his ability to come up with something so quickly.

"Clever." It was unclear whether or not the constable was being facetious.

"What did you find down inside the underground chamber?"

"There was some kind of magic down there. There were glowing words asking...me a question." He had barely stopped himself from saying *us*.

"What was the question?"

"It asked me what I would use the treasure for." Jacob wasn't sure why he lied.

"And how did you answer?"

"I said the first thing I would do would be to pay off Juniper's debt. Then I would..." He was going to talk about Shelu and Korga but figured he probably shouldn't make the constable aware of their existence if he wasn't already. "...I would buy a ship. I would pay a crew, and we would be a merchant ship or something like that."

"And the chamber could hear your answer?"

Jacob shrugged. "I don't know how magic works."

The constable seemed satisfied with this answer, nodding and pursing his lips to the side.

"Then what happened?"

"The treasure chest raised up out of the floor, magically."

"Okay." The constable scratched his temple with his fingertips. "That treasure chest is heavy as shit. How did you manage to get it all the way back here by yourself?"

"I used the rope." There was no harm in telling the truth, but Jacob had already started down the path of lying, and this just seemed easier to explain. "I made a makeshift pulley system. I learned about that kind of thing from the people who worked for my father."

"Who's your father?"

Jacob had come to this island with a made-up surname because he wanted to leave the past behind him and start anew. But the prospect of jail scared him out of his mind, and the ruse no longer mattered.

"My father owns the First Frontier Trading Company."

"*The* First Frontier Trading Company?" The constable asked, unbelieving. "One of the biggest companies in the League of Islands?"

"Yes."

"And your father owns it outright?"

"Yes. He is the owner and sole proprietor."

"And you left that to come here and buy a failing pub? Then you risk everything to find a treasure with riches that probably wouldn't even equal a quarter of your family's wealth?"

"Yes. But it's not that straightforward."

"Is there something wrong with you?"

"There must be." Jacob hung his head and stared at the floor.

"Alright. Anyway. So, you get the treasure out using a rope. But how did you get it back to the pub?"

"I had a cart. I borrowed it from Yandro, the young man who brings supplies to the pub. I mean, I took it without him knowing, then returned it when I was done. He had no idea it was ever gone."

"And you pulled that heavy treasure through sand and up hills, all the way to town by yourself?"

"Yeah. I'm stronger than I look. More determined than I look, too."

"That's impressive." Again, it was hard to tell if this was sarcasm or not.

"Hmm." Jacob continued to gaze at the floor.

"Then you dig a hole yourself and bury the treasure without one of your friends finding out?"

"It was very late when I got back. Cora and Tadrick were at their homes, and I assumed Juniper and the kids were asleep. I was as quiet as possible."

"And what was the plan from there? Were you going to tell them you had found the treasure? How would you have explained having so much money?"

"I hadn't thought that far ahead. Didn't think I'd ever find the treasure, to tell the truth."

"And are you?"

"Am I what?"

"Telling the truth." The constable's stare pierced Jacob's soul. He knew. He absolutely knew.

"Yes." Jacob wanted to say more, but it would only make his lies more obvious.

The constable sighed as he stood. "Alright, then. Please stay here while I talk to the others." He looked at the treasure chest. "I don't think I need to tell you this, but it would be really, really stupid of you to try and run away."

"I know." He did know, but he felt like the chances he would do it anyway were fifty-fifty.

CHAPTER 30

Juniper's Story

The constable marched straight to the door Juniper had gone through. He gave it a gentle knock before cracking it open and saying, "Hello?"

When he did, Jacob heard a strange echo, as if he was hearing the constable's voice from two places at once.

Juniper answered, and again there was an echo.

The constable entered the room and closed the door.

"I'm sorry about all this hassle, but this is serious business." The constable's voice was as clear as if he was still in the same room as Jacob. It sounded like it came from the wall behind the constable's desk. Jacob turned and examined the wall, finding four circular holes cut into it at ear level. The constable must have created some kind of system for him to eavesdrop on people in those rooms.

"I want to tell you straight away that I am not a monster." The constable's voice sounded from the hole on the far left, only slightly muffled. "If I find that it was you who is responsible for taking Mr. Lowell's treasure, I won't send you to jail. You're a single mother, and I simply won't take you away from those kids. Mr. Lowell will just have to deal with that. I will, however, confiscate the treasure, and I will have to shut down your business, too."

"I understand." There seemed to be relief in Juniper's voice—a soft note of hope.

"So, tell me what happened. How did the treasure find its way to the yard behind your building?"

"Well," Juniper said, "it seems to me that you have your solution, already."

"What do you mean?"

"If you offer me up to Mr. Lowell, but refuse to lock me away, I'll lose my restaurant and the treasure."

"Yes."

"Let's just say that, hypothetically, you pin it on Jacob instead. The treasure still gets confiscated, and I still don't have enough money to pay Mr. Lowell, so I still lose my restaurant."

"Okay."

"So, the end result is the same for me, only in the latter scenario, my friend goes to jail."

"But what if Mr. Lowell uses his influence to have me fired and throws you in jail?"

"You said that he'd just have to deal with it."

"Yes. I did. But there's always the possibility that I have misjudged my standing in this town and that he would have me fired in order to see you punished."

"I don't think you make much of a habit out of misjudging things."

"No. I don't. But it has happened before, and I'm sure it will happen again someday."

For the span of several bounding heartbeats, there was silence in Juniper's room.

"What are the chances you're wrong?" Juniper asked.

"Probably one in one hundred." His answer was surprisingly fast.

"And let's just say you were wrong and he did fire you... Maybe if I had a bit of a head start before you went and told him, I could get myself and the kids off island?"

The constable made a sound that was indiscernible without facial expression and body language.

"I want you to pin it on me," Juniper said.

"That is honorable of you," the constable replied. "Unwise, but honorable." He cleared his throat. "But the truth is, I don't need you to tell me what to do. I need you to tell me what happened."

More silence.

"Okay, the kids and I went to the beach to build sandcastles. Eventually, it turned into a search for little creatures amongst the rocks. You know, sea stars and that kind of thing. So, we lose track of time and distance a bit, and we end up over by this strange rock tower, not knowing we were on Mr. Lowell's land." She paused. "Do you have kids, constable?"

"No, ma'am."

"Well, if you did, you'd know that they can get into all kinds of trouble if you so much as look away for a moment."

"Okay."

"I turned back to see that my kids were climbing that rock tower, and were damn near at the top."

Another pause.

"You wouldn't give me that look if you knew the climbing abilities of faun children." Now Juniper cleared her throat. "I yelled at them to get down, but they were already at the top. So, I climbed up after them, and that's when we discovered that trap door. We were curious, so we opened it and went inside. It opens up into this big underground chamber with somewhat familiar faun magic seeming to run the whole place. It asks us why we want the treasure, and I give this disembodied voice my whole sob story, from my husband's death to the decline of business at our restaurant. Then this treasure chest pops out of the floor. The end."

"How were you able to get it out of the chamber and home?"

"I used magic to make it float behind us."

"You used your own magic for that?" He sounded incredulous.

"Yes. And you wouldn't ask me that if you knew the magical abilities of fauns. Would you like me to lift you off your seat right now as a demonstration?" Jacob was shocked at the tone she was taking with him. Maybe it was nervousness or a strange tactic he didn't understand. Whatever it was, he hoped it worked.

"No, ma'am." There was the slightest tinge of mirth in his words. "I won't need a demonstration."

"Okay, then."

"So why did you bury it in the back of the pub?"

"I had a moment of weakness. I figured if you or Mr. Lowell's henchmen tracked it down, they wouldn't be able to pin it on me."

"A moment of weakness." It wasn't a question. And if Jacob wasn't mistaken, there was a hint of reverence in his voice. "Alright, I suppose I'm done with your questioning. I'm trying to make this as quick as I can so you can get back to your young ones."

"I appreciate that, constable." Juniper's voice dripped with honey.

"Please stay here until I come back to get you."

CHAPTER 31

Cora's Story

When the constable came out from Juniper's room, Jacob had his head down on folded arms atop the desk, as if he hadn't just been on the edge of his seat listening to the hole in the wall.

"You doing alright?" the constable called.

Jacob lifted his head and gave the constable a sleepy nod.

After another gentle knock, the constable entered Cora's room.

"Hello, ma'am," he said, and the next hole over projected his words from the wall.

"Hi." Her tone was flat, as if she had already given up.

"I just want to get your honest account of what happened last night. I know you know I'm no dummy, so you can dispose of any ideas about telling me a tall tale. Not that I'm saying you would do such a thing."

"Okay."

"So, how did you and your friends find the treasure?"

"My friends had nothing to do with it."

Jacob's eyes opened wide.

"So, you found the treasure yourself, then?"

"Well...do you know Yandro?"

"Yes. The delivery man. Good kid."

"He and I are, kind of, together, now."

"Oh yeah? What does that have to do with any of this?"

"He and I were out on the beach...engaging in a Ringlight tryst." Her delivery was so awkward. "We went for a walk along the beach to the north and...we were making out and stuff. Do you know what making out means?"

"Yes. I am a living, breathing person, too, you know."

"Okay. Well, we were making out when he rolled onto a sharp sea shell that stabbed into his butt cheek."

"Hmm."

"So that took him out of the romantic mood. Plus, he had to go home because it was getting late and he had to get up to go to work early." Cora seemed to find new life in her story. Her tone went from completely flat to somewhat lively in the course of a few lines.

"Okay."

"I wasn't tired, though, so I stayed out on the beach. I like to sit out there and listen to the waves and look up at the Ring. I was doing that when I noticed this rock tower thing that I'd never seen before. So, I decided to go take a look at it."

"Mmm hmm." The constable obviously wasn't buying anything she was trying to sell.

"When I got to the tower, I jumped up on top of it and—"

"Jumped?"

"I used a little ciguapa magic to help boost me. Do you know much about ciguapa magic?"

"Very little."

"So up on top there was this trap door thing, so I got curious and opened it."

"What was inside?" The constable seemed to be doing nothing more than going through the motions, now. His voice was monotone.

"A ladder that led down into this giant underground chamber. There was this glowing writing on the wall in the human tongue asking a question. It said something like, "You have two choices: Give two-thirds of the money to people you don't know, or take everything for yourself."

"What did you choose?"

"I chose to give most of it away."

"Commendable," the constable said.

"To tell the truth, I thought it was a trick question. Although I probably would want to help people out with the money, anyway."

"Then what happened?"

"This treasure chest comes up from the floor."

"And how did you get the chest from the chamber to a hole in the ground behind the pub?"

"I used ciguapa magic to transport it there."

"Directly into the ground?"

"Uh...no. I transported it to a spot in front of the firewood, then buried it when I got back."

"Using what?"

"To bury it?"

"Yes."

"Ciguapa magic again. We can do pretty much anything with it."

"I see you've got five rune tattoos," the constable said.

"Yeah." Cora's voice was suddenly much more nervous.

"And you've got jumping, transportation, *and* digging spells among the five. Pretty convenient."

"Yeah. I guess you could say it was...or is."

"Hmm."

"For what it's worth, I'm sorry about all the trouble I've caused by finding that stupid treasure. If I could take it back I would. Not the part on the beach with Yandro, but the rest of it."

"But you're still willing to take all of the blame for it? To face Mr. Lowell alone?"

"I was the one who found the treasure, so why wouldn't I take the blame?"

"Indeed." A chair squeaked as the constable stood. Jacob quickly returned to his position with his head down on the desk. "Please stay in here until I come back to get you. It won't be long."

CHAPTER 32

Tadrick's Story

Jacob looked up as the constable exited Cora's room. The man had a befuddled expression on his face.

"One more to go," he said to Jacob with a sigh.

Jacob nodded.

The constable strode across the room, knocked on the jail area door, and slipped inside.

Jacob quickly learned that sound from the jail traveled through the wall just like in the two offices.

"Hello," the constable said, "I've already talked to all the others. I've been able to take all their stories and get a real understanding of what happened. So just give it to me straight and we can wrap this up."

"Sure." Tadrick's voice sounded defeated, too.

"So, how did you find out about the treasure?"

"From the Fenton poem. When Mr. Davies sold the pub to Mr. Bright, he included his original copy of the poem. Jacob shared it with us and we tried to figure it out together."

"But what about the last clue, the one that led you to the actual treasure? Tell me about that."

"It directed us to the farthest point on the northwest of the island."

"You keep saying *us* and *we*. Who went with you to the northwest tip of the island?"

"Nobody."

"Really?"

"Yeah. We had tracked down the other clues together, but when it came to this one, a greedy urge came over me, so I went to try and find the treasure myself."

There was a silent pause.

"I took a small sailboat I had found unattended at the docks and sailed to the part of the island the clue led to."

"You're a sailor, then?"

"I know enough to get myself in trouble." Tadrick's laugh was extremely nervous. "My dad can sail, and he says that a lot. But really, I can get by."

"So?"

"So, I land out near the point and find this tall rock formation."

"So, you found some clever, improbable way to get up there. Then you found a trapdoor that took you down into an underground chamber."

"Yes."

"So, what's your version of what the faun magic asked of you down there?"

"It asked me if I was sure I wanted to take the treasure by myself."

"How did you answer?"

"I broke down right there in the chamber. I realized I didn't want to hoard it all to myself. I told the magic wall that I had changed my mind. And apparently, that was the right answer, because the treasure chest rose up out of the floor as soon as I was done talking."

"That treasure chest was heavy. How did you get it back by yourself?" The constable asked questions as if crossing them off a checklist he found extremely boring.

"It was imbued with faun magic, too. Made it really easy to haul it up the ladders. I tossed it down from the rock formation and carried it to the boat, which was anchored in waist-deep water."

"Hmm."

There was a stretch of silence. The only sounds were of someone tapping on a table.

"You live with someone, correct?" the constable asked.

"Yes.... His name is Darian."

"Did he know what you were out doing? Does he know anything about the treasure?"

"No to both questions. He thought I was working late at the pub. Been doing a lot of that lately."

"I figured you might answer that way."

More silence.

"So, you're going to stick with the answer that faun magic helped you single-handedly carry that treasure chest up two ladders, into a boat, and from the beach to the pub?"

"Well, actually, I used the creek behind the pub as an easier way to get the treasure close. I walked alongside it while pulling the boat upstream."

"Mmm hmm. But you carried the chest up the ladders by yourself, correct?"

"Yes."

"Hmm."

CHAPTER 33

The Constable's Decision

The constable came out from the jail area with Tadrick following close behind. He marched across the room and opened the two doors on the other side, beckoning Juniper and Cora to come out into his main office.

When everyone had gathered around, he spoke.

"You may be the worst liars I've ever had the pleasure of interrogating," he said, his face and voice impassive. "But you surprised me, which isn't easy to do.

"Usually, when this kind of thing happens, the people whom I question all try to point the finger at someone else. But you lot...each of you tried to take the blame yourself, even though it was obvious you were full of shit." He chuckled. "It was the reverse of what I expected. So... well done in that regard."

He stopped and looked to the ceiling, stroking his mustache with thumb and forefinger.

"This whole thing, although ridiculous, was refreshing in a way. It did my heart good to see people from all stripes of life banding together as you did. Each of you put the well-being of others ahead of yourselves. I was starting to worry that kind of sentiment was a thing of the past. I don't want to sound too grandiose about this whole thing, but you kind of restored my faith in humanity. Er...I should say my faith in.... What's the collective name for people of all different races?"

"People, sir," Tadrick offered.

"Yeah. I suppose you're right. You restored my faith in people. Not their overall intelligence, because those stories were laughable at best. But in our potential for kindness and self-sacrifice, I suppose."

The constable continued to look up, continued rubbing his mustache.

No one said a word. Jacob held his breath until he couldn't any longer. He took a breath and ground his teeth instead.

"I have decided to prosecute no one." The constable dropped his gaze to meet the group's eye level.

The relief in the room was palpable. Everyone un-tensed at once, letting out loud rushes of air.

"I will have to confiscate the treasure, but you're all free to go. Mr. Lowell will have to live with that. I do have *some* power on this island, as trivial as it may be. I intend to flex that this morning. He won't be happy, but I'm probably too difficult to replace, so he'll have to bend to my will this time."

"Thank you!" Jacob said, way louder than he planned, with knees wobbling so hard he thought he might tip over.

The others echoed his appreciation.

"I thank *you*," the constable replied. "One, for giving me a good laugh with those stories. And two, for the whole faith in people thing. I've been spending way too much time with the rich and powerful, who are, in my experience, absolute pricks. I almost forgot what it was like to be around people like you."

"I don't suppose you could throw us a few gold coins so we could pay off Juniper's debt, could ya?" Jacob had to try.

"No. That's a bit too far. I'm not going to personally hunt you down for what you already might have taken and spent, but I'm not about to be party to taking from the treasure myself. I've got to maintain some sense of self-preservation, here."

"Worth a shot," Jacob said.

"I wish I could help you." In this, the constable seemed genuine. He turned to Juniper. "By the way, you've got two days to pay Mr. Lowell or I will have to terminate your lease. I'm sorry."

CHAPTER 34

Chopping Firewood

By the time they got back to the pub, the sun was coming up. Jacob was mentally and physically exhausted but wasn't in the mood to go to bed.

The range of emotions was wide. On one hand, the threat of one of them being thrown in jail for an unknown stretch of time had been miraculously thwarted at the last second. On the other, Juniper's business and home were going to be taken away. She insisted she and the kids would be fine. They would find another place to live and she could get a job on the fish lines. It was far from ideal, but they would survive.

"So, each of us tried to take the blame," Juniper said, trying to shift the focus away from herself.

"I can't believe you tried to take the blame for us." Cora rubbed the side of her face. "You have so much more to lose than we do."

"To tell the truth, the constable told me I wouldn't go to jail. He said if I was found guilty, he would take away my business, but he wouldn't take me away from my kids. So, I figured I should be the one who took the fall. If it had been any of you, there would have had to be jail time. I couldn't bear that idea." She paused, looking at the ground. "What warms my heart is that you all did the same thing, even though you *would* have gone to jail."

"Not knowing about the deal the constable made with you, I didn't want you to be taken from your kids," Cora said. "Tadrick has Darian, and Jacob has his fresh start at the pub. It was the choice that made the most sense. I'm young. I could do time and still have a life afterward. I hoped, anyway."

"But you have Yandro," Jacob said. "That's one of the reasons I couldn't let you take the blame."

"I don't know if I *have* Yandro, exactly."

"But the potential for something wonderful is there. I don't have anyone like that at the moment."

"You will," Tadrick said. "You're a good man. It's only a matter of time before someone sees that and wants to be with you in that way." Tadrick made eye contact with Jacob. "I couldn't allow you to take the fall. I figured you would try, but I couldn't let that happen. You've given me so much."

"I haven't given you anything," Jacob said.

"You gave me room to be myself. You gave me something outside of home that I could take a little pride in."

"I appreciate the credit. But if I'm telling the truth, making you and Cora equal partners was a business decision. I figured if you had a stake in the pub's success, you'd step up and make it work. I *was* able to learn a few things from my family."

"Okay, boss." Tadrick flashed him a knowing and somewhat patronizing smile.

Jacob looked down and kicked an imaginary rock.

"I'm going to go run the numbers," Jacob said. "Maybe we missed something. Maybe we have enough money to save Juniper's house and business after all. It's worth a look."

"Good idea." Cora rubbed her arms. "I'll make a fire. It's a little chilly this morning."

Jacob sauntered to his office and sat down at the desk. He took the money they'd saved from the safe and began counting. Both Cora and Tadrick had taken very little for themselves since becoming partners. They were remarkably selfless. The goal for all of them had been to save enough to pay off Mr. Lowell.

When the last copper was counted, the grand total came to three gold, one silver, and ninety-seven coppers. They were short by at least a gold and a half.

"Shit." Jacob sat with his head in his hands, staring at the stacks of coins. They had come so far but fell woefully short of their goal.

He wondered if they had focused on the treasure too much. How much could they have earned if they'd poured all their energy into the pub? The sting of having overlooked that option was difficult to take. The treasure had been so damned appealing, though. It had almost seemed like destiny that they would find it and save Juniper's livelihood. The adventure of it all may have clouded his judgment. When they started to run afoul of the law, he should have reassessed the situation. Hindsight brought out a lot of *what-ifs,* but it was too late for any of those.

Dejected, he sat and did nothing for a while. Cora had started a fire; the scent and warmth didn't take long to reach Jacob's room. Sighing, he stood and rejoined the others.

"We're a gold and a half short." He couldn't look at Juniper as he spoke.

"Wow," Juniper said. "I can't believe we, or you, made three gold so quickly."

"It had *a lot* to do with you," Jacob said.

"I'm sorry," Cora added.

Tadrick put an arm around Juniper's shoulders.

"I'll be fine." Juniper did her best to sound confident, but couldn't hide her fear completely.

Jacob didn't know what to say. They all stood and watched the fire.

"We're going to need more firewood," Cora finally said. "I'll go split some."

"Can I do it?" Jacob asked, raising his hand.

"Sure." Cora showed a half-smile.

"Thank you."

Jacob hurried out back. He found the axe behind the firewood cover. He would have liked to forget about the treasure, but he had to navigate around the hole the constable had left in the ground in front of the firewood to get logs to split.

Once he had retrieved several logs from the cover, Jacob set one of them up on the stump where Mr. Davies used to cut wood.

He raised the axe overhead and brought it down in one smooth motion, splitting the log in two.

Jacob had always enjoyed chopping wood. There was a certain satisfaction every time his axe split a log. It was a sense of accomplishment, however small. It was doing something that needed to be done. Watching the blade bite into the center of the wood, seeing it split perfectly in two, knowing that his actions manifested change in the world, however small. When he kept his head down and focused on the work, it was satisfying.

There had been little cause for satisfaction lately.

Actually, when he thought about it, there had been immense satisfaction with the pub and the thrill of the treasure hunt, but all that had been for nothing. Juniper was still going to lose her home and business. Aspen and Ceda would have to stay with someone else while Juniper worked grueling hours processing fish. All their satisfying work hadn't changed a thing.

A parrot squawked at him from up above while he swung the axe, causing him to strike the side of the log he was trying to chop and send it tumbling off the stump.

"What?" Jacob said to the parrot, only partially aware he was speaking out loud. "You're gonna pile on, too?

The parrot squawked again.

"I'm almost done. Then I'll stop bothering you."

As he picked up the log to place it back on the stump, Jacob pondered what they would do next. Juniper hadn't lost her place quite yet. Things weren't looking good, but he wasn't about to quit.

He kept chopping, wracking his brain for any kind of solution, but finding none.

Mrs. Covington and Arthur waddled out from their door. Arthur immediately lay down in the dirt, while Mrs. Covington went to have a look at the pond. Jacob examined her from afar, wondering how he hadn't noticed her protruding belly before.

The parrot squawked.

With a half smile, Jacob split the last of the firewood and wiped his brow.

"See," he told the parrot. "All done."

The parrot gave a final squawk before flying away.

Mrs. Covington munched on grass while Jacob gathered the wood in his arms.

He was about to bring it inside when Juniper, Cora, and Tadrick burst outside through the back door.

"We have an idea!" Cora shouted, her face positively glowing with renewed hope.

CHAPTER 35

Save the Nacias

"I'm done," Tadrick called, lifting the sign he'd painted so everyone could see.

It read:

NACIAS ARE IN DANGER OF DISAPPEARING!!!

COME HELP SAVE THE BUSINESS THAT BROUGHT YOU THIS WONDERFUL CREATION!

A FUNDRAISER TO <u>SAVE THE NACIAS</u>!!!

TONIGHT

STARTING AT 6!!!

<u>Nacias Available by Donation</u>

. . .

"Perfect." Cora gave him an overhead hand slap.

The *Save the Nacias* fundraiser had come together very quickly out of necessity. Ever since they had come up with the idea, Juniper had been mass-producing corn chips as fast as she could. Cora had volunteered to go find Yandro and make an emergency cheese, chicken, and vegetable order. He had come through for them, delivering everything they needed in less than two hours. The crew—including Yandro, who had volunteered to stay and help— gathered in Juniper's kitchen and helped her prepare seasoned chicken and chop the vegetables.

Tadrick drew up flyers, and Cora posted them all around town. Tadrick also asked Darian to gather Bilge Rat for a last-minute performance. They agreed immediately, even offering to play for free.

The last touches were the sign and the donation jars, which were two large clay pots Tadrick had found at the market and decorated with lifelike paintings of nacias.

With an hour left to go before the official start time, everyone scrambled to get ready. Chairs, tables, and dishes were moved over from Juniper's restaurant to accommodate the (hopefully) over-capacity crowds.

When Darian and the other members of Bilge Rat showed up, Darian walked directly up to Tadrick, in front of everyone there, and embraced him. Jacob was in a position where he could see Tadrick's eyes go wide as he tentatively embraced back. Tadrick looked to Jacob and raised his eyebrows in surprise. Jacob, not knowing what else to do, put a hand up and mimed doing an overhead hand slap. Tadrick smiled and closed his eyes.

After the unexpected greeting, the band set up to play outside under the cover.

Everything in the pub was arranged, then rearranged to allow for the most people possible to be comfortable.

Everything was ready. All they had to do was wait and hope.

∼

The clock struck six and no one had shown up yet. A nervous tension arose as the group of friends waited for the rush of people they had prepared for. Bilge Rat played instrumental versions of their songs to empty chairs.

It was a relief for most when the first customers came through the front door, but not for Jacob. The first two people in were the shady-looking men with the crossbow case.

They were cordial enough—smiling and dropping small handfuls of coppers into one of the clay jars as they took their nacias. But then they waved Jacob over to their usual table in the corner. Reluctantly, Jacob made his way to them, wary of their every movement.

One of the men opened the crossbow-sized case on the table.

"Hello, sir," the man said. "My name is Rick, and this is Neal. We've been meaning to get you alone for a few minutes, but that task has proved to be pretty difficult."

"I'm Jacob." Trying to be nonchalant, he glanced at the opened case, seeing it was full of little green vials. He didn't know what to make of that, but it was definitely better than a crossbow.

"Do you have any problems?" Neal asked.

"Like itchy skin, sore back, toothache, depression, or problems in the bedroom?" Rick added.

"Uh..." Jacob did a quick self-assessment, wondering what they were getting at. "I'm tired a lot." He shrugged.

"Perfect," said both men at once.

"Have you ever heard of the healing powers of dragon oil?" Rick asked.

"No."

"Well, that's a little shocking. The stuff is all the rage on Paradise Island, and spreading through the islands like a brush fire."

"Oh."

"You see, it's so popular because it's a miracle cure-all for whatever ails you." Neal took a green vial from the case and handed it to Jacob. "There is nothing—"

"Where do you get it from?" Jacob asked. "There aren't any dragons around."

"True." Rick lifted a finger in the air. "But there were dragons long ago. You see, those dragons have been found in the ground and their oil was extracted through a painstaking process."

"And people believe that?" Jacob said.

"Yes. Why wouldn't they?"

"And they believe it can cure anything?"

"Yes. Because it does."

"No thanks," Jacob said to the men. "Not right now. Thank you for your donation, though! I hope you enjoy your nacias."

"No?" Neal was incredulous. "You're walking away from a miracle?"

Jacob smiled at them and walked away. When he first arrived in New Dawn, he'd been so anxious about those two, automatically assuming ill intent. Then, the entire time he'd been here, he was too timid and uncertain to simply ask anyone about them. He could have avoided a lot of stress when there wasn't anything to worry about.

Jacob shook his head, smile growing wider. Two months ago, he would have let those guys take him for some serious coin. He would have been unable to say no. But he felt a newfound resolve thriving within him. He could be kind, and also not let anyone take advantage of him. His kindness was not weakness.

"What are you smiling about?" Cora asked when he came back.

"Nothing much." Jacob would have elaborated, but a small group of people came in before he had the chance.

That group was followed by another, and before long, there was a steady stream pouring in single file. The dull thuds of coins on clay were replaced by the metallic tinging of coins on coins. Nacias were being served as fast as they could be made.

Eventually, people started singing with the band, and the place had a lovely, lively atmosphere.

Shelu and Korga ducked in through the front door, eliciting nervous whispers among the patrons in line.

Jacob's heart went out to the orcs. It must be dispiriting to draw that kind of reaction wherever they went.

Cora must have felt the same way. She hurried around the serving table, squeezed through the line, and made a show of greeting them with handshakes and smiles. Her actions seemed to ease the tension in the room. The people in line no longer kept constant watchful eyes on the orcs as they got their nacias. Just like Jacob, all they needed was a small interaction; an indication that orcs weren't the monsters they'd heard about in childhood stories. It was a shame it had to be that way, but at least things seemed to be moving in the right direction.

When it was their turn, Shelu and Korga each donated a couple of coppers into the jars.

"You didn't have to do that," Jacob said. "You're saving up to go home. We could have given you plates for free."

"This is more...urgent," Shelu said. "Juniper gave us work when not many others would. She does not deserve to have her place close."

"Thank you." Juniper came around the serving table and gave them both big hugs.

Jacob was impressed with their selflessness. Being in their situation, and elongating it by giving money away, couldn't have been easy, but it was the right thing to do, so they did it.

"Jacob," Juniper said after the orcs had gone through, "could you run over and heat up the next batch, please?"

"Sure." Jacob welcomed a small break from smiling and interacting with customers.

Over at Juniper's restaurant, a tray was filled with plates of already-made nacias. Jacob slid the tray into the oven and closed the door.

Laughter rang out from the seating area, so Jacob peeked out from the kitchen. Aspen and Ceda were sitting at a far table folding paper. They hadn't even noticed Jacob was there. Their focus on their work was intense, but still interspersed with giggles. Their laughter was so great to hear.

"Oh!" Jacob ran to the oven and opened the door. Luckily, the nacias were only burned in a few tiny places.

When he came back and set the tray on the serving table, a shock of dread shot through his chest as the constable entered the pub.

"Shit," Jacob said aloud while handing a plate of freshly-warmed nacias to a random customer. "I mean, I'm sorry. Please enjoy. And thank you so much for your donation." The customer walked away confused.

Jacob's mind began to throw out all kinds of questions. Why was the constable here? Did he change his mind about prosecution? Did Mr. Lowell force his hand in the matter? If so, who was he coming for?

The constable held a hand out over one of the ceramic jars and let several coins fall in. At least one had a silvery flash.

"One order of nacias." He flashed a warm smile. "And a beer, please."

Jacob could have melted into a puddle on the floor. He let out an audible sigh and handed a plate to the constable.

"Thank you." Jacob hoped his eyes conveyed at least a part of the gratitude he felt.

"Again, thank *you*." The constable looked each of them in the eyes. "All of you."

He took his plate and his beer outside and ate at one of the tables while watching the band.

"Well that was terrifying," Cora said when he was gone.

"I almost threw a plate of nacias at him," Tadrick added with a smile from his place at the beer tap.

"I think he has a good heart," Juniper said.

"But he's still gonna take away your home if this," Tadrick spread his palms, indicating the entire fundraiser, "doesn't work."

"I think it's working." Cora pointed around the pub.

"We'll see." Juniper gave them a half-smile. "It's a lot of money we need to raise."

Just then, a tall, beautiful, and somewhat familiar ciguapa woman walked in. Jacob tried to remember where he knew her from.

"Hello, Mrs. Juno," Cora said.

It was the woman from whom they had stolen Arthur.

"Hello, Cora," she said with a genuine smile. "Where's the capybara you all heisted from me?" Her smile became decidedly playful.

"Arthur is out back in the pond with Mrs. Covington. Would you like me to take you back there?"

The woman hesitated. "Sure. Why not?" She donated a few coins, took some nacias, and followed Cora through the back door.

Jacob eventually made another trip to warm up nacias. They got a rhythm going, getting perfectly-melted nacias to patrons as they came through.

About ten customers later, Cyrus entered the pub. Jacob could hear him before he saw him. His voice could be heard above the band and the din of the gathering crowd as he regaled Jenny with some kind of seafaring tale.

"...then the Kraken's one staring, soulless eye fixed on me and..." Cyrus looked up at Jacob. "Hello, young man!" he bellowed. "We'll take two orders of this wonderful creation." He dropped a handful—which was a considerable amount when factoring in the size of the man's hands—of coppers into the jar.

Jacob handed them each a plate. "Thank you so much!" He tried to match Cyrus' intensity.

"I'm just wonderin'," Cyrus said, "I don't want to hold up the line, or make anything about me, but have you had a chance to ponder our little conversation on my ship?"

"I have," Jacob answered. "Quite a bit, actually."

"Well, good. Like I said before, it's plain to see you've come a long way since then."

"I have to agree with you."

Cyrus and Jenny rounded the table to allow the people behind him to be served.

"I'm happy to hear that." Cyrus's expression turned more serious. "I have a confession of sorts, but I'll make it quick. It's something I think you should hear since you've got a natural leadership ability."

Jacob doubted his leadership ability but was extremely interested in what Cyrus had to say.

"When I started out as the captain of a ship, I was a right bastard. I ruled my crew through fear and intimidation. It was the way I was brought up, and I thought it the only way for a time." He looked to the line as if trying to assess if Jacob's absence was slowing it down.

"They'll be fine without me for a while," Jacob said.

"Alright. So, the thing was, I slowly began to realize that the way I carried on was detrimental to our whole operation. My crew did the bare minimum to avoid my ire, and nothing else. There was no trust, no camaraderie. We all felt like we had to watch our backs at all times. And all of that was on me. I was the captain, the leader. It was my job to foster the culture I wanted on my ship. So, one day, I tried something different. I tried to mix in a little kindness. Just a bit at first, but eventually, I allowed it to completely replace fear. And the difference was night and day. It was only

226

then that we became a genuine crew. I don't want to go on for too long but suffice to say, absolutely everything was better from then on."

"It's hard to imagine you as a bastard," Jacob said.

"Oh, I was. Believe me. And it's a good thing I was cured from it because Jenny wouldn't put up with one second of that bullshit."

"No, I wouldn't." Jenny's voice was raspy and melodic. Jacob wasn't positive, but he thought that may have been the first time he'd heard Jenny speak.

"Well, our nacias are in danger of getting cold, and I've rambled on enough. Just wanted to drop that little story on ya since, in my mind, you're destined to be a great leader someday. Not that there was any chance you'd be a right bastard like I was."

"Thank you, Cyrus," Jacob said. "I really hope we see each other again."

"Aye. Me, too. I'll be setting sail tomorrow, but rest assured I'll be back. Can't bear being away from Jenny for too long, ya know."

The two men shook hands. Jacob matched his firm grip, looking him directly in the eyes. Jenny and Jacob said goodbye to each other, and the couple strolled over to the band.

Jacob returned to the serving table to find Yandro giving out nacias alone.

"Sorry about that!" Jacob said. "Where'd everyone go?"

"Juniper ran to her kitchen to warm up some more nacias in her oven. Cora is still out back with her last…suitor's mom, and Tadrick's stuck on the beer tap."

Juniper came in through the back door carrying a giant tray of freshly-warmed nacias. Cora, who had held the door for her, followed Juniper into the pub.

Juniper set the tray on the table, and Cora stepped right up to Yandro and kissed him on the lips.

Jacob's mouth hung open; his eyes wide. He turned away to avoid staring as Yandro flashed Cora the biggest smile he'd ever seen on anyone.

Juniper tugged on Jacob's sleeve, turning him toward the line of customers, which was slower, but still present.

It was then that Mr. Lowell's ciguapa henchman, Mali, entered the pub with his hood up over his head. Jacob tensed, searching the hench-man's face for any signs of ill will.

As Mali approached the table, he removed his hood. Both Cora and Yandro had noticed his presence and turned to face him, hand in hand. Yandro widened his stance, almost imperceptibly.

For a moment, no one spoke. Mali simply stared into Cora's eyes.

"You were a formidable opponent," he finally said, his voice low and unnerving. "The illusion you used was quite clever. It threw me off your trail just long enough for you to get the treasure. I tracked down its loca-tion not long after you left." He cleared his throat. "If I'm ever pitted against you again, I will win. But you and your friends bested me this time."

He gave them a solemn nod, then cleared his throat again.

"I would have made the journey over here to tell you this anyway, but I have other business, as well. Mr. Lowell has sent me to shut this whole thing down." He spread his arms, indicating the entire operation, a hint of mild regret in his expression. "You have not filed the required permits for a fundraiser of this sort through the proper channels. All events with more than fifty people in attendance must be pre-approved by the New Dawn City Council, of which Mr. Lowell is the commissioner."

"Shut it down?" Jacob said. "This," he indicated the entire pub, "is business as usual. And the constable literally just came by and participated."

"I'm afraid the constable isn't the final authority in this town."

The constable, who had been enjoying the band, rushed over to the serving table. "What's going on here?"

"I have been sent by the New Dawn City Council to shut this fundraiser down, as they have not filed the proper paperwork," Mali said.

The constable paused, twirling one end of his mustache. "You're absolutely right," he replied. "If they didn't do it the correct way, I'll have to shut this whole thing down right now. Rules are rules."

Jacob audibly gasped. He thought the constable had changed and would stand up to Mr. Lowell and his men. Was it possible Jacob had misjudged him?

"All I need is the signed cease and desist," the constable continued. "You have that with you, right?"

"No. But..." For the first time since Jacob had met him, Mali seemed unsure of himself.

"That's no problem," the constable said. "Per City Ordinance 137, all you'll have to do is bring the proper paperwork, signed by at least two members of the city council, and I'll be able to legally enforce it."

"I..." Mali stuttered. "I'll have to confer with Mr. Lowell." He spun on his heels and headed for the door.

"Hold on!" Cora called, drawing the attention of everyone nearby.

Mali turned back around.

"You're saying you were sent by Mr. Lowell to shut down what we're doing here when all we're doing here is trying to raise enough money to save a restaurant in this town?" She was looking around the pub and annunciating loudly, clearly playing to the crowd.

Mali nodded.

The confrontation had drawn a lot of attention. Even the band had stopped playing.

"Why would Mr. Lowell want Juniper's restaurant to fail?" Cora demanded. "Is it possibly because, I don't know, he values money and influence over the best interest of this town?"

The enrapt crowd was mostly quiet, but there were some grumbles and nods throughout.

"You know, when I was a little girl, I always thought that someday I would be married on the hill under the Ceiba tree like my parents were. Back then, Mrs. Fenton was happy to host their wedding. She even attended it and brought them a wedding gift. But Mr. Lowell is no Mrs. Fenton." This statement drew a lot more nods. "She did her best to respect everyone on this island. I believe she truly cared about all of us. But it's clear to me that your boss only cares about himself."

Mali started to turn away, but Cora continued.

"We're just trying to be contributing members of this community." Now she pointed around at all in attendance. "And look! They have come together in a wonderful show of support. They have gathered here to help pick up someone who has fallen on difficult times."

Without a word, Mali turned away.

"Aren't you going to get some nacias?" Cora asked.

He continued outside without looking back.

Without missing a beat, Cora looked to the band and said, "Let's get this going again."

They smiled and started back more or less where they had left off.

The nacias line continued on.

"I would like to give you a hug," the first person in line said to Cora.

"Well, alright." Cora rounded the table and embraced the human woman. She looked at the rest of the line. "Don't expect that everyone gets hugs. This isn't that kind of fundraiser."

The people in line laughed and the tension, it seemed, was dispelled.

Later, when the line of customers was much sparser, Juniper approached Cora and Yandro, who were still hard at work. "I think it's slowing down," she said. "You two go ahead and have some fun. Thank you for all your help today. I appreciate it more than I could ever say."

"You're welcome." Cora gave Juniper a long hug, then she and Yandro practically floated away, hand-in-hand.

Aspen and Ceda skipped into the pub as Cora and Yandro left. They both held a hand behind their backs.

"What are you hiding?" Juniper asked them with a motherly tone.

"Something for Jacob," Ceda said.

"Oh yeah?" Jacob was intrigued to see what they had made.

Slowly, and with a wonderful level of showmanship, the girls brought their hands out from behind their backs.

"We made them for you." Aspen held a paper bird out to Jacob.

"I made a tiger." Ceda held up her creation, too.

Jacob grinned and took both paper animals, studying them closely. They were basic but fantastic. He wasn't sure if he could recreate them if he tried. The designs were original and so damned creative. Aspen's bird had long individual feathers on its wings, and Ceda's tiger had a wonderful spiraling tail. Jacob was thoroughly impressed.

"These are amazing," he said to them. "I can't believe how good you two are at this!"

The kids' faces reddened as they thanked him.

"Thank you so much," Jacob continued. "I'm going to find a place to display these in here."

"You're welcome!" the girls said together before rushing off to find the capybaras.

Jacob continued to enthuse over the paper creations, still unable to believe the kids had come so far so fast.

"They really took a liking to you," Juniper said.

"I took a liking to them, too. They're great kids."

Juniper nodded knowingly.

"You know, you could take a break, too," Juniper said. "Go sing, or have a beer. You earned it. I think I can handle it from here."

There really weren't many customers to speak of anymore. Jacob peered into the clay jars, hoping for good news. They were both about half full. Most of the coins were copper, but there was an encouraging amount of silver sparkling throughout.

"You know what?" he said. "I think I might just do that."

"Which one?"

"The beer first. Maybe two. And then I'm going to sing."

"Sounds like a great plan." Juniper squeezed his shoulder. "But before you do that, I wanted to thank you, too. I really couldn't have asked for a better neighbor."

The beginnings of tears formed in Jacob's eyes. "I couldn't have either."

They embraced, but only for a moment.

"Alright, go get your drink." Juniper shooed him away in a very motherly way. "I'm looking forward to hearing you sing." She flashed him a playful smile.

Jacob quite possibly had the time of his life singing with Bilge Rat. He let all of his inhibitions, his self-doubt, and his fear go. He sang his heart out, working the crowd like a seasoned professional. His voice was a bit off-key, but he made up for it with a flair he didn't know he possessed. Many times throughout the song, he and a woman in the crowd met eyes. She had wonderful dark eyes and long black hair with a blue flower attached at her temple. Her beautiful smile gave him a big enough confidence boost to really go for it.

When the song was over, the crowd cheered, and Jacob walked right up to the woman and asked for her name.

An Offer

When the last customer left, the crew locked up, and everyone started in on the monumental task of cleaning.

"If you all don't mind, I'm going to go count the money," Jacob said.

"Please do," Juniper replied.

Jacob took the ceramic jars back to his office bedroom. He pulled a sheet of parchment and a pen from his desk and began counting. The coins were overwhelmingly copper, but there were several silver coins mixed in, as well.

Sweat dotted Jacob's brow as he counted. A feeling of dread buzzed uncomfortably in his stomach. What if it didn't add up to enough? Juniper would lose her home and business in a matter of hours.

Eventually, Jacob got lost in his task, collecting coppers in stacks of ten.

Cora poked her head into the room. "Are you done, yet?"

"Getting close." Jacob kept stacking without looking up.

"Is it looking good?"

"Just let him count," Tadrick called from across the pub.

"Fine. Sorry." Cora's head disappeared.

As he neared the end of the pile, he knew it was going to be close. They needed seven more stacks of ten to get to the magic number they were shooting for.

His hands got progressively sweatier as he stacked the next three. He noticed how dry his mouth was as he made the fourth stack. It was going to be *very* close.

A loud knock sounded from the front door.

Jacob paused, tilting his head to listen. The door creaked open and a cacophony of elevated voices filled the main pub area. He knocked over several stacks of coins as he pushed up from his desk.

"Let's all keep calm," the constable said as Jacob burst from the back room. "He's only here to make you an offer."

Mr. Lowell and his two henchmen stood just inside the door. The constable stood between them and Jacob's friends, arms outstretched to either side, trying to keep the peace.

"We're not interested in any offers," Cora said, spittle flying from her mouth.

"My offer isn't for you." Mr. Lowell showed an aggravating level of calm. "It's for Jacob."

Jacob's heart pounded, his chest tingling.

"I would like to buy this pub from you," Mr. Lowell said. "I'm prepared to give you twenty gold right here and now."

The oversized human henchman tossed a bulging coin purse onto the nearest table, creating a jingly thud that echoed through the quiet pub.

"No." It wasn't even a question in Jacob's mind.

"No? From what I understand, that's twice what you paid for this place."

Jacob said nothing.

"Alright." Mr. Lowell opened his own coin purse. "Thirty gold. Although paying that much goes against my better judgment."

"No." Jacob didn't care if he offered the entire Fenton Treasure. He would not be bullied or bought. Money was not everything.

"You could pay your friend's debt, though." Mr. Lowell said the word *friend* as if it pained him.

Jacob considered Mr. Lowell's words. It was true that he could save Juniper's restaurant if he accepted the offer. And he wasn't sure if they'd made enough in the fundraiser, yet. Would rejecting the offer mean putting himself first and hiding behind high-minded concepts about money? Jacob had a wealthy family to fall back on. Juniper had the fish lines.

Juniper must have sensed his hesitation. She stepped forward and said, "Not this way, Jacob."

Steeling himself, Jacob turned to Mr. Lowell. "The answer is still *no*."

Mr. Lowell narrowed his eyes and yanked closed the drawstrings of his coin purse. He turned to the constable. "I need to collect the final payment on the faun restaurant right now, or you will have to shut it down."

Juniper's face went pale. She seemed wobbly on her feet, so Jacob pulled out a chair for her. With a sleepy nod, she sat down.

Without a word, the constable looked down and away from Mr. Lowell.

Jacob's eyebrows pinched. This was not the reaction he expected, or hoped for, from the constable. He had never seen the man break eye contact before, let alone be rendered speechless.

For several breaths, the constable stared at a spot on the floor. All eyes were on him as he stood motionless.

"I need the money owed to me," Mr. Lowell said, "or the restaurant must be shut down. This is not negotiable."

The constable faced Mr. Lowell, standing up to his full height. "She has until tomorrow to make the final payment."

"I don't think you understand. I'm saying I need it now."

"I understand perfectly well what you're saying. The fact remains, the due date is tomorrow."

Jacob and Cora shared a look, both of them wide-eyed.

"But you must not fully grasp the influence I have on this island." Mr. Lowell spoke as if admonishing a child. "If you did, I daresay you wouldn't have resisted me when I told you I wanted one of these people to be punished for taking the treasure from my land, and you wouldn't be resisting me now."

"I grasp that, as well," the constable said, straight-faced. "And this seems as good a time as any to tell you that I've written to the Governor on behalf of my office. I've explained to her both the alarming insufficiency of having one constable in this town and the corruption that has seeped onto this island since, frankly, your arrival. She has sent people from the capitol to investigate. They should be arriving any day now."

Mr. Lowell's face turned a deep red. "You've crossed the wrong man." He glared at the constable. After a few exaggerated breaths, his glare shifted to Juniper. "And you...the full amount of your debt is due tomorrow morning. If you're a half-copper short, I will take the building and turn it into a...foul-smelling tannery. They use dog shit in the tanning process, you know. Not the ideal neighbor for an open-air pub." He smirked at the idea, then turned and stormed off, his henchman following close behind.

CHAPTER 37

Mrs. Covington

The scene as soon as Mr. Lowell fled was one of celebration and appreciation for what the constable had done. Jacob was extremely thankful, but he couldn't keep his attention on anything other than counting coins.

"Excuse me," he said after shaking the constable's hand, "I've got to find out if we earned enough at the fundraiser."

"Of course," the constable replied. "Get to counting."

Jacob hurried back to his office and started stacking coins again. After restacking the first four, his eyes flicked back and forth from the fifth stack to the pile of remaining coins. He didn't think it was looking good, but kept at it, trying to keep hope alive.

As he made the sixth stack, optimism started to push its way in.

By the time he put the last coin on top of the seventh stack, his heart raced as if he'd just sprinted from Shelu and Korga's cave.

"We did it!" he shouted. "With only four coppers to spare!"

The others rushed into his office and began making all kinds of strange celebratory noises while jumping up and down. Tears were streaming down Juniper's face, which made the rest of them cry tears of joy along with her. There were more overhead hand slaps and hugs than Jacob could count.

They moved out into the main pub area, where the constable had been waiting, and poured celebratory beers, crashing them together in toasts so enthusiastic they threatened to break the mugs. After some not-so-gentle coaxing, the constable even joined in.

The excitement took a while to wane. When it finally dropped below manic, Jacob started to think about the orcs, Shelu and Korga. He wished they had made enough to get them home, too.

As if reading his mind, Juniper said, "If only we could have raised enough for those wonderful young orcs to get home."

"Yeah." Cora made an exaggerated but genuine frown.

"What if we give this money to them instead?" Juniper asked.

"For one thing," Jacob said, "you've got little kids who need their home. And for another, that money was raised by people who were donating to a specific cause. I'm not sure if it'd be right to appropriate it somewhere else."

"But if they're the greater need..."

Jacob contemplated the idea. He was about to speak when a loud, horrible, and indescribable sound came from behind the pub.

"What in the world was that?" Tadrick stood up from his chair.

The crew hurried out the back door and found Mrs. Covington lying down in the middle of the yard. She was making a noise Jacob had never heard from her before—a guttural moan of misery.

As the group approached the uncomfortable capybara, the reason became clear. She was giving birth.

Cora softly clapped her hands in front of her face. "How exciting," she whispered.

"Let's give her space." Juniper stretched her arms out to her sides.

The crew backed up several steps.

After a few more moans, the first pup emerged into the world. It lifted its head and looked around in a daze, then let out a long squeak.

Mrs. Covington panted on her side, then began to moan again.

"So," Cora said to Jacob, "whatever happened with that woman I saw you talking to last night?"

"Really?" It seemed an incredibly awkward time to discuss such things. Jacob's face warmed considerably.

"What? They can have a litter of up to eight sometimes." She looked to Mrs. Covington, who was pushing out baby number two. "I mean, I'm fascinated by the miracle of birth, but I was just kinda curious about that woman, too."

"Okay, her name is Ana. She's a teacher, who has actually had Aspen and Ceda in her class before. She likes music and dancing and sword fighting. That's about all I know."

The second baby capybara was born.

"That's great," Cora said. "Do you have plans to meet up or something?"

Jacob hesitated, still feeling awkward about discussing his love life while Mrs. Covington gave birth ten feet away. "Well...she did say she would give me a sword fighting lesson sometime. I've always wanted to learn."

The third baby entered the world. Then the fourth. As the fifth baby was born, Mrs. Covington stood on unsteady legs and began giving them tongue baths.

"So, it's a litter of five," Juniper said.

Cora restrained herself from running over and picking up one of the babies, but just barely.

"What should we name them?" she asked.

"If one is a girl, I'd like to name her Eleanor, if possible," Tadrick said. "It was the name of my imaginary friend growing up." He gave an embarrassed shrug.

"Eleanor it is," Cora said. "And if there's a boy, I want to call him Steve."

"Why?" Jacob asked.

"I don't know. It's funny. A capybara named Steve." She held her hands out, palms up.

Jacob tried to think of a name but came up blank.

The babies awkwardly rose to their feet and gazed up at the world around them.

One of them let out a tiny but forceful squeak.

"Let's call him Mr. Squeak!" Jacob said, quite proud of himself.

Another baby lay down and closed its eyes as if it was already in need of a nap.

"We could call her Sleepy?" Cora pointed to the tired little one.

The tiniest, cutest little snore issued from the sleeping baby before her mother woke her up with a tongue across her face.

"How about Snorri?" Juniper offered.

"Perfect!"

"That leaves one more." Jacob rubbed a hand across his chin, eyes skyward.

The yet-to-be-named baby suddenly took off in her best attempt at a run. She made it about three steps before tripping over a small stick and rolling to her back.

Very tentatively, with eyes trained on Mrs. Covington, Tadrick knelt near the baby and rubbed her belly. "How are you, you clumsy little dingus?" he said in a soft voice.

"Dingus?" Jacob scrunched up his forehead.

"You never heard that before?" Tadrick continued to scratch her belly.

"Can't say that I have."

"How about Dingus?" Cora threw her hands out to her sides, again.

"Why not?" Tadrick looked down at the content little capybara, who seemed to love the belly rub. "Hey there, little Dingus."

The baby they had named Mr. Squeak, fresh out of a tongue bath, meandered over near Tadrick, then turned around to look back at his mother.

Tadrick tilted his head and brought it lower to the ground. "Uh... I'm no expert, but I think Mr. Squeak might be a Miss."

"Oh." Jacob frowned. "We can still call her Mr. Squeak, can't we? I'm already kinda attached to that name."

"I'm fine with it."

"Me, too."

"Great." Jacob grinned.

Tadrick stood back up and joined the group. Dingus and Mr. Squeak made their way back to their mother, joining the others in a huddle just underneath her.

"What's that thing around her neck?" Juniper pointed at Mrs. Covington.

Jacob could just make out what Juniper meant: a metallic strand visible on the capybara's left side.

Cora gasped. Her hands shot to her chest, eyes wide, mouth hanging open. She stood frozen in place, staring at Mrs. Covington.

"What is it?" Yandro asked her, looking more than slightly concerned.

"I didn't drink *that* much, did I?" Cora said, mostly to herself.

"Huh?" Tadrick looked from Cora to the capybara, and back.

"I can't believe I forgot about that." Cora hadn't moved anything but her mouth.

"Forgot about what?" Tadrick was losing patience.

"The night we came back with the treasure, and we celebrated in the pub..." She blinked. "I must have blacked out, but I vaguely remember, now." There was an agonizing pause. "We were all playing around with the treasure. There was this jewel, as big as a peanut. It was a brilliant aquamarine, the same color as Mrs. Covington's dress. It was attached to a pendant, on a thin silver chain. Do you remember when I put it on her?"

"Yes," Juniper replied, eyes wide.

"Well, when we put everything back in the chest, I kinda forgot about it...I guess."

"So, there's a jewel as big as a peanut around Mrs. Covington's neck right now?" Tadrick asked.

"I think so."

Tadrick crept up to Mrs. Covington as she tended to her newborns. Very carefully, he unhooked the clasp and removed the chain from around her neck. The capybara was only slightly annoyed by this. Grinning, Tadrick held up the chain for everyone to see. The bluish jewel sparkled brightly in the Ringlight.

Victories

Shelu and Korga waved from the rail of a ship called *The Sea Dragon* as it sailed away from the docks of New Dawn.

Jacob, Cora, Yandro, Tadrick, Juniper, and her kids all waved back, shouting goodbyes over the calm waters of the bay.

"I still can't believe you know a smuggler," Cora said to Tadrick as they waved.

"Yeah." Tadrick shrugged. "Simon's an old friend of mine. I almost got into that line of work with him, but I didn't have the nerve for it."

Tadrick's smuggler friend had been able to sell the jewel in the underground market. The money they made was enough to send the young orcs home to their parents but not much more.

Shelu and Korga were extremely grateful but insisted they be allowed to work in exchange for the money. After a short discussion with Juniper, Jacob and his co-owners decided to have a door put in between Juniper's kitchen and the pub, which would make selling nacias much easier. While they were at it, the orcs also expanded the faun family's living area and soundproofed the walls so Juniper could sleep on You Sing nights.

When the *Sea Dragon* wasn't much more than a smudge on the horizon, Jacob turned to his friends.

"Well, we pulled it off," Cora said, hand-in-hand with Yandro.

"We did," Tadrick agreed. "Although it would have been nice to keep the whole treasure."

"Would it, though?" Cora gave him a serious expression. "I mean, what do we need that we don't already have?"

"Fair point," Tadrick said. "I guess."

Jacob considered what he'd do if they were able to keep the massive treasure. He still longed to buy a ship and try his hand as a sailor, or even a captain someday. But that could wait.

"You know," he said, "maybe the real treasure is the—"

"I think whatever you were about to say is probably better left unsaid," Cora interrupted. "Let's just revel in the victories of Juniper's home and the orcs' homecoming."

"You're right."

Cora flashed him a smile. "So, you're supposed to meet that woman from the pub today?"

"Yeah." Jacob's face flushed. "In about an hour from now. My first sword fighting lesson."

"That's fantastic." Cora wrapped her arms around Yandro's neck. The two of them had been unable to keep their hands off each other for nearly a week.

Tadrick playfully rolled his eyes at the affectionate couple. "I suppose I'll head back to the pub. Wouldn't want to interrupt all the love in the air this morning."

"Oh, it's too early for much business, anyway," Cora said, still tangled up with the eternally-smiling Yandro. "Go sit in the pub and finish your damn book."

Tadrick was very close to the end of his dragon story. Jacob looked forward to reading it when it was ready.

"Alright." Tadrick started to turn. "I'll—" His finger shot into the air. "Oh! Speaking of books, I got something for you." He was looking at Jacob as he felt around in the knapsack he had strung over one shoulder.

"You did?"

"Yeah." He pulled out a thick book with a leather cover. "It's *Griffin the Unrivaled*," he said. "The book you tried to read when you were younger."

"Really?" Jacob took the heavy book. "Thank you. That was really kind of you."

"No problem. I think you're going to like it. It's got a lot of adventure and chivalry and stuff like that."

"Alright." Jacob thumbed through the pages, excited about jumping into it.

"Anyway," Tadrick said, "I'll go back and check on the pups, too."

"Give Steve a scratch under the chin for me," Cora said. "And the others, of course."

Tadrick raised a hand over his head. Cora broke her embrace for half a second to slap it. When Tadrick turned to Jacob, hand still in the air, Jacob did the same without even thinking about it.

"Goodbye, Juniper. Goodbye, kids." Tadrick waved to them as he backed away.

"Don't we get one?" Aspen asked.

"Oh! Yes, of course." Tadrick gave modified hand slaps to Aspen and Ceda, then a higher one to Juniper.

"Hey, Uncle Jacob," Ceda said. "I can teach you how to sword fight right now." She held an arm-length stick up in front of her.

"Where'd you get that?" Jacob asked.

Ceda used her stick to point to a section of sand near the dock where a tangle of seaweed and several sticks had washed ashore.

Jacob set his new book down gently in the sand, then hurried to the pile and plucked three suitable swords from it. He tossed one to Aspen, then turned to Juniper, holding another out with a shrug.

"Kids against adults!" Juniper called as she took the stick.

The girls smiled at each other, then charged.

Acknowledgments

To Alicia, for making my life cozy.

To Kaden and Ashton, for reminding me of the importance of fun and coziness.

To Mom and Dad, for fostering a mostly cozy childhood.

To Rob, for enhancing the coziness.

To Sara and Lilly, for making my jump into the book community cozy.

To Nathan Hall, for being very tough and always right. You made this book so much better.

To Daniel Wekellis, for the wonderful cover art, interior art, and postcards.

To these wonderful book bloggers, without whom I would have never got this project funded:

H.C. Newton (The Irresponsible Reader)

Sue Bavey (Sue's Musings)

Jodie Crump (Witty and Sarcastic Book Club)

Tabitha Tomala (Behind the Pages)

Starr K (Pages and Procrastination)

Shazzie (Fantasy Book Critic)

Esther (Cozy With Books)

and Fantasy Book Nerd.

To Sara Quinn at Tumbleweird.

To all of these fantastic people who gave this book life:

Jared Leys
    Sean Gibson
    Adam Holcombe
    Timothy Wolff
    Jess Moon
    L.L. MacRae
    Barbara Seiders
    Erika McCorkle
    Justin Aaron Gross
    Michael J. Sullivan, author
    Nicole May
    Margaret Harrison
    Colin Shoemaker
    Emily B.
    Helen Ellison
    J. Shelby
    Carol Dascanio
    E.M. Middel
    Emma Adams
    Ratty
    Robin Sutton
    Ariane Beauparlant
    Becky C.
    Jonah Gutierrez
    Adriana

J.K. Swift
Roman Pauer
Emily Lantzy
Alix Scarborough
Melodie Patton
Naticia
Melissa Crook
Heather A. McBride
Candice L. Boysen
Andrea Hirsh
Lani Weaver
Rosie Pease
Tyrel Souza
Jenn Peters
Diane Hart
Richard Novak
Chris Bowman
Su Penn
Hampus Jarleborn
Terri Connor
Caroline Scott
Sab
Ellie Meister
Oscar Vest
John Idlor
Dawn Therin
Dawn Schmidt
Kat James
Charlie Fairchild
Jen and Andrew
Eddie Black
Kristy Van Wyhe
Heidi Bailey
Nancy Hutchins
Misti Dunnuck-Strycker
Dundi Thompson
Lydia

Emily Boydston
Dakota VanLinden
Jessica Cline
Ryan Scott James
Sonse Cahuni
Kelsey F.
Sydney A. Baker
Micheal Lederer
E.L. Sapp
RoxMart
Emmy
Debbie Scott
Bryan Miller
The Cunninghams
Bettyetters
Kevin Brady
Jeanna Simmons
Marian West
Elizabeth Lindsey
Matthea W. Ross
Joe Rixman
Alex Carpenter
AnaMaurin Victoria Conley
Alderbeez
Brookestar
AingealWroth
SimonC
Jean Sitkei
Kathryn Craig
Ricardo Monascal
Ryan Lane
Heather Hewitt
Vicki Hsu
Suzanne van der Heide
Natascha Neve
Christina Getzen
Megan Krantz

Jen Ruiz
Melissa T.
SaraBeth Roberson
M.A. Phillips
Melanie B.
Kim Roueche
Cedric Kulacz
Megan Allen
Katie Pawlik
Madeleine J Frey
Trip Space-Parasite
Katie Van Riper
David Lars Chamberlain
Rachel Liliane
Dave Baughman
Rachael Besser
Rafi Spitzer
Cassey Eisch
Katie Dresel
Ashlee DesRosiers
Emma S.
Becky B.
K. Coleman
René Fuentes
Alexandra Romero
Alyssa Emmert
Christine Wells
K. Windler
H. Kirch

And all those who supported this book but chose to remain unnamed in these acknowledgments!

I really can't thank all of you enough! I would love to have nachos (and a beer if you're so inclined) with every one of you :)

About the Author

K.R.R. (Kyle Robert Redundant) Lockhaven started out writing humorous fantasy (hence the stupid name) but finds himself being pulled in the direction of Cozy Fantasy.

His first book, The Conjuring of Zoth-Avarex: The Self-Proclaimed Greatest Dragon in the Multiverse, received a starred review from Kirkus.

His fantasy trilogy, The Azure Archipelago, was published by Shadow Spark Publishing.

Website: krrlockhaven.com